PRAISE FOR STEPHANIE KEYES

The greatest strength of this story is the development of the relationship between Pippa and Finn. "Internship" is the journey of two characters as they learn to trust and love despite emotional roadblocks and self-sabotage. "The Internship of Pippa Darling" is a great start to the Summer Abroad Series and leaves the reader craving more!

— GWENELLEN TARBET, IN'DTALE
MAGAZINE

"Each turn of the page brought something different, and I found myself sometimes laughing out loud; other times, I wanted to crawl into the book and follow these beautiful characters to the end of their story. The Internship of Pippa Darling will leave you ready for more hot Irishmen and lots of laughs."

— MOLLY EDWARDS, READERS' FAVORITE

Cover Design by

Najla Qamber, Najla Qamber Designs

Editorial Services by

Ashley Turcotte, Brown Owl Editing

The Internship of Pippa Darling

THE SUMMER ABROAD SERIES
Book One
By Stephanie Keyes

To my grandfather, Carl Dunn, who was the gentleman I've always modeled my heroes after. I'll miss you forever, Pap.

PIPPA

*"Dreamers sway in the night under waxing moonlight,
transfixed by the weight of their own futures."*
—James Black, *To the Ends of the Earth*

*P*ippa Darling was in love. She couldn't get
Jake out of her mind. It didn't help that he
was all long legs and lean muscle and brooding expres-
sions. His girlfriend, Cassidy, was even cuter, if that were
possible. Her funky golden locks and hippy-esque personality were sweet. Pippa couldn't wait to see how Jake and
Cass came together, how they would kiss and cuddle and
make love, and face the tough times with their heads
raised to meet the danger—whatever it might be. She
couldn't wait to discover every intimate detail of their
lives.

The discovery was the very best part about writing a
book.

Which was why Pippa had gotten zero shut-eye the
night before. Instead, she'd torn a notebook from her

nightstand drawer and started jotting ideas until three a.m. She didn't mind the exhaustion. Writing gave her permission to create new and exciting worlds—worlds far more interesting than her own. Writing was her life.

But she wasn't writing just then.

Instead, Pippa sat coffee-less in the dean's waiting room that April morning, kicking her umbrella back and forth between her feet while Johnny Cash played over the ancient radio. *Johnny Cash.* Ugh.

I fell into a burning ring of fire
I went down, down, down
And the flames went higher

Dean Montgomery didn't say why he wanted to meet that morning. His exact words were: *The matter is time sensitive. How early can you stop by?*

The dean's office was much more . . . posh than any of her professors'. Overstuffed chairs in pale yellow and blue brocade flanked a gleaming cherry console table. On it rested a spray of daffodils. Their light spring color clashed with the old money vibe going on. Behind the front desk, an aging secretary pounded on a keyboard, threatening to hit the speed of about two words per minute. She didn't really fit with the whole sophisticated office vibe, but Morris College of Creative Arts seemed to hire people at birth and keep them on for life. At least if the staff in Financial Aid was anything to go by. Or the dining hall. Or the mini-post office.

Her eyes drooped as Johnny played on. Shaking her head to clear it, Pippa reached for her bag and tugged out her well-worn copy of *To the Ends of the Earth*, her favorite book ever. At some point last year, she'd taken to carrying it around with her. Her best friend, Uma, called it her literary security blanket. Pippa called it motivation. If an unknown writer could craft something so beautiful, then so would she. One day.

Before she read to the end of page one, a door opened, and Dean Montgomery, head of Fiction Studies, popped out. He reminded her of an owl with his white hair, eyebrows that pointed out to the sides, and large, gold-rimmed glasses. "Pippa?"

"Sir," she stood, smoothing her pencil skirt for the hundredth time.

His smile widened as they shook hands. His was cold and clammy, Pippa's as hot and sweaty as a teenage boys' locker room on game day.

"This way, please." He led her into his office and gestured to a wide, leather chair in a faded seventies-era rust color with cracks running along the arms. It looked like it'd been in that exact spot longer than Pippa had been alive. The dean left his door partially open as the pair of them sat. Johnny filtered into the office.

I went down, down, down
And the flames went higher

Resting her messenger bag on the floor, Pippa extracted a small notebook and pen from the front pocket. *Always be prepared.* That was her motto—or somebody's motto, but borrowing it was just good thinking.

"This summer is it for you, huh?" The dean took a seat across from her and sipped his coffee. He didn't offer her a cup. Pippa probably would have settled for instant at that point.

"Yes, sir. I have to turn in my manuscript by the first

week of September, and then that's it." Pippa tried to inflect some enthusiasm into her voice, but finding the time to finish her novel would be the toughest part.

"You're one of the most talented students in our Creative Writing program. Winning the Blue Ribbon contest last year only cemented that in our minds." He smiled, but it wasn't one of those fake deals. It seemed genuine.

"Thank you, sir." The blue ribbon win had been huge. Not only was it an incredible honor, but it paid her past two semesters' tuition.

"What would you say to working somewhere more *interesting* for your last semester, out in the real world?"

"What do you mean?" To Pippa, "the real world" meant summers schlepping guests' dirty laundry up and down four flights of stairs at Dad's B&B.

Dean Montgomery sipped more of his coffee. Would he notice if Pippa just snatched it out of his hand?

"There are a number of esteemed graduates from our Master of Fine Arts program. Many have gone on to become New York Times best sellers."

This she was painfully aware of. Seeing her name on that list had always been Pippa's dream. A writer who'd made "the list" was *a writer*. She couldn't imagine a better source of validation. It didn't just have to do with getting away from the B&B. There was more to it. To have that many readers *knowing* her characters and getting hooked on worlds she created . . . she closed her mouth to keep from salivating. "Yes, sir."

"One of our graduates is none other than Finn Burke.

You've heard of him?" He winked, like he was letting her in on some sort of secret.

"Who hasn't? He's famous."

Even that was an understatement. Burke was the Morris star who landed an agent and a six-figure deal—all in the same week. After he dropped out of school, Morris awarded him an honorary degree six months later.

She also knew the truth. Finn Burke's book *sucked*.

Dean Montgomery smiled. "Yes, his popularity has grown. When he was a student here, he penned one novel. *Lost* hit number one on the New York Times list its first week out. It's an absolute best seller."

Bullshit. Burke's main character was a bastard. The other characters were miserable and boring. Pippa had abandoned the story by chapter ten. Why did every book that people fell in love with have to be a depressing piece of garbage? Couldn't someone write a "happy book"?

"Obviously, he picked up a few things while he was a student here." Dean Montgomery beamed—as though he were personally responsible for Finn Burke's sales figures.

"Yes, sir." She bit her tongue.

"I don't know if you're aware of this, but for the past two summers, Finn's taken on an intern. It's grunt work and it doesn't pay much. Mostly, it involves organizing and proofreading his files, that sort of thing, but Finn also works with the student on his or her manuscript throughout the summer. And for this year's intern . . . he's chosen *you*." The dean beamed at Pippa.

"Wow. Really?" *So* not what she'd expected the meeting to be about.

"And if you take Finn's internship, you'll have all summer to write, plus you'll receive feedback from an industry professional. You really can't buy that kind of experience."

It was just her luck. She'd landed an internship with the one author whose work she hated. She'd have to decline. It wouldn't be right to accept the post.

But not accepting would mean going home and spending the summer being overrun with tourists. Hot and sticky days in her non-air-conditioned bedroom, with only small windows of writing time. She'd be lucky to finish her manuscript. "What would be involved with the internship?"

The dean sipped his coffee, eyeing her over the rim. The scent of French roast tickled her nose. "Finn has property in Ireland. A castle, of all things. You'd spend the summer there. You'd have your own guest house, plenty of time to write, free room and board, and, like I said, a small salary. No tuition since this isn't being run by the school. He will also pay for your airfare, which, if I may say so, is quite generous."

Room and board in Ireland, plus airfare? *Ireland.* She'd always wanted to go. After all, it was what had made her pick up Burke's damn book in the first place.

Dean Montgomery cleared his throat, cutting into Pippa's internal monologue. "I should also add that we've had two other students who've interned for him. He's been very influential in their success."

He named two writers from previous classes. Though she'd never met either, both had good book deals to their credit already. And there she was, being given the same shot as those writers. It was a dream, really.

"Take some time and think about it—but not too long. I'll need to find a replacement if you can't take this on, all right?"

"Certainly, sir."

Dozens of questions flittered in and out of her mind as she shook the dean's hand, thanked him, and then headed out of the office in a daze.

Back in the waiting room, another country song played—something about an *achy-breaky heart*. Pippa opened the door and then shut it behind her, silencing the music.

A summer in Ireland with Finn Burke.

It was the last thing she'd expected, but maybe the summer would end up being the best ever. Or the *worst*.

2

FINN

*"I sank the punch into his jaw. Fat drops of blood splattered the
pavement. That shut his mouth, all right."*
—Finn Burke, *Lost*

The close, Florida heat clung to Finn Burke with
every step. His T-shirt hugged his wiry body.
He should have known better than to wear black. Yet it'd
been years since his last visit to Florida, and the weather
shocked him the same as it had when he'd first arrived on
campus as a student. At least he'd been able to combine
his visit to Morris with one at Ma's. After that morning's
meeting, he'd be on a plane home to Ireland. He couldn't
get there fast enough.

A wave of air conditioning pummeled him as he
stepped inside the administrative building. He breathed in
the artificial cold. Thank *feck* for the AC.

His MacBook under one arm, he jogged up the steps at
a furious pace, getting in his exercise where he could, and

yanked the door handle to the hallway. A soft, curvy body shot through the door and smacked into him.

"Oomph!" Finn staggered backward, banging into the railing behind him. His hands shot up as he lost his balance. The MacBook slipped from his grasp and flew over his shoulder. "Whoa, whoa!" He spun, gripping the railing as he tried to catch it, but he was too late.

The MacBook crashed to the steps below. "For *feck's* sake!" Finn whirled past the person who'd collided with him, tearing down the stairs.

He spotted the MacBook lying on the steps, neatly split into two pieces. *Jaysus.* Phillip had been on him for two years to buy a laptop and quit using his "damn typewriter," as he'd referred to it. He finally had, and this *shite* happened.

Finn jerked his head up and spotted a woman, a wisp of a thing no taller than his chest, standing on the landing above him. She was all curves and spitfire. Right that instant, she was looking at him with legitimate concern. But compassion didn't trump stupidity.

"You bloody *eejit*!" he cried, thrusting the pieces of his MacBook into the air. "Look what you did!"

The woman cleared her throat and tipped up her chin. A fire brewed in her eyes that he could spot even from one floor below.

"Technically, I didn't do anything. I walked through the door. Why don't you have a protective case for that laptop? It's a Mac, for crying out loud. They're worth more than my car."

She had a point. He should have bought a case for the damn thing months ago. Instead, he'd carried it around, as though the technology might self-destruct at any moment. But she didn't need to know that.

"My entire manuscript was on there!" he said.

"Look, don't panic. Take it to the IT department. They can probably copy your files off the hard drive." She bit her bottom lip. "That is, if that part hasn't been, uh, destroyed." Her eyes widened in horror. "But you back up your work, right?"

"I don't have a backup of *that*." He thrust a finger at the destroyed MacBook.

"I'm really sorry. I'm a writer, too, so I understand." She shouldered her own bag a little more securely, as if he would reach up and take it. "I didn't mean for that to happen."

"Clearly you're a klutz as well as an *eejit*."

The woman's eyes flashed. "Maybe you should have been watching where you were going?"

"Maybe *you* should have," Finn said, trying not to notice how the flush in her cheeks combined with the thunderclouds in her eyes.

His anger kicked in again. "And that's supposed to make up for the destruction of a three-thousand-euro laptop, eh? Maybe I should sue you for recompense."

She frowned. "You want to sue *me*? It was an accident. Get over yourself." Her words increased in velocity until they ran together in one, messy string.

Finn cradled the broken pieces of his MacBook in his arms as he climbed the stairs until he reached her level. She sure was something to look at. Yet, the way she glowered, with her eyebrows practically touching the tip of her nose, made Finn think she contemplated throwing *him* down the stairwell.

Without waiting to find out, he pushed past her, reaching for the handle of the door she'd come through. "Maybe you should get the hell out of the way."

"Why don't you go to hell, Mr. Crabby?" She muttered the words as she took to the stairs leading to the exit.

"I'll join you there, darling!" he cried.

The instant the door slammed shut behind her, Finn roared with laughter. Mr. Crabby, indeed.

3

PIPPA

"The land, this earth we call home, is all that really matters in the end."
—James Black, *To the Ends of the Earth*

*P*ippa waited until the door slammed behind her, then rested her head against it. Who the hell was that guy?

He'd been a dangerous sight. A *hot*, dangerous sight, with his heaving chest and his intense glare. He'd had some sort of accent, though she couldn't place it. Like he'd come to this country and the Floridians' dialogue sucked some of it out of him. Too bad he'd had the personality of a troll to go along with that sexy voice of his.

That guy had called her *darling*. Had he known her name? Or had he meant it as some sort of warped endearment? The rain began to start up again. First, it misted, but the light drops quickly turned heavy, pelting her heated skin.

In a matter of seconds, it seemed well on its way to a

full-scale thunderstorm. Pippa reached into her bag for her umbrella. Not there. Oh, no. She'd left it in the dean's office. Freaking fabulous.

Hunching her shoulders, she placed her bag on top of her head. She'd just have to deal. Nothing was worth another run-in with the owner of the broken MacBook. If she never saw that jackass again, it'd be too soon.

The humidity had gone up, in that special way it did in Florida. It was possible to be cold and sweaty at the same time in the state, when the weather called for it. That morning, the slick, rain pelted Pippa's skin, even as the thick air stole her breath.

Morris was like a mini-city in and of itself. There was even a Main Street, but instead of storefronts, the buildings held space for classes. A huge open green separated the dorms from the classrooms. Students biked or walked everywhere they needed to go. Pippa ran down one of several paved trails that connected the two parts of campus. The school was surrounded by tall, stainless steel fencing that had been spray-painted green. It wasn't designed to keep students in, but alligators out. That was Florida for you.

By the time Pippa reached the townhouse she shared with Uma on the other side of campus, her clothes, hair, and bag were drenched. She wasn't sure who she was angrier at. Herself, or the jerk-wad in the hall that made her not want to go back and retrieve her umbrella.

She opened the door to the smell of coffee and the warm glow of a lamp on a low table. Mornings had always been her favorite writing time, but *later* in the morning. Whenever she could force herself out of bed, anyway. Half of her class got up at five a.m. It would have been nice if she could get on that kind of schedule. She barely managed eight o'clock.

"Uuum, ya home?" she called from the kitchen as she retrieved her favorite mug, which read, *I am a writer—watch it or you'll end up in my book*, and then added the coffee. The first sip was heaven.

"Hey, Pippa. Be down in a few minutes. Shower's yours if you want it," Uma called from her bedroom.

"Do I ever," Pippa said, taking her coffee to the bathroom, after making a detour for a short stack of dry clothes. Stripping off her wet things, she hung them on the towel rack on the back of the door and climbed into the shower. The hot spray was heaven after the chill of the heavy rain. She took her time cleaning up before shutting off the water and toweling dry. By the time she'd thrown on her favorite yoga pants and a hoodie, Uma waited in Pippa's room, coffee in one hand, a thick book in the other. Uma was a poet. She had this innate rhyming sense that Pippa could only dream about. It probably came from her inhaling poetry volumes the way Pippa did coffee.

Uma glanced up as Pippa walked in and plopped down on the bed beside her. "What did the dean want? Are you in trouble or something?"

"Nope. Not in trouble." She drank the remainder of her lukewarm coffee, draining the cup, and already wanted a refill. She leaned over and pulled a pair of thick socks from the dresser beside her bed and slipped them onto her frigid feet. Her Comparative Lit class wasn't until three p.m., so she had plenty of time to warm up. "Dean Montgomery offered me an internship."

Uma's brown eyes widened, a smile stretching over her pale skin. "That's great. Details, please!"

"With Finn Burke." Pippa meant to add more, to transition into that news in a way that wouldn't send Uma into shock. She failed.

Uma froze. "*The* Finn Burke? Of *Lost* fame?" she asked, closing her book and setting it on the bed. "But we hated his book. I'm not talking mild dislike, Pippa. We hated it."

"Yeah. Tell me about it." Pippa stretched her legs and hopped off the bed. Uma trailed her as she took to the steps and made her way into the tidy kitchen of their townhouse. She waited as Pippa poured another steaming cup of coffee into her mug, draining the pot, and then began to set things up for a second.

"Is that all you're going to say? We're talking the same Finn Burke you were ranting about a couple of weeks ago?"

"Yes." Pippa climbed onto one of the two tall stools at their kitchen counter.

Uma took the other, nudging Pippa in the side as she did so. "The author of the book you claimed worked best as a *coaster?*"

"I did say that, didn't I?" Pippa cringed. Of course, those comments had followed on the heels of several rejections from literary agents. She hadn't been in a good place.

"I'm surprised you didn't pick up some spray paint and graffiti it all over the student union." Uma stretched her arms toward the ceiling and yawned. "What did you tell the dean?"

"That I needed time to think about it. He told me not

to take too long, though. I promised I'd let him know as soon as possible.

Uma bounced her foot on the bottom rung of her barstool. The pink lines on her white shoes matched the pink in her black and pink leggings. Uma never color-coordinated on purpose, it just worked out that way. Like some innate instinct took over the moment she opened her closet door.

"Burke has a castle—in *Ireland*. I'd have my own living space and plenty of time to write. If I go home . . ." Pippa shrugged the rest of her answer.

"You'll be working fourteen-hour days and taking an undesired break from your manuscript and *not* in Ireland?" Uma offered. "A castle? Really?"

"Yeah." Pippa slumped against the back of her stool. Nothing about the decision was easy. Or maybe it would have been if she'd been a different person.

"Is the internship paid?" Uma asked.

"Montgomery mentioned a salary." That was another thing that appealed to Pippa. Not only would she get writing time, but she'd get paid to do it. How often in her life would she get that chance again? The odds weren't her friends.

"I think you should take it." Uma shrugged, sliding her arms into her worn hoodie. "It's kind of a no-brainer, Pip. I mean, you get out of working at the B&B, plus you get paid, your own place, and tailored advice from a best-selling author."

Huh. "You don't think it's wrong to accept? Since I don't enjoy his work, I mean?"

Uma shook her head. "You don't have to like someone's work to learn from them; you just have to respect them."

That was true. No one said Pippa had to like Burke's writing, but maybe he *could* teach her. It would certainly give her a leg up.

Pippa rolled her eyes. "I suppose, but he's no James Black." She patted the side of her messenger bag, where the canvas bulged in the shape of her favorite book.

"Excuse me? No one could live up to him, not even James Black himself. You're, like, in love with that guy and you know nothing about him. He could even be a *she*, for all you know." Uma patted Pippa's arm. "I'll miss you, but it would be such a cool experience for you. We could FaceTime and you could send pictures . . . Promise you'll think about it. "

"I promise." A lump formed at the base of Pippa's throat. It was the first year that she knew she wouldn't be seeing Uma in the fall. Uma was a year behind Pippa, and then planned to continue her studies after that. Pippa had been choking up about her impending graduation a lot lately. She leaned forward, wrapping her arms around her roommate and best friend. "I love you."

"I love you, too."

Uma patted Pippa on the back, and they broke apart. "Let me know if you want to talk about this later, but for now I've gotta run. Class in ten."

"See you later," Pippa said as Uma headed out for the morning. She had her phone out and the number dialed by the time the door clicked behind Uma. It only rang once before someone picked up on the other end.

"Yankee Hollow Bed and Breakfast, Jim Darling speaking."

A rush of homesickness filled her. Gettysburg seemed far away right then. Dad would have been standing at the front desk, behind the polished mahogany counter. The wood would've been shining because he'd just polished it, like he did every Monday. Even the spokes on the wide, curved staircase would've been gleaming. "Hi, Dad."

"Pippa!" His voice changed instantly, filled with even more warmth than when he first answered. "How's it going?"

"Good. Miss you." Her bottom lip trembled, and she bit it to still it. The old guilt about coming to Morris settled on her shoulders, and she did her best to shrug it off. "What would you say if I didn't come home this summer?" Slowly, she exhaled, waiting for his reaction to travel to her end of the line.

There was a pause as Dad processed her words. "Not come home? Why? Whatcha got cooking for the summer, Pip?" But his voice had turned wary. His mind would already be in motion, contemplating how he'd replace her, who he could hire that would accept Pippa's modest hourly rate. His concern wasn't because he wanted to manipulate her, or even take advantage of Pippa's willingness to help. Dad was a small business owner. He had to think that way.

"I got offered a paid internship. In *Ireland*."

"Pippa! That's amazing. What an incredible opportunity." His excitement poured through the phone.

No, she couldn't go. It was wrong, leaving him to deal with everything alone. The school year was one thing—

the winter months had always been leaner on reservations. Not the summer.

"What's wrong?" he asked. "You don't sound as excited about this as I'd expect."

"I don't want to leave you in the lurch."

"Don't worry about me. I can rent out your room— make a little extra money. I'll be fine and so will you." But Dad wouldn't be fine. Pippa would only be making things more difficult for him.

Low voices broke into Pippa's thoughts. "Hey, Pip, I've got a guest here. Talk to you later, okay?"

"Sure, Dad. I love you." She waited, listening to the familiar background noise until the last second, when he hung up with a click.

Pippa stared out the front window of the townhouse. Rivulets of rain traveled down the glass. She wished her guilt about not going home would wash away so easily. But it wouldn't. If she wanted that internship, Pippa had to take it and swallow her feelings.

Snatching her phone from the counter, she navigated to the dean's contact info and pressed the number link in his signature. She really was going to Ireland.

4

FINN

*"Love is a convenient lie we tell one another to excuse ourselves
from acting like assholes."*
—Finn Burke, *Lost*

Finn Burke stacked stones around the foundation of the ruins of Teármunn Castle's keep. The stone structure was all that remained of the once-glorious castle. Finn and his neighbor, Bob Hannigan, were determined to do as much of the restoration on their own as possible. Though Finn doubted they'd be able to work for much longer. Once the stacked foundation grew too high, he'd need to hire someone with the right equipment. That would take time and money he wasn't ready to invest. Especially, after the expense of building his modern living quarters on a nearby portion of his land.

In the meantime, he enjoyed the manual labor and the sweat on his forearms from an honest day's work. Of course, that wasn't the only reason he was outside working at the keep instead of inside writing.

He'd been avoiding dealing with the brand-new MacBook sitting on his dining room table. He hated the thing already. Not only did it cost a fair bob, but he didn't know how to use it the way he should. Not really.

He hadn't bothered to learn all the ins and outs because he just happened to like working on his type-writer better. Also, he was a bit superstitious as a rule. Hard drives were fickle creatures; paper, he could trust. Unfortunately, his literary agent, Phillip, had insisted. Get a laptop and get into the twenty-first century.

Finn had. He'd bought a MacBook, loaded it with the best writing software, and had gotten to work.

"You gonna pick up the pace, there, boyo? You've been holding that stone all day." Bob Hannigan stood on the opposite end of the keep ruins. His arms were loaded with two stone blocks. Finn's own hands ached from carrying one at a time. "We can go for a pint when we're done, if it's talking you're after."

Finn grinned. "Or we could go for a pint now." He reached down and held up the small cooler Bob's wife, Zoe, had packed them. "Courtesy of your lovely wife."

"She's a catch, that one. I'll be up directly." Gripping the walls of the keep as he clambered up the hill, Bob joined Finn on the highest part of the cliff.

Sweat dripped into Finn's eyes, despite the cool weather. Early May in Ireland wasn't frigid, but it was not exactly what a body would call warm, either. Not an ideal day for stacking stone. The sea was rough that day, and it still carried with it the bite of winter. Truth be told, it could pack more of the same in June. The only thing predictable about the weather in Ireland was its unpredictability.

Finn opened the cooler and extracted two cans of Guinness. Bless them for the tiny sphere full of CO_2 and nitrogen Guinness added to every can to ensure a smooth pour.

Clearly, Bob didn't feel the same. The older man shook his head. "Cans. A travesty, that."

"What'd you expect, a tap in here?" Finn handed Bob the can.

The older man accepted it, popped the tab, and then drank deeply. The wind whipped the gray strands of Bob's hair. "You want to tell me why you're out here today and not working on that novel of yours? Didn't your scheming *fecker* of an agent set a deadline?"

"That he did."

Finn had just never expected a little vixen to show up and cause him to drop his work down a stairwell. Finn had driven to the Apple shop in Dublin for a replacement. Six hours of driving, round trip, and over €2700 later, he had a new laptop. He said as much to Bob over their afternoon pint.

"*Jaysus*, that's a pain in the *arse*." Bob nursed his Guinness.

Finn took a pull from his own beer, watching the blue water glitter to green under the moody sun's rays.

"The store supposedly recovered my files and put them on the new machine. Everything *should* be there, but I'm dreading booting the bloody thing up. If my manuscript's on there, I'll be one lucky bastard." Finn shrugged and took another drink, letting the full stout, as heavy as any meal, slide down his throat.

"Talk about some random thing. Running into that woman? Dropping your damn computer Lord knows how many feet?" Bob tapped his fingers against his can. It seemed more rooted from his need to keep moving and working than impatience at listening. Zoe always claimed Bob could be the best listener when it suited him.

"It's that damn woman who plowed into me. A menace, she was—whipping around like a race car driver." It didn't matter that she had the look of a fairy and the body of a dancer in one compact package. "If the woman couldn't walk, she should've stayed clear of the doorway."

"I had a woman run into me once." Bob's lips quirked.

"You did?" Finn drank again, mimicking Bob's actions. "What happened?"

"I married her." Bob burst into laughter, the rumble in his chest contagious. Something about Bob Hannigan had always relaxed Finn. Perhaps because he'd been Finn's da's friend. That connection to Jack Burke meant a lot now that Finn had no more people in Ireland. Da was dead, and Finn was hours from the county he'd grown up in.

Finn shook his head. "Back to work with you."

Bob took the empty from Finn's hand. "Back to work with *you*. Inside to sort it all out."

Finn would've preferred to argue, but there was little point in that with Bob. He would only needle Finn until he got the job done.

"Fine." Grabbing his shirt, he tugged it back over his head. "G'bye."

Bob waved as Finn hopped down and onto the nearest

walkway—the one that led to his living quarters. The sound of the sea matched his stormy mood as he strode through the woods, but once he stepped inside his house and shut the door, the rhythm of the waves dimmed. It was only Finn then, and what he had to do.

He moved to the dining area, a room surrounded by windows and light, and sat at the table. Bob was right. He had to get this laptop situation sorted. His new intern, Pippa Darling, would be arriving soon. He'd need to hit the ground running with his manuscript in order to make Phillip's deadline. He couldn't do that without help.

An image of Phillip's email swam in his mind.

Have the entire first draft to me by September 1st, or we're going to have a serious talk, Finn.

Phillip was a bastard, there was nothing for it. Yet, he was Finn's agent and he'd gotten Finn the publishing deal that allowed him to live his current lifestyle. One Finn wasn't interested in changing, particularly since he'd wiped out his advance on the house and the castle keep. He was living on royalties, and that was risky business as far as he was concerned. Readers were fickle.

Though Phillip, he supposed, had some right to be impatient. Finn had missed his last four deadlines. But what Phillip meant when he'd said they'd have a serious talk, Finn didn't know. Finn hadn't missed those due dates from lack of trying. He was simply struggling. He'd written his first best seller with luck. He wasn't sure if he had a second in him.

Sitting down at the table, he unpackaged the MacBook

and plugged it in. He pressed power. After a moment, it booted and loaded. Crossing his fingers, Finn went to his desktop. Thank God. His files were there. His work hadn't been destroyed.

He opened his writing software and chose the same options he always did: File and Recent. Several minutes later, his stomach plummeted. No files were listed. How could that be? He'd always accessed his files that way before.

He closed the software and returned to the desktop, hovering his cursor over each file in turn, reading each filename. The files he wanted weren't there. He'd lost a month's worth of work. How had that happened?

Easy. It all came down to that petite woman with a penchant for colliding with unsuspecting authors.

Maybe looking at some of the work he did have would jar his memory. He double-clicked one of the damn files, it opened, and then Finn's mind blanked.

He remembered writing the pages in front of him, but anything before or after seemed gone, lost within the depths of his mind. It wasn't the first time something had slipped Finn's mind. He forgot things all the time. Things like eating, his car keys, if he'd paid the electric bill . . .

If the everyday got lost in his thoughts, he was the better for it. But to forget his own writing . . . Writing was all that mattered.

The scattered notes in his journal didn't offer any clues, either. Maybe forgetting his earlier draft was for the best. What he'd written hadn't been very good. He was certain he could do better.

But what if he didn't? What if it bombed and he ended up a failure? It would be just like *before*.

Finn didn't think he could stand that.

Bollocks. Like he had time for more delays. It was bad enough he had a deadline to meet. Now he had to redo everything.

Pippa Darling would be his savior. She'd help him get it all in order. That other woman, the uncoordinated one who seemed to get off on destroying a man's laptop, could roast in hellfire for all he cared.

5

PIPPA

*"Traveler, traveler run. Follow the call of the sea, the hum of the
train, the relentless pounding of the horse's hoof."*
—James Black, *To the Ends of the Earth*

The flight to Dublin was long. Painful. Pippa
was surrounded by a senior tour group. One
member, a lady with a large mouth and tight red curls,
kept shouting at Pippa to stop sleeping and look out the
window. Of course, there was nothing to see but night
and ocean. Pippa didn't feel particularly excited about
either—especially, the ocean. After several demands from
her seat neighbor, Pippa tugged down the shade and
popped in her headphones.

Once she landed, someone named Zoe Hannigan
would pick her up. Pippa hoped Zoe was a nice, normal
person, because, from there, they would drive three hours
to Finn Burke's home in County Donegal. Teármunn
Castle was the name of the place, though Pippa hadn't

been able to find anything more than pictures of ruins online. Hopefully, she wouldn't be spending her internship in a pup tent.

A rush of homesickness hit her. It would be the first time she'd spent the summer anywhere but at home or at school. No matter how much time she'd spent away, she'd always been able to count on going home—even if only for a little while. Things were about to change.

She still had no idea what Finn Burke even looked like. She'd Googled him and found nothing. Nothing other than press pieces and undeserved rave reviews. How was that even possible? The guy must have been some kind of recluse. Or the next Unabomber?

Oh. My. God.

Breathe, Pippa.

Eventually, she'd given up her research after reading some snooze-fest interview about his writerly inspirations. It was probably better that she hadn't learned much. She didn't want to skew her perception any more than it already was. Especially since his work was a depressing hole of darkness.

By the time the plane touched down, it was late afternoon in Dublin. The sun's rays splashed across Pippa's face as she opened the shade. There wasn't much of a view from her spot on the runway. She couldn't wait to get off the plane and scope out Ireland for herself.

The airport wasn't too difficult to navigate. Her bags popped onto the carousel way faster than she'd expected. Thank God. It would suck to end up in a foreign country with only the clothes on her back. Once she'd located her banged-up, trusty suitcase, she had nothing to do but wait.

She scanned the entire baggage claim area, narrowing her eyes to make herself look mean to any potential attackers. The frown hurt her face, and her right eye began to twitch. Apparently, looking mean wasn't Pippa's forte.

"Are you all right?"

Pippa whipped around as a fifty-ish woman moved to stand beside her. She was dressed in jeans and a hoodie, her dishwater blond hair done up in a bun, though it was hard to say whether it was for style or convenience. Since she wore no makeup, Pippa guessed the latter. That's when she spotted the sign hanging limply in the woman's hand. It read, *Pippa Darling*.

Pippa pasted her most welcoming smile on her face. At least, she hoped it was welcoming. After the commute she'd been through, that was questionable. "Hello." She held out her hand. "I'm Pippa."

The woman grinned, her rosy cheeks bunching up. "Of course you are. Sorry I'm late. Parking was murder." She shook Pippa's hand with enough enthusiasm to pump her arm off. "Zoe Hannigan. I'm the sometimes housekeeper and more times neighbor of Mr. Burke. Welcome to Ireland."

"Thank you. It's nice to meet you, Zoe, and it's no problem. My plane just landed." No need to mention she'd already been working on a self-defense plan.

"Good, good." Zoe held the door for Pippa. "I imagine it's a relief to be off the plane. How long was your trip?

Seven hours?" They entered the car park and then took to the stairs.

Pippa latched onto the question. "Twelve if you count getting to the airport and waiting around for a really long time."

"Goodness. Well, we've got you now." Zoe led her outside to an old, teal wagon that looked like it had hit its prime in the eighties, and popped the hatch. She snatched Pippa's oversized bag from the ground before Pippa could offer and tossed it in. Her duffle and laptop bag followed.

It was just after four o'clock, but all traces of the sun had gone, hidden behind thick, dark clouds. The misty rain sent chills skating over Pippa's skin. It was May. Why was it so cold?

Zoe gestured for Pippa to climb in on the passenger side. It only took Pippa a couple of moments to remember she had to sit on the opposite side of the car. "Let's get you to where you'll be staying for the summer."

For the summer.

Her words sounded as final as a dungeon door slamming closed.

"It's really a three-hour drive?" Pippa asked.

Zoe grinned. "It might be around two hours with myself at the wheel. You'd best buckle up."

PIPPA SOON LEARNED Zoe hadn't been exaggerating. Once she navigated onto a highway called the M3, they might as well have been on the Autobahn. Trees flew past them on either side. Pippa gave up on trying to see anything.

Though Zoe pointed out several *loughs*, or lakes, there wasn't much to look at. Except green. Green everywhere, and sheep. Lots of sheep.

The rain kicked up as they continued northwest, bringing fog with it. Soon, even the sheep disappeared, replaced by thick, white wisps that surrounded them. Zoe didn't seem bothered. Pippa, on the other hand, kept a close watch on the strip of road in front of them.

Pippa answered Zoe's questions about her writing and school, who her "people" were, and what she hoped to do after graduation. In turn, Zoe shared that she cooked dinner for Burke every night, but also did all the shopping and cleaning. Pippa would be seeing her at least once every day. She also had a husband and a son, Caden, who was twenty-two and at university.

After a stop at a McDonald's drive-thru, Pippa decided to broach the question bouncing around in her head. She cleared her throat, hoping she wouldn't sound as awkward out loud as she did in her head. "What's Mr. Burke like? I tried to find something about him online, but it's like he's a social media hermit."

A chuckle burst out of Zoe's chest and Pippa relaxed. "Social media hermit. I guess that would be a fitting description. Burke *is* a little eccentric."

Okay. "What do you mean by eccentric?"

"He's one of those hipster types. You know? One of those ones who are trying to get the typewriter to make a comeback. He just bought his first laptop, or rather, his *bollocks* of an agent strong-armed him into it."

Pippa thought about her sleek laptop and tablet,

resting in a padded messenger bag in the trunk. "He sounds like an absolute delight."

"He can be. Or he can be a right crotchety bastard—like an old man in training, I suppose."

Wow. This guy was just getting better and better. She couldn't wait to meet him.

Zoe patted her arm. "Don't mind me. I like to give Burke grief every now and then—it's good for his soul." Zoe laughed.

"And is he married? Dating?" Why had she asked that question? It wasn't like she cared. She didn't even know the guy.

"There was a woman once . . . but that was a long time ago. Now Burke lives like a monk, never sees any women. Believe me, it would be easy enough for me to know. The guy almost never leaves his house." Zoe threw a sideways glance in Pippa's direction. "You aren't after a shag, are you? You know, a bit of fun in the bedroom?"

Pippa blushed three different shades of red. "No. No, I just—"

"I'm just messing with ya. Burke's a ride, but if he's not celibate now, I'll eat Granda's bible."

Oh my God.

Pippa's face continued to flame as she faced the window. She stored Zoe's information away. It was better if Burke was celibate. At least she wouldn't have to worry about being stuck in the Irish countryside with some horny stranger.

After about ten minutes or so, they pulled onto a road that looked like it could accommodate one car at a time.

"The house on the right is mine," Zoe said, gesturing to

a homey-looking cottage with a thatched roof. Tea roses in shades of red and pink stood out against the white-washed exterior. An explosion of other flowers covered the postage stamp-sized lawn.

"It's beautiful," Pippa said. The flowers and the white picket fence combo reminded her of Yankee Hollow. She forced the thought down.

"Thanks. We've put a lot of effort into turning that junk heap around." There was an unmistakable note of pride in her voice.

Zoe eased the car onto another road, just before a small sign that read Teármunn Castle. The instant they made the turn, the ground grew uneven. It was rutted—so deep in some places that Pippa expected they wouldn't make it. After they passed a carved wooden sign labeled *Burke*, she realized they were on a private driveway.

"Where are we? The sign mentioned the castle, but this road—"

"Burke isn't into visitors and Teármunn isn't much of a castle. Not yet, anyway." Zoe pulled over to the side of the road and parked the car.

Pippa stared ahead, but all she could make out were trees. Lots of trees, with rays of light filtering through the branches. She had no idea where they were. Pippa had no choice but to follow Zoe.

Shoving open her door, she stepped out and onto the ground. Immediately, her boots sank three inches into the mud. Great. So much for her new boots. Disaster.

Gripping the side of the car for leverage, she tugged one foot free, barely escaping with her boot. Shaking as much of the sludge off as she could, she rounded the side of the car where she found Zoe waiting. Pippa's luggage sat on a patch of dry ground beside her.

"Here we are, Pippa. Come on," Zoe said, waving her on as she guided them from the gravel road and onto a wooden walkway partially hidden by trees. It was new—that much was obvious from its relatively unblemished texture. The wood glistened from the recent rain. Still, the sturdy surface gave Pippa the chance to shake off any loose mud from her shoes. As for her outfit, the whole thing was a mess. Mud trailed up the fronts of her jeans and had shifted the color of her boots from black to brownish gray.

Pippa hadn't planned on having to wheel her suitcase through the woods. Yet, that was exactly what she was doing, hoofing it down a path in the middle of nowhere. They trooped along for about a minute, before the trees opened up. Then Pippa halted in her tracks, taking it in.

"Holy crap!" She froze, her mouth dropping to form an O. Whatever she'd expected Finn Burke's home to be, it wasn't that.

The ocean lay spread out before her. No guard rails, no warning signs or protection. It was just *there*. To her left, on a raised bit of earth, sat the remains of a castle. Really, it was only a wall that had been recently rebuilt. More like a castle-in-progress than an actual *castle*.

"Please tell me that isn't where I'm staying." Pippa suppressed an eye roll as she jerked her head toward the ruins.

"There? You think you're staying *there*?" Zoe burst into laughter. "Come on, you."

Pippa gave one last look at the castle ruins before

following Zoe down the ramp and into the woods. The salty air kissed Pippa's lips as they walked. On and on they moved, until they reached another clearing. That one was a great deal larger, with tall trees surrounding it like ancient guardians.

Three large, round buildings sat at various points within the clearing, all joined by elevated wooden walkways. Each had a raised roof that reminded Pippa of a tepee. Lights blazed from the wide windows of one of the structures. Pippa glimpsed gleaming hardwood floors through the sheer curtains of the closest one.

White lights adorned a large gazebo in the center. They weren't lit. Though it was nearly eight o'clock, daylight didn't show signs of giving up any time soon. She could envision the place at night, however. Fireflies would play hide-and-seek among the trees, the glowing bodies of the little bugs flashing in the darkness. Burke's property was more appropriate for a wedding reception than a private home.

It was infinitely better than the castle, picturesque though it might have been. As her understanding of the full layout of the place began to take shape, she had to admit Burke's property was utterly charming and beyond cool.

"That will be your building," Zoe said, gesturing to one of the darkened units. "Why don't you leave your luggage outside the door? We'll go and meet Burke."

As Pippa parked her luggage outside her new door, she inspected the building. Vine-covered trellises hugged each window, giving the impression that a woodland princess lived behind its walls.

No, not a princess. Just her, Pippa.

Zoe led them from Pippa's cottage and down the walkway toward the lighted gazebo. A modest fountain spit water into the air, oozing tranquility. It made Pippa feel like she had to pee. They were only a few feet away when she spotted a man with short-cropped, brown hair sitting alone at a table inside the gazebo. His back was mostly to them, though there was enough of him in profile for Pippa tell he'd been chewing on that pen he'd jammed between his teeth.

Every once in a while, he'd stop to write something down on a piece of paper pinned under his laptop. Then he'd return to his typing, pounding his fingers furiously on the keyboard. Muscles lined his arms, and it was obvious from the way his shirt strained over his torso that he was ripped. He also had a full beard that screamed hipster, as Zoe had implied.

When he didn't acknowledge them, Pippa's stomach began to tie itself into a tight knot. That guy was going to be her boss for the summer? He looked kind of intense. Was he ignoring them on purpose? Maybe he was just antisocial. The Unabomber storyline ran through her mind again.

"Finn," Zoe called.

He didn't answer. He seemed like he either hadn't heard or didn't want to. His energy led Pippa to believe him capable of both.

"Wait here," Zoe said before climbing the steps to the gazebo and touching the man's arm. He jolted, as if woken from a dream, and then jumped to his feet. "Sorry, Zoe. I didn't hear you come up."

"Here I am, all the same. And I've brought Pippa," Zoe said, gesturing to where Pippa stood.

Then Finn Burke finally spun around, and she met the familiar, light green eyes of the MacBook guy from school.

Shit.

6

FINN

*"If you want praise, die. If you want blame, marry. That's what
Da always said."*
—Finn Burke, *Lost*

It had been a fine day. He'd gotten in a good run, followed by 750 words. That was an exceptional day for him. Most mornings, he'd sit at the keyboard and barely reach 500. At least that's how things had gone since *Amélie* had gone. She'd taken with her all of Finn's inspiration. *Shite* and all if he knew how to get it back.

And then he'd turned around and discovered that lunatic on his property—his new intern. "You," he said, his voice shifting to a growl. Before him stood the one who'd ruined everything. Who could still be the reason he didn't meet the September deadline Phillip had set for book two.

The woman stood straighter and forced her shoulders back. The action was so immediate, it seemed ingrained in her, as though she'd done it many times or practiced the posture in front of a mirror. She thrust a tiny hand in his direction. He glared at it but didn't accept.

They'd already met.

"Yes. Hi." She cleared her throat. "I'm Pippa Darling. I'm your summer intern."

He couldn't believe it. Not only did she recognize him, for it had registered instantly in those brown eyes of hers, but she acted as though nothing was wrong. As though she hadn't nearly ruined his life.

He scowled. "You're not. You've just been fired. You knocked my *feckin'* laptop over a railing. Get this woman out of my house."

"I'll do no such thing." Zoe crossed her arms in front of her chest.

"*Now*, Zoe." He expected Zoe's normally calm expression and found a thundercloud instead. Didn't she realize this woman had cost him a month's worth of work? Surely if she had, she wouldn't seem as pissed at Finn right then.

Pippa's mouth dropped open, her pink lips forming an O. "But you hired me."

Finn shrugged. "I'll be rescinding my offer, if it's all the same to you. You can stay the night, but you'll need to be leaving in the morning."

"Excuse me?" She jutted her chin out. "You can't do that. I need this internship. I'm not going anywhere."

Unbelievable. He stood and took two steps closer. Some sort of fancy perfume or body lotion tickled his nose—something with a flower in it, or possibly a fruit. Her toiletries were not his concern. She'd refused to leave, and Finn liked nothing better than a challenge when it suited him.

"Is that so? Well, if you won't go, then I'll carry you." He took another step toward her.

She thrust one of her impossibly small hands against his chest. "Like hell."

"If I want you gone, you'll be gone. This is private property. My property."

Pippa's cheeks flushed. First a pale pink, that switched to a red after cycling through every color in between.

"I'll pay your way home." Writers were usually poor—especially writers in college. He reached for his wallet.

"Listen," she said, holding out a hand to stop him. "I don't want your money. I want this internship."

"That's not possible," Finn said, reaching into his pocket anyway. "I don't need an employee who destroys thousands of dollars' worth of equipment in seconds. Especially ones who give themselves stupid pen names."

She locked her jaw. "Excuse me?"

Fine. If they were going to go there, she might as well have at least one lesson from him. "I mean"—he threw up his hands—"Pippa Darling? What kind of name is that anyway?"

Pippa glared at him, her eyes shooting daggers in his direction. "It's my name, jackass. My *real* name."

When she continued to stand there, tapping her foot, Finn's eyes widened. "*Jaysus*. I'm sorry. Really, I am." He tried to shift his facial expression so that he at least looked sincere. He'd probably managed a grimace at best.

"You have to hire me," Pippa said.

"Really, and why is that exactly?" It was Finn's turn to

cross his arms. She must have quite the explanation coming. This would be good.

"There's no way you'll be able to request another intern via *carrier pigeon* in time to get any work done. I mean, we *are* in the middle of nowhere—"

"I thought you were meant to be convincing me?" he asked.

"And," Pippa continued, as though he hadn't spoken, "classes have already ended for the semester."

"She's got a point there." Laughter filled Zoe's eyes, as she threw a sly look Finn's way. Cheeky neighbor.

Damn. The campus would be closed until mid-summer session. Even the offices had shut down. He wouldn't be able to get ahold of Dean Montgomery in time to contact a second choice. Hell, he hadn't even made a second choice.

He'd have no one working with him, and Finn had learned that he needed someone to keep him in line. Otherwise, he'd get lost in the tempting world of revisions and never get anything done.

He could ask Zoe. She'd helped him with *Lost*, after all. Still, she'd told him it would be a fine day in hell before she helped him again. He was too much of a "crabby bastard" for her.

"Even if you find a replacement, that'll take a couple weeks. You probably have a deadline. I'm betting you don't have a couple weeks to spare." Pippa stood, waiting, arms crossed over her compact body.

The same body that had slammed against his in the stairwell, shocking him into throwing his novel, encased in brushed aluminum, over the railing.

Shite. Finn shouldn't have been noticing her body. He shouldn't even have considered thinking of that moment. He was responsible for her—or he would have been if he'd decided to let her stay. Which he definitely hadn't.

"I can have someone else here by tomorrow morning."

"And who might that be, *Mr.* Burke?" Zoe cocked an eyebrow.

Traitor Zoe. "I know people. I can make it happen." He hoped. He'd been about to say more, some line designed to send Ms. Darling packing, but the words faded from his mind when he spotted something familiar jutting out of the side pocket of her bag. Without thinking, he reached forward and tugged it free. He turned the tattered copy of *To the Ends of the Earth* over, examining it.

His body had gone numb. He hadn't held a copy in years. Not since he was nineteen and it had shown up by special courier. With care, he opened the book, revealing the dedication he'd known would be there.

For Amélie, my moonlight. My everything.

Finn's throat ran dry. He'd tried to make himself forget and put it out of his mind, and then an entitled American showed up with a copy that looked as if she'd bludgeoned it and then backed over it with a tractor. If nothing else, it held promise as a good advertisement for Sellotape.

"It's my favorite book. By James Black. He's never written anything else. Just this one." Pippa stared at the book as Finn flipped through the pages. "It's out of print."

Yes. It was. And for good reason. He shoved the book into her waiting hands. "Looks like *bollocks* to me."

"Really?" Zoe asked, glaring. She was pissed—something he'd certainly hear about later. Either from her or Ma.

Pippa scowled, pursing her pink lips. "Excuse me, but I know good writing and this"—she shook the book in front of him, like an old granny telling him to get off her lawn—"this is *great* writing."

Finn stared at Pippa, flabbergasted. Was it possible she didn't know who he really was? True, people had never beat down doors to find James Black, but she seemed completely unaware of his dual identity. The right thing to do would be to tell her the truth, but the last thing he needed was to dredge up the past. Some things were too painful.

"If you say so." Those were all the words he could manage, anyway. No one he knew had ever felt that way about *To the Ends of the Earth* before. Even Amélie. *Especially* Amélie.

Pippa's eyes fought for his attention, drawing his thoughts from the book. She was trouble. A small smile tugged at the corner of his mouth. "You're very stubborn."

"So are you." She didn't smile in return.

Weariness washed over Finn, and he still had hours of work ahead of him. "Fine." He ran a hand through his hair. "We start at five a.m. Right here. Don't be late." Reaching into his pocket, he pulled out a key and tossed it to her.

By some miracle, Pippa caught it. "Thank you for the opportunity. Thanks, Zoe." Whirling away, she headed for her cabin, her boots making a clicking sound on the wooden walkway.

"Don't mention it," Zoe said. But as soon as Pippa had gone, she made a clucking sound, her mouth flattening to a disapproving line. "You weren't very nice to our Pippa."

Finn could yell at Zoe, could order her to leave. Technically, she worked for him, but she was also his friend, and his ma's friend, which meant she was family. "She destroyed my laptop, Zoe. Do you even know how much work I lost because of her?"

"Maybe it's a fitting punishment that she helps fix things. Ever think of that, *James*?" Zoe patted Finn on the shoulder. "Why didn't you tell her?"

He didn't need any further clarification to know what Zoe was referring to. "I've a right to my privacy, Zoe. There's a reason no one can link me to Black. I've seen to that."

Besides, he'd frozen at the sight of the book. It had once meant the world to him. Right then, he'd have been fine never laying eyes on the thing again.

"Then maybe it's time you either confronted him or buried him for good." Zoe turned away then, following the same path Pippa had taken, leaving him only with his thoughts and the roaring crash of the ocean.

The whole James Black issue aside, Pippa had spirit. He might actually enjoy working with her. Salvaging the internship would either be the smartest thing he'd ever done—or the stupidest.

7

PIPPA

*"The deepest loneliness comes only from crossing the line
between what we know and the unknown."*
—James Black, *To the Ends of the Earth*

ippa pushed open the door of her cabin. She
didn't need the lights on, but flicked the
switch anyway. A glaring overhead light shot on, bright
enough to illuminate an airport landing strip. The light
was entirely too bright for any time of day. She couldn't
imagine waking up to that.

The room was some sort of minimalist deal. It was
new, that much was obvious, but the gray floors and bare
walls were the opposite of inspiring. Like, if the terms
"modern prison cell" and "inspirational space" duked it
out, inspirational space wouldn't have stood a chance.

The cottage was small, circular—big enough for a twin
bed, a desk, and a puny dresser for her things—with
windows running along the top of the wall in a complete
circle, stopping before they reached the ceiling. They

were plentiful enough to let in light, but high enough that she couldn't see through them. There was no TV. She scanned her phone. There was a strong Wi-Fi signal. She'd be able to stream shows from the internet, at least.

The entire cottage almost sparkled with cleanliness. A faint lemon verbena scent filled the air.

Because of the almost-Spartan accommodations in the bedroom, Pippa didn't expect much from the bathroom. Yet, terracotta-colored tiles covered the floor and one wall of a glass-enclosed shower big enough for two, as if that were an option. Tall windows flanked the vanity overlooking the woods. Hopefully Finn didn't have any close neighbors. The last thing she needed was some perv peering in while she was showering.

There was also a large tub with what looked like jets. Her muscles twinged in response. Oh yeah, there was definitely a bath in her future. The tile continued there, running along the walls, forming an uneven surface that jutted out at random intervals. Despite the rocky start she'd gotten off to with Finn, the place had awesome potential.

Another door stood opposite the bed. Pippa tried the knob, and it opened with ease, revealing an illuminated hallway and a downward-winding, spiral staircase.

Forcing her worn-out legs to move, she took to the steps, following the stairs until she reached the bottom. Pippa gasped.

She stood inside an enormous underground room. If she'd taken the entire first floor of the B&B and doubled it, she could fit it all inside this space. Another spiral staircase stood at the opposite end of the room. She walked all the way to the end and glanced up through the steps. A closed door was all that awaited her up top.

Burke's room, possibly, or some other space. Backing down the steps, she inspected the room again.

Pine-colored flooring ran the length. Large desks bordered one wall. Another held a whiteboard bigger than Pippa's used Volkswagen back home. An enormous printer took up one corner. A long, fluffy-looking couch in tones of muted green filled another wall.

"Cool." The printer alone was a huge deal. Printing manuscripts on her little inkjet had always ended in disaster. A model like that one could probably issue hundreds of copies without breaking down.

Pippa spun in a circle, taking it all in. The space should've seemed cave-like, but it didn't. Four large skylights embellished the ceiling. Even on rainy days, the place would have exploded with natural light. The space above the room must have been the open area between Pippa's building, the gazebo, and possibly one of the other cottages she'd spotted when they'd first arrived.

Finn Burke might have been a jerk, but his house, compound, whatever he wanted to call it? Seriously cool. Maybe living and working there through the summer wouldn't be the hardship she'd been expecting.

She picked up her phone, thankful she'd paid extra for a plan with international calling. Within seconds, the sound of the phone dialing filled her ear as she climbed the steps back to her room.

"Yankee Hollow Bed and Breakfast, Jim speaking. How can I help?"

Warmth filled Pippa's soul at the sound of Dad's voice.

Ever since Mom died, they'd grown closer, not further apart. Guilt about not helping out that summer swept through her once more.

"Dad, it's Pippa. I'm here!"

"Pippa! Thank God. I was wondering if your flight had gotten in safely. Tell me everything. How is it?"

Pippa contemplated telling her father that Finn had already fired her, but she didn't want to give him hope that she'd be coming home early. "It's nice. Different. I'll send you some pictures of my cottage soon."

"Did you meet Mr. Burke yet?"

Oh yeah, she'd met Mr. Burke. But she wasn't ready for that line of questioning. "For a minute. I'll get to work more with him tomorrow."

"Do you think you're going to like him?" A bell rang on the other end of the line, signaling someone entering the B&B. She wouldn't have Dad's attention for long. It was the nature of the business. Sometimes guests had to come before family, or the family would find themselves without guests.

"Right now, I'm too tired to think about it. Can I call you tomorrow?"

"Of course you can, Sweetie. I'm just glad you got there safe. I love you, Pippa."

"I love you, too, Dad." She ended the call, but part of her heart remained with him.

By the time Pippa finally crashed, it was about ten o'clock at night. She would have gone to bed even earlier, but she'd taken a bath. The jetted tub had turned her legs to Jell-O.

After a quick text to Uma, Pippa stuck her phone on

mute, set the alarm, and went to bed. It wasn't her bed from home (a shame) or the one she slept in at school (a bonus), still it was more than comfortable. Not too hard, not too soft. Her eyelids slipped closed and she drifted to sleep.

Beep! Beep! Beep! A moment later, or what felt like it anyway, a loud beeping sound filled the room, sending Pippa's head pounding. Her eyelids shot open. "What the hell?" She jerked to a sitting position and stared at the clock. How could it be 4:45 already? She'd just gone to sleep.

She slammed her palm on the Snooze button. Blissful silence. Pippa then proceeded to spend at least five minutes staring at the numbers with suspicion, waiting for them to turn back. Why the hell did Finn Burke want her to meet him at five in the morning?

Grumbling, she picked out a pair of jeans and a light sweater. Fortunately, it was one of those mornings where her hair wasn't standing on end when she woke up. She tamed her chin-length tresses with her fingers and a comb. She reached for her makeup bag, and then decided against it. This was her summer vacation, or as close to one as she was going to get. She would be makeup free.

There. Ready to work.

Grabbing her hoodie and laptop bag, she opened the door to her cottage and stepped outside. The sun was just about to rise, and a wash of pinks and purples filled the horizon. The salt air hit her immediately, overpowering and calming at the same time. The sound of waves crashing filled her ears. Pippa followed the wet walkway, using the white lights she'd admired when she arrived to guide her. Wet leaves covered the glistening wood and Pippa had to take care not to slip.

Finn sat at the long table under the shelter of the gazebo, frowning as he sent his fingers traveling across the keyboard. He wore a hoodie with the Morris logo on it. It was like the one she'd grabbed from her room, though his was older, more tattered. A chunk had gone missing from the right wrist, like he'd gotten hungry and bitten off a piece.

Curiosity hummed through her. She wanted to know more about the land, the castle, all of it. Chances of Finn speaking to her, let alone responding to any queries she might have, however, seemed slim. With care, she navigated the slick steps, relieved to find the chairs had escaped the fate of the wooden walkway. She chose one opposite Finn, then took a seat on the dry surface.

He didn't look up. The sound of crickets and the stray hoot of an owl competed for attention with the crash of waves against the shore. As Pippa waited to be acknowledged, she scanned the area around them. All woods.

Had Finn been out there working in the dark? How could he stand being in the open like that? If Pippa had been outside on her own, at night, she would have been imagining a million eyes trained on her. Heck, she already was.

Finn still hadn't spoken. She set her bag on the table, shrugged into her own hoodie, and zipped it. Then she took out her notebook, opening it to the first page.

Sliding a pen from the pen holder inside her bag, she wrote *INTERNSHIP NOTES* at the top of the page. There, she was ready for her first day on the job.

"Do you plan on making a habit of being late to work?" Finn popped his head up from behind the laptop, his eyes narrowing.

She'd jumped when he'd spoken, but after taking a slow breath, she glanced at her cell phone. "You told me 5:00. It's 4:58. I've been here for a minute already."

"Early is on time. On time is late," he muttered as he returned to his typing.

"Which would mean I'm still on time."

"In your dreams."

Five after butt crack in the morning and he was already getting on her case. That guy had to be the biggest asshole on the planet. She scanned the gazebo. Where was the coffee? An empty teacup rested on the table next to Finn's laptop.

Tea. But where was the coffee?

She could risk asking him, but he'd probably protest and call it a coffee break.

"Do you have something you'd like me to do?" she asked, willing herself not to get fired again. "Or did you bring me out here before dawn to complain about my alleged inability to tell time?" Oops. She shouldn't have said that.

"Don't talk to me when I'm writing, Darling." His voice sounded even, despite his abrupt words. She couldn't help but remember the haunting green of his eyes. Pippa couldn't see them anymore, though. They were hidden behind a laptop and a bad attitude.

"Here we are." Pippa jumped as Zoe came bustling into the gazebo, wearing a purple fleece and a matching scarf. "Morning tea."

Oh God, really? Tea? "Zoe?" Pippa swallowed, feeling terrible. "Is there any . . . coffee?"

"Entitled American. You think you're owed everything." Finn spat this out, even as he accepted his tea from Zoe with a smile. "Thank you."

"Anytime." Zoe patted Finn's cheek.

"Excuse me. The last time I checked, you went to school in America," Pippa said. Oops. There she was, already telling her new boss off again, and she was three minutes and twelve seconds into the job.

Finn's eyebrows furrowed. "You're fired. Get your things. Zoe can take you to the bus station."

Zoe let out a massive sigh and planted her palms on the table. "You can't keep firing her every time she puts you in your place. If you do, it's going to be a long summer." Zoe scolded him, but at the same time kept her tone motherly, warm.

Finn's green eyes darkened. "It's not your business, Zoe."

"You know I'm right. And how happy do you think that fancy agent fellow of yours is going to be if you push back on your deadline? Again?" Zoe crossed her arms, positioning herself at an angle beside Pippa.

A tiny ball of warmth blossomed in Pippa's chest. She had an ally.

He shook his head, his eyes locking onto Pippa's in such a way that it sent shivers through her. "She stays." He thrust a finger toward Pippa. "But be punctual."

Pippa scowled in response. They were back to that again? "I was—"

His unrelenting glare silenced Pippa's protest. They were close in age, but he acted more like a temperamental old codger than a hot, twenty-something writer. "Fine. Thank you for the second chance. Sir." She suppressed the urge to salute him.

Finn's lips twitched, and for a sec she thought he might laugh, but he faced the laptop instead. "Good. Glad we're in agreement."

Zoe snorted. "Now that you two have made up. I'll be happy to bring you some coffee, Pippa, but be warned. This one"—she jerked her thumb at Finn—"doesn't believe in coffee. He claims it taints the body with evil."

Pippa partially rolled her eyes, stopping mid-roll. She'd almost gotten fired, after all. "If you could point me toward the body-tainting coffee, I can make it."

"Nonsense. How do you take it?" Zoe asked, bouncing on her heels as she waited for Pippa's reply.

"Black." Pippa didn't bother to suppress her grin. Beautiful, wonderful coffee—balm for the writer's soul— exactly what she needed to turn her already disastrous day around.

"Excellent. You're a lovely, low maintenance sort of house guest." Zoe's rich, warm laugh dug into her gut as she strolled away into the dark woods.

"Are you ready to do some real work? Or are you going to keep pissing around on my dime?" Finn stared directly at Pippa, perhaps for the first time that morning. His eyes were focused on her, his dislike clearly visible, as he sipped his tea.

She refused to let her temper take over. "What can I do?"

"For starters, you can—" His eyes flickered over the screen of his MacBook and he froze, gripping the sides. "Don't do this to me. Please don't do this." He stood, jamming his hands into his hair. "Don't 'effing do this!"

"What is it?" Pippa jumped to her feet, peering around his shoulder in time to catch the pop-up window on his screen. The too-bright square announced Finn's file had corrupted and would be closing. "Oh, I'm sorry."

Finn gripped fistfuls of his hair as if he meant to pull it out. "You should be. You're the one who made this happen!"

"Me?" This guy was a lunatic. Certifiable.

"You talked to me. With you distracting me, I forgot to save everything." He slammed his body into the chair, his eyes narrowing in a look of disgust.

Before she could offer up an epic retort, he moved to reopen the file.

"Don't!" She thrust out her hands, palms up. "Don't touch that file."

"Don't you be telling me don't. It's my laptop." He moved for the touchpad again.

"Your writing software crashed. I might be able to get the file back and save your work, but if you open it now, you may lose your changes."

Again, those eyebrows of his peaked across his brow. "Yeah?"

His expression seemed so hopeful, it reminded Pippa of a little boy's. Of course, if she botched things, he could end up firing her, *again*. If she salvaged his work, however, things between them had a chance of improving. They certainly couldn't get any worse. "Trust me. I've been there. I almost lost a ton of work last year when this exact same thing happened to me. I've picked up a few things."

His eyes bored into hers. It was as if he was somehow seeing straight into her soul. After a moment, he stepped away from the laptop and shoved his hands into his pockets. "Then earn your pay, Miss Darling." He stepped back to allow Pippa access—trusting, considering he blamed her for the destruction of his last machine. "If you do anything to my work, I'll leave you in the woods for dead."

Okay, not so trusting, then.

"Thanks." She took his seat at the table and let out a slow breath. His desktop was littered with dozens of documents. Most of the titles had been cut off. She opened Finder instead and browsed his desktop files there. Only one file, *Untitled*, had been modified that day. Pippa opened a blank document and chose the File and Open options. Mentally crossing her fingers, she chose Open and Repair from the drop-down list and waited.

Finn tensed beside her, his knuckles white against his cracked red teacup.

The file opened. Thank goodness for that. Using a series of shortcuts, she highlighted all the text, copied it, and then pasted everything into a new document. "This file only has 900 words in it." Was he working on an earlier version of the book? Where was the rest?

Finn cocked an eyebrow. "900 words I've lost because you've cursed me with your presence."

Pippa rolled her eyes as she saved the file with the title,

followed by the current date in the name. "Never mind. I'm sorry I asked." Pippa stood up, backing away from the table. "Here you go. You're all set."

Finn's eyes widened. "You're serious?"

"Yep. It's right here." She gestured to the file she'd just created. "I saved it under the same name with today's date in the title. It will make finding your files a little easier if you name them that way."

A huge smile lit Finn's face, transforming him from his crab-ass self into someone almost . . . pleasant. He set his cup on the table. "You're joking."

"Nope." Pippa smiled, too. It was hard not to at the sight of his obvious relief. "If you work from this copy, you should be good."

Finn stared at Pippa as though she'd reached into the sky and dragged down a star. Before she realized what might happen, Finn grabbed her hand, tugged her toward him, and crashed his lips down upon hers.

8

FINN

"Women torture us weak-minded men. We're pansy-asses."
—Finn Burke, *Lost*

*I*f he'd been pulled into an interrogation room, he'd never have been able to explain it. How one moment he stood in front of Pippa Darling and the next he was kissing her as if his life depended on it. But she'd saved his file, his work from that morning. After all of the rewriting he'd had to do after losing his laptop, he'd been overcome with relief.

And then all he could think about was Pippa. She tasted of honey and something darker that he couldn't define, but he wanted to. He ran his tongue along her bottom lip, and she opened her mouth against the sensation, finding his tongue, meeting it with hers in slow, tentative movements. She slid her hands around his neck. Finn groaned as he deepened the kiss.

It had been so long since he'd kissed someone. Too

long. From the way Pippa's lips met his own, it must have been a long time for her, as well.

Or was he acting like an overbearing *arse*, kissing his intern on the first day. Kissing her *at all*. *Jaysus*.

Drawing on all his resolve, he broke the kiss, taking two steps back. Pippa staggered, almost losing her balance. He gripped her upper arms to steady her, and then jerked his hands away as though he'd been stung. What had he been thinking kissing her?

Easy. He hadn't been thinking at all.

"I'm sorry. That was . . ." He released his breath in one long stream as he tried to find other words. The ones he needed to make things right. But just like the words he couldn't capture for his second book, they evaded him then, too. "That shouldn't have happened."

Pippa locked eyes with Finn, pinning him in place with her hooded gaze. As if they were both trapped. Both unable to shatter the tension hanging between them like the close Florida air.

"Here you are, Pippa. A nice, piping hot cup of coffee." Zoe bustled into the gazebo with a tray containing a carafe and mug.

Pippa's cheeks turned pink, and she tore her eyes from Finn's to accept the tumbler of coffee. "Um . . . thank you so much." She drank from the cup even as a flush rose on her neck.

A flush he had put there.

"If you show me where the coffeemaker is, I can make it in the mornings." Pippa kept her eyes downcast.

Zoe waved her away. "Nonsense. It's no bother at all to make up some coffee while I'm brewing tea for this *shite* over here." She gestured to Finn, throwing him a glare as she passed by.

Feck. She'd seen. And his ma would hear all about it. One phone call from Zoe and Lila Burke would be calling him.

He wasn't certain he even liked Pippa Darling. He liked parts of her. Like her mouth—that sweet little mouth that'd met his, again and again. Of course, he wasn't sold on that same feature when she used it to argue with him.

"But I did put a coffeemaker in your room, with some supplies. Us coffee drinkers have to stick together." Zoe smiled at Pippa before turning to Finn in a salute. "Happy writing."

Finn nodded, still wordless and unable to do any more than stare at Pippa. It mattered little how her kiss had tasted, or even how her body had felt, pressed against his own. She was his employee. She was working for him. He couldn't put either of them in any more of an uncomfortable position than they were already in.

"That shouldn't have happened, Pippa. I'm sorry, I—" He broke off. She had this rumpled, tired look to her. One that made him want to sweep her off her feet and take her to bed. She'd made his body burn. That unsettled him. "You're working for me. I want it known that I'm not expecting anything from you. I just—"

He was making a bungling mess of it all. *Feck.* He didn't see how he could possibly make it worse. She was well within her rights to pack up and leave that very day.

"I understand. You were excited that I was able to save your manuscript. It's okay. We writers are passionate."

She took another sip of Zoe's coffee, closing her eyes for a moment. Recalling their kiss—no savoring the caffeine, more like. "I would have done the same."

Finn couldn't help the grin that spread across his face. "You would have? Well, that'd be something to remember."

Pippa stiffened, her face reddening even further.

Finn cleared his throat. No more of that. It was time he got to work. Phillip's damn deadline wouldn't meet itself. "Do you think you can print off a copy of this manuscript? I'll be wanting you to start reviewing it, but we'll talk about that later."

"Yeah. Which printer should I print to?" She gestured to his laptop, all business again, the way he should have been. She picked up her notebook and pen, poising utensil over paper.

He rounded the table to point it out, but the instant he'd come within inches of her, memories of her kiss assaulted him. It would have been so easy to catch those sweet pink lips in his again . . .

Pippa's breath caught from somewhere beside him. If he could just . . . *bollocks*. He would show her a few things, and then he would deliberately put distance between them. He had to. It would be the only way he'd survive the summer.

He moved in close, taking care not to touch her. He had no cause to be touching Pippa Darling ever again. "Right here," he said, gesturing to one of the two printer icons. "This is the downstairs printer. The other is in my office."

"Got it." She didn't move. Instead, she gripped her

coffee cup white-knuckled, as though it were the elixir of life. "Is there anything else you need me to do? Get the mail? Answer your email? Stuff like that?"

"There's no mail service here. I have to go to town to pick it up. I'll take you there this week. For now, this would be good."

"Got it." She nodded, her back still ramrod straight as she scribbled notes in that pad of hers.

"I'm knackered. I'm going to take a shower and then have a lie down." More like he'd be taking a cold shower. *Jaysus*.

"But why did you have me get up so early if you were going back to bed?" She sputtered out the question, her mouth frowning into a near-pout. Not a full one. Pippa Darling wasn't one for feminine wiles, he could tell that already. At least not intentional ones. No, she preferred to share every thought that entered her head rather than play at mystery.

"Back to bed? *Shite* and all. I never went *to* bed." He snatched his teacup from the table, downed the rest of the once-hot liquid, and then set it back on the tabletop. "This here is your time to write. Work on your stuff. I'll critique for you after I wake up—around eleven. Then you can do the same for me."

"Oh, okay. Sure." Her entire face flamed, her skin tinged with a most flattering shade of pink. It gave him more than a little satisfaction to know he'd put it there.

"Later, Darling," he said, before turning and heading back to his lodgings. That woman and that kiss. Damn it all, it would be a long summer. If Pippa Darling didn't cause the death of him first.

9

PIPPA

"I search inside myself, past the flaws which mar my soul, to the deepest feelings within."
—James Black, *To the Ends of the Earth*

*P*ippa didn't like Finn Burke. She detested his morbid, dark writing that made her want to throw his book across the room, kick a puppy, and drink an entire bottle of vodka in one go.

But, somewhere in the space of a second since he'd first brought his lips to hers, that dislike dimmed.

The coarse whiskers of his beard had scratched her chin and tickled her lips, leaving behind the sensation that she'd been branded. Before she'd met him, she'd imagined Finn to be some tortured, miserable recluse. But after spending minutes in his presence, she'd glimpsed his energy, his passion. There was a gentle streak in Finn Burke, too. She'd felt it in his kiss. Swift and intense, yet .. . tender. He would never hurt her. That much she knew.

No one had ever kissed her like that. Not Branden, her

high school boyfriend. Definitely not the shortlist of guys she'd dated in college. Not even Zack—her recent friend-turned-nothing crush.

She shouldn't have enjoyed Finn's kiss. Yet her fingers kept moving to her lips, remembering.

Of course, she'd expected the first words out of Finn's mouth to be some excuse. Some proclamation that their kiss shouldn't have happened. Instead, he'd stared at her as though she'd slapped him, not kissed him back. *Then* he'd apologized and claimed it shouldn't have happened.

She sipped her coffee. Hopefully, the caffeine would wind clarity and some long-forgotten common sense into her brain.

It took no time at all to print Finn's manuscript. It was unfinished, after all. She collected the pages from the printer, making a mental note that they were low on paper, and then closed his laptop. With Zoe's coffee pumping through her veins, she was less zombie and more Pippa.

The gazebo really was a sweet setup. It had a fridge, outdoor power, and comfy chairs. She'd spotted rolled tarps tucked tidily along the inside ceiling and a standup heater. She'd lay odds Finn worked outside all year round.

The sun peeked over the trees, layering the gazebo and the surrounding lawn in varying patches of gold. Birds chirped as they dive-bombed the ground for worms. There were no other sounds. No neighbors. No cars. No civilization. It was as if the gazebo was her own private island. She was untouchable there. At least by anyone but Finn.

God, *Finn*.

What was wrong with her?

Pippa was acting like Finn's kiss meant something. It didn't. He'd gotten caught up in the moment. It was just that Pippa didn't think stuff like that happened in real life, only in her head.

It was silly to think he'd kissed her because he was into her.

And the way his eyes lit when she'd tried to tell him it was okay, that she would have done the same . . . had he been imagining a scenario in which she'd kiss him first?

Come on, Pippa. Enough fooling around.

He'd given her an assignment. He wanted her to write. Pippa's jet-lagged brain couldn't remember where she'd left off, so she pulled up her notes and opened her working file.

"Oh, shit." The chapter she needed to write was a sex scene. "Really?"

And if she had to pick out the only memorable thing in Finn Burke's writing, it was his sex scenes. They were mesmerizing, all consuming. A lot like the man himself.

Memories of Finn standing behind her as he'd helped her find the printer flooded her mind. His breath had whispered along her neck. She'd tensed, waiting for his lips to brush her skin. They hadn't.

Holy inferno of awkwardness.

She'd *kissed* her boss and she liked it. A lot. A lot, a lot. She should try to avoid him. Maybe even quit. That would've been the responsible thing.

But no. The honest-to-God truth was, she didn't want to do any of those things. Regardless of what a black hole his books were. She was in Ireland. She had an amazing internship. And she'd liked the kiss, welcomed it. How could she blame him for his reaction when hers was just as questionable?

Pushing him out of her mind, she turned her attention to her work. That morning's chapter was a love scene between Jake and Cassidy, her two main characters. She used to love writing their story, but lately they hadn't been cooperating. Their relationship seemed *forced*. She couldn't pin them down, no matter what tact Pippa took. It would be their first love scene—at least if she stuck to her careful plotting.

The birds' chattering filled her ears and sent her head pounding. Shoving in her earbuds, she queued up her playlist and sat back against the chair, fingers poised. Time to write.

Jake and Cass. They'd kiss first. She just needed to focus on writing one part of the scene at a time. The kiss. Some boob action. Some clothing removal. No need to write a love scene in the vein of Finn Burke, where his characters engaged in some kinky, X-rated moves Pippa couldn't even think about without blushing. Besides, she couldn't imagine trying something like that, what with the whole closed-door, fade-to-black approach to love scenes in so many young adult books.

Besides, this wasn't Finn's love scene. It was hers. She needed to write it her way, in her voice. But it didn't help that her mind kept reverting to images of Finn's kiss, to memories of his lips on hers. Unbidden, she recalled the first sex scene in Finn's own book. Okay, maybe all of the people *were* unhappy, but that scene? His characters needed to be together—they were *past* ready.

That sent her mind churning. Huh. Maybe the reason Pippa couldn't write a sex scene was that her characters weren't ready to . . . *do the deed*? God. She blushed at her own internal monologue. When had she become such a prude? It wasn't like she hadn't had sex. She'd been raised to be smart about sex, not ashamed of it.

But maybe there was something to the whole not ready angle—as in the scene should be a kiss, and not sex? But a kiss could be as hot as sex.

Finn's kiss had been. Heat rushed into her face. Heck, yes, it could be that hot.

Setting down her coffee, Pippa began typing. The pages unfolded before her as if a movie played out in her mind. She pushed forward, shoving her cowardice aside to finish the chapter. Her fingers wouldn't move fast enough. And if Jake's actions mimicked Finn's a little too closely, it was a coincidence. If Finn wanted to read something into her words, then that was his prerogative.

Several hours passed before she collapsed back against her chair, creatively spent. She'd need to read through everything she'd just written, but first, coffee.

She refilled her cup and returned to the pages in front of her. As Pippa began reading her work, pride surged into her. She'd written a solid scene. Thank God. She'd finally started to figure out her characters.

10

FINN

*"She was quite a ride, and she kept me up half the night
imagining her—in my bed."*
—Finn Burke, *Lost*

*H*e'd tried to sleep. Perhaps the trouble came in
the fact that he couldn't get those lips of
Pippa's out of his mind, or the way they'd moved over his.
Christ, it had been too long since he'd been with a
woman. Wasn't it just his luck that one had moved under
his roof, sporting a foul temper and a hot body to boot?
Jaysus. It would be the hardest summer yet. In more ways
than one.

He climbed the steps to the gazebo, tea in hand. He
didn't bother to hide the scowl he knew filled his face.
There was nothing for it. He kept to his schedule whether
he got sleep or not. As Da had always said, you call off
work when you're dead.

One look at Pippa and Finn knew he hadn't yet died.

She sat in front of her own laptop, fingers pounding

on the keys as though she couldn't pull the words out of her brain fast enough. Tiny earbuds poked out of her delicate ears. Pippa could only be described as a petite thing. He'd had to bend down to kiss her.

Next time, he'd be sure to pick her up, so he didn't get a crick in his neck. Wait. Next time? Christ almighty, there wouldn't be a next time.

Get a handle on yourself, Burke.

Reaching into a storage cabinet, Finn freed a bottled water from the small wine fridge stashed on one of the shelves before digging out his electric kettle. When he stood, Pippa jumped with a squeal.

She tugged her earbuds free. "I didn't see you."

"So it would seem. Morning." Finn shook his head as he added the cold bottled water to the kettle and plugged it into one of the outlets. He'd done everything he could to give the gazebo all of the comforts of home. He loved the outdoors—the way the wind whistled through the trees, the crash of the waves on sand. Sitting in the gazebo and writing each day was a gift. One he remembered to appreciate daily. "How's it been going?"

Pippa stood and stretched. The hem of her sweater rode up, exposing a slice of too-pale skin. He had to fight to keep himself from staring.

"I got a whole chapter done. I like working out here." She sounded surprised.

The kettle shut off, so Finn added a ball of imported tea leaves to an insulated tumbler and poured the boiling water overtop it. Ma would have been on him for drinking the fancy tea, but some indulgences were worth it. "You've never worked outside?"

"No. Maybe once or twice." She lowered her laptop lid and poured more coffee from the carafe Zoe'd left her.

He set the wind-up timer on the cabinet top for five minutes and they sat in silence while the brew steeped. Pippa stared off in the direction of the sea, the wind lifting a few stray strands of her hair.

Once the timer beeped, Finn removed the ball of tea leaves and added a pinch of sugar along with a generous helping of milk into the tumbler before stirring the mixture. He capped the container and took a long, scalding drink that bordered on burning his tongue. Ah, just right.

"Milk? In tea?" Pippa wrinkled her nose.

Finn snorted. Where had this woman come from? He couldn't help but feel bad for her. An American, on Irish soil. Clearly, she'd be needing an education. "Let me guess, you take it weak and overloaded with sugar? *American.*"

Her entire face changed, she held out both hands, as though she'd just caused an international incident. "Sorry. I didn't mean to offend you."

"Sure you did." He shot her a grin.

Again, shock registered on her face. "I didn't realize you had a . . ." She tossed him a puzzled frown.

Perhaps she was attempting to edit her words before setting them free? Either way, Finn, who normally liked silence, found himself wanting to know. "A what?" he asked. "A sense of humor?"

A small smile crossed her smart face. "A *teasing* side."

"Ah, I suppose I deserve that. I'll have you know I have many sides. You've already seen several of them." *Bollocks.* Doing a great job of not bringing up their kiss, he was.

"Look, I really am sorry about before. The kiss. I was sleep deprived and very relieved, but rest assured it won't happen again."

"Oh, I'd forgotten about that." Yet she rested two fingers against her lips, as though remembering his mouth on hers. *Christ.*

"So I can see." He forced his smile away and settled at the table with his tea. "Now let me see what you've been working on while I've been catching up on my beauty sleep." He held out his hand for her laptop, waiting. "Give me the chapter you just wrote."

Again, she hesitated. He had been known to be a moody bastard at times. Maybe she was worried about getting his feedback. That was understandable. Most people seemed to expect a glowing review every time.

The old expression always went, *The devil is in the details*. To Finn, the devil was in people's expectations. They spent so much time drumming things up in their minds, that the outcome could only be a disappointment.

"You don't want to start from chapter one?" she asked, reddening.

"Chapter ones are always tough. I'd rather start in the middle or somewhere and work my way backward."

Pippa avoided his eye as she handed over her laptop. "These are the pages I wrote this morning."

Finn nodded, taking another swig of his tea, the anticipation buzzing through him. "Okay. Any problem if I start a few chapters back? To get a sense of the characters?"

She shook her head. "Go for it. I'll take anything you want to give me."

Finn's eyes locked onto hers, holding them for a

moment. Either she had a talent for double entendres or for putting her foot in her mouth. He couldn't be sure yet. Finn turned his attention to the document before him.

Once he'd positioned the cursor where he needed it, about two chapters ahead of where she'd shown him, he began to read. Pippa's prose was strong, for the most part. The only problem was the characters. They had the emotional depth of a teaspoon. The last chapter she'd written, that morning's project, was a kissing scene. Interesting. It didn't spark so much as a hard-on with him. He read:

> Jake slid his hands through Cassidy's hair, gripping a section of the strands at the root. "You're every dream I've ever had. And if this is a dream, I don't want to wake up." He slid his mouth over hers. His mind and body exploded with want and he pulled her close against him.

What the devil kind of *shite* was that? Finn wasn't much into reading romance, but he knew a few things about women. That sort of thing wouldn't work. Bending over the keyboard, he made more suggested edits.

> Jake slid his hands through Cassidy's hair, gripping a section of the strands at the root. **Sounds like he's a caveman. Women don't get horny by having their hair yanked. Soften this. Example: Jake slid his hands through Cassidy's hair, the pads of his thumbs grazing that sensitive point on her scalp, above where her head dipped down to the nape of her neck. Also, slow the scene down—the pacing's too fast.**

"You're every dream I've ever had. And if this is a dream, I don't want to wake up." **Bollocks. What guy utters shit like that? Example: *'I want to fuck you.'***

He slid his mouth over hers. His mind and body exploded with want and he pulled her close against him. **What does that mean? Are her panties wet or what? Show us her need.**

Finn continued marking up the manuscript. Pippa wouldn't like it. They never did. Each of his interns had pranced in, expecting nothing but the glowing reviews they'd gotten from their MFA program mentors. Finn, however, didn't believe in lying. Writers didn't need falsehoods. They needed guidance.

Finally, Finn slid the laptop away from him and stood. "Okay. It's all yours."

Pippa had been biting that bottom lip of hers. She was nervous, just as all the others had been.

"Should I read this now?" she asked, sliding the machine toward her.

"Sure. That's part of what this experience is all about. You write. I critique. We talk. You *grow*." He waved his hands with a flourish. He hated corporate jargon and the like, but the truth was, he found himself plain exhausted and far too frustrated with the quality of Pippa's writing. The *shite* she'd given him didn't come close to touching the short story that had won her the internship in the first place. Writers had rough patches, though. He was smart enough to realize that morning's work could be part of one for Pippa.

Pippa nodded and leaned forward, a wrinkle forming

on her brow. He sipped his tea as he waited for her to start shouting. She didn't disappoint.

"I want to fuck you? Really?" she asked, her voice spiking.

"What?" Finn shrugged and took a long drink of tea as he positioned himself against the gazebo railing. "That's what a guy would say."

"This is a young adult book." Pippa's hands seemed to have glued themselves to her hips. She sure was ready for a fight.

"So? I know what I was thinking about when I was a bloody teenager. Why beat around the bush?" Finn smirked. "Course, I guess that's the point. He wants to beat the bush. Get it?"

Shut up, Burke. Now.

She slapped her palm against her forehead. "I thought you were going to give me *real* feedback. I can't waste time on . . . this."

He should have fired her. That would've made the most sense. Clearly, they wouldn't work well together, but he couldn't help his own curiosity. Pippa Darling intrigued him, and when something interested him, he paid attention and saw it through.

Finn stood straighter, abandoning the railing, and set his cup on the wooden tabletop. "This *is* real feedback." He gestured to the laptop and Pippa's marked up work in progress. "Exaggerated, possibly, but my point is that if a man wants a woman, he's not going to grab her hair. He's not going to say things like, 'If this is a dream, I don't want to wake up.' If you're going to write male characters, make them *men*. It doesn't matter if their seventeen or twenty-seven."

Excitement had begun to spark within him. He could help strengthen Pippa's writing. That was certainly something he could do—something he was very good at. No, he wouldn't fire her. It would be far more interesting to watch how Pippa Darling's internship played out.

*"In such swift meetings and partings, we drift past one another
—close enough to touch, yet far enough to dream."*
—James Black, *To the Ends of the Earth*

*P*ippa couldn't see anything but an ugly, red haze that clouded her vision. Her temper whipped through her like a snake. She searched her brain for something she could possibly say that wouldn't get her fired, but come on!

I want to fuck you? That had been the amazing Finn Burke's earth-shattering literary critique? She'd come to Ireland hoping to approach the experience with an open mind, to give Burke and his lousy writing the benefit of the doubt, and he'd already proved that a lost cause.

Finn must've read how pissed off she was, because the smirk slid from his face. "I'm meaning no disrespect, but this scene, it's forced. Show us what they're feeling, thinking, or if they aren't capable of thinking. A good love scene like this should . . ." Finn took a step toward Pippa.

His scent, soapy with an undercurrent of pine, filled her nostrils.

"A good love scene should evoke the physical as well as the emotional. If you can elicit some sort of physical reaction in a reader, you know it's a good sex scene."

"It's not a sex scene yet." She cleared her throat, as though she'd forgotten how to speak. "Just kissing."

"Kissing is . . . foreplay. It should make the reader want sex as much as the character does." His voice, the Irish lilt to it, combined with its timbre, sent chills skating across her skin.

"But I don't know how to do that," Pippa said.

"Think about it from your characters' perspectives. Maybe he doesn't say . . . 'I want to fuck you, Cassidy.' Maybe he says, 'Do you know how much I want you?'"

Oh. My. God.

Pippa's heart slammed against her rib cage, erasing every conscious thought with its cadence. Finn was going to kiss her again.

He couldn't kiss her again.

God, he has to kiss me again.

With him standing so close, fresh memories of their kiss raged to life. It was wrong. He was her mentor. He should never have kissed her. True, she wasn't some green college freshman being taken advantage of. She was a woman, and it wasn't like Finn had been her first kiss.

"See what I mean?" Before she could process his words, he stepped back and took another sip of tea.

"Excuse me?" she asked. Had ten buckets of cold water just been dumped on her? God. He was such an asshat.

Finn, however, didn't seem to be bothered in the

slightest, one eyebrow quirked as he waited for her answer. "Your scene. Does that help?"

Pippa had to work to even her breathing before she answered. "I'll have to think about it."

"Good." He seemed to have been expecting that answer. "Oh, and just to improve your accuracy for when you do your rewrites. I used more tongue than that when I kissed you." He tapped the laptop screen for emphasis, smirking.

Horror flooded Pippa. "That scene . . . had absolutely nothing to do with you." Her voice morphed into high-strung mode. She wasn't convincing anyone.

"Whatever you say, Darling." He winked.

Oh my, God! I just died.

Ugh. He really was a piece of work.

12

FINN

"The bitch was after my money."
—Finn Burke, *Lost*

inn was having the worst writing day of his life. For starters, he was bone tired. Losing sleep over Pippa Darling cost him, just as losing his laptop in a stairwell accident had. He kept trying to rewrite the scene he'd written the day Pippa destroyed his laptop. But no matter how he approached it, he couldn't recreate the same energy he'd had from that first draft.

When an email came over from Phillip, reminding Finn that he still hadn't seen a single page of book two, well . . . that just made it. Phillip had a unique gift Finn was certain all literary agents possessed. He had the ability to make Finn feel guilty without saying a word. That took skill. Phillip had it in spades.

Then, *Herself* had taken a seat across from him, with *his* pages and *her* little red pen, to give him her feedback. He'd asked her for high-level comments only, but he couldn't help noticing that she'd taken to writing an awful lot. He was no stranger to feedback, but that many notes . . .

There had to be millions of them, all written in her tidy hand. She even had a schedule for when she'd review each group of pages. It was all mapped out in that notebook of hers.

He gritted his teeth, forcing his attention from Pippa. Yet, the more she wrote, the more his temper built. On and on, she noted her thoughts in red ink, that little minx. Finn hadn't written a word. He hadn't realized that he'd taken to staring until she rested pen on paper.

She jerked her head, her brown eyes locking onto his. "What? What's wrong?"

"Nothing," he said. "Just thinking."

Pippa's face reddened, as though she could imagine just fine what he'd been thinking. She cleared her throat, a little *huh-huh* sound that seemed fairy-like on its own. If he didn't know better, he'd think Pippa Darling had a place among the Good People, as the fairies of folklore were known in Ireland.

She slid the pen behind her ear. "Do you want my feedback now or later?" Irritation coated her voice. He couldn't be sure if the reason was the writing or himself. It seemed a safer bet to go with both.

"Now's fine." He extended his hand, accepted the papers, and plopped the pages onto his lap. He immediately found himself blinded by a sea of red. *Jaysus.* What was all that about? He tore through the contents, notes jumping off the page.

Not enough emotion. This is a big deal. What is she feeling?

Women don't think like that. I've never heard women compare penis length in church.

This is so cold. What can you do to make these people more real?

Finn snapped his head up, throwing the papers onto the table with a thwack. "What the hell is this? I said high level."

Pippa frowned. "It *is* high level." She sipped her coffee, pretty as you please, with no more than a cock of an eyebrow to show for her impertinence.

"It's *bollocks*. That's what it is. *Bollocks* and lies!" Finn smacked the table for emphasis.

"Look. You write what you want, but I'm telling you, real women don't think like this." She tapped his manuscript for emphasis. "If you want to write from a woman's point of view, then you'd better make it real. Unless you want to write porn."

The pressure in Finn's chest grew with each passing second. She'd gotten his Irish up and all on the first day of work. The last thing he needed to do was unleash his temper. For words, once said, were something he could never take back. "Of course I'm not after writing pornography. I'm a Catholic." Or he was on Christmas, anyway. Most years.

She rolled her eyes as she stood, taking one, two, three steps toward him. "Real women don't want to be told what to feel, how to act. Women want to be heard. They want to talk." Damned if she didn't take his hand in hers, sliding her thumb across his palm, staring up at him through hooded eyes. "They want *all* the right words."

The scent of her pervaded his nostrils—something

floral, musky, and one hundred percent woman. Pippa dropped his hands, pivoting in a flash to return to her coffee. When she turned toward him, a smirk covered her face. Damn it to hell. He'd been played. Played at his own game by Pippa Darling, and very well, he might add.

"Fine." Finn had to work to make the word come out at all. He drained his teacup, for fortitude. "Just so you know, this is all your fault. Every last word of it."

"What are you talking about? I didn't write that. You did."

"After you destroyed my laptop. Do you know when I got my new one back, half of the book was there? I've got an agent breathing down my neck and a deadline on September first that I don't know if I can meet. Tell me whose fault this is now." Finn's shout rang across the gazebo as he brandished the papers at her.

"Only half the book?" She frowned, a little divot forming in a crease in her brow. "That doesn't make sense."

He gripped the edge of the table so hard he might have splintered it. "What are you—"

"Hear me out. They were able to save your old hard drive, right? I mean, otherwise you would have gotten your new machine with nothing on it at all."

"So they said."

"Then they would have moved everything on the hard drive over." She bit her bottom lip, the action somehow sexy and innocent at the same time. "Do you mind if I see your laptop?"

He gritted his teeth. "Fine." He stopped pacing and set the machine in front of her.

Pippa slid her own work aside. For several moments, *too many* moments, she clicked and *hmmphed* and *hawed* about it all. Finn left to get more bottled water for the kettle. His cottage was bright with ~~morning~~ early afternoon light when he entered. He relaxed straight away, the solitude calming him, as it always had. Though that morning, things were different because Pippa was there.

He tried to force Pippa from his mind. His fingers had itched to take her tiny wrist in his hand, to trail his thumb down the inside and watch the goose bumps he knew would raise on her skin. But he couldn't think about her that way—not if he wanted to keep his "give back to Morris" program going. The school had given him so much. A direction, a purpose after Amélie. He'd landed on his feet again because of Morris.

When Finn returned to the gazebo, Pippa's fist rested against her forehead, as though she'd been punching herself. Either way, that didn't bode well for the future of his manuscript. "What's the matter? Why're you looking like that, Darling?"

She jerked her head up, her face reddening again. No need for that. He'd only called her that because it was the name her bloody parents had given to her. "You save each chapter in your book as separate files?"

Finn scowled, his bushy eyebrows angled so that they almost pointed to the bridge of his nose. "And why wouldn't I?"

She shook her head, letting out a sigh. "Because you're not supposed to."

"Oh." Finn missed his typewriter. The new software Phillip had thrust on him had been so complex, he hadn't known where to start. He'd just made his way and done the best he could. He hadn't thought about what would be involved in putting the book all together. He'd had to write it first.

"You have 567 files here. They all have single chapters and weird names. Some of them are AutoSaves." She drank more of her coffee and seemed more jet lagged than since she'd arrived. "They were in four or five different folders."

"What's an AutoSave?" he asked.

"Didn't you learn this stuff in elementary school? How old are you, anyway?"

"Twenty-five." Finn scowled, resting the ball of tea leaves inside a carafe of hot water. "I did learn it all in school, but I don't like it."

"They have classes. For free. That you can take. They'll show you how to use it." Pippa stared at him like he'd gone soft in the head.

"All the way in Dublin. As if I'd go there any more than I absolutely have to." He kicked back more tea, savoring the hot liquid and wishing he'd thought to add a drop of whisky for patience.

"Okay, fine. That aside, I think we can fix this, but it's going to take time. Is what you lost really worth saving?"

Hope began to build in his chest, in the form of a warm ball that he didn't want to let his brain acknowledge. He didn't want to jinx himself. "It is." Sure, he'd change it all once he got his hands on the files, but it was the jumping off point he needed.

"Then I'll help you. But first, pull up a chair. Let's talk about cloud storage."

Finn did as she said, taking a seat beside her. He reached for his tea and settled in. He hated technology. How cell phones let people track you everywhere and provided constant dings and jangles, sounds he didn't want or need at all hours of the night. Yet, if technology could help him retrieve, and keep safe, what he'd lost, it just might be worth a listen.

For September was many months away, but it would come. Faster than he could ever imagine.

13

PIPPA

"I stand under the heaviness of the moon, its rays a comfort in
that I don't walk alone."
—James Black, *To the Ends of the Earth*

The weeks running into June were rainy. Though Ireland had the ability to represent all four seasons in one day, the gazebo wasn't prepared for it. It certainly wasn't waterproof, for two or three holes had appeared in its roof, probably by-products of the heavy rain, salt air, and a bad thunderstorm that had rocked the coast the previous week. They'd herded water onto the tabletop in a constant stream. Another, larger opening directed water onto the chairs, drenching the cloth. All of that meant Finn and Pippa retreated to the underground workroom most days.

Reassembling Finn's manuscript had been slow going. Each chapter had ten or more partial duplicates linked to it. From what she could guess, it looked like someone tried to organize the files. Badly.

Finn had had a cloud storage account set up, but only part of the manuscript had been backed up. He'd created separate documents for each chapter, so there were dozens to sift through. The whole thing had sent her head spinning.

She'd reorganized his cloud storage file system. Through a series of searches and just plain digging, she'd assembled all of the files in one place and had begun sorting through them and removing the duplicates. More research had shown her that chapters ten to thirty-five had been the most impacted by the destruction of Finn's laptop. After that, it would be up to Finn to decide what order they went into.

In the meantime, Finn had taken to writing the last twenty chapters of the book. He'd seemed satisfied that she would locate everything he'd lost.

All in all, it was the most awkward job she'd ever had. He rarely spoke. When he did, his criticism of both her writing and her critiques of his own work stung. When she'd arrived, Pippa would have called herself optimistic. With the constant rain and her lack of a car isolating her from the rest of the world, negative thoughts set in. It was entirely possible she'd made the biggest mistake ever in coming to work for Finn Burke.

She had, however, settled into life in Ireland, despite it all. She'd decorated her bedroom with prints of antique cars and writerly quotes. She'd added a vase of dried flowers. Finn took her to the village once a week. Anything she couldn't get there, she'd ordered online.

"Pippa? Pippa, are you listening to me?" Uma's voice cut through the room, ending her daydreaming.

She positioned herself in front of her laptop for a moment, so the webcam could pick up her face. She smiled. "I'm sorry. I am listening, just getting some laundry put away. Keep going."

"Are you gonna give me the rundown on how things are in the wilds of Ireland? Every time I've asked, you change the subject." Uma laid down on her side, propping herself up on one hand.

"What do you want to know?" Pippa kept her voice light, but she fisted her hands, her short nails biting into her palms.

Uma chuckled. "You're hedging. How's it going?"

She could lie, could pretend that every moment of it had been awesome. Yet, she'd already been in Ireland for two whole weeks and she didn't feel any closer to knowing Finn Burke than before. She was, however, getting to know his suck-fest of a manuscript. Intimately. "It could be better. Working with Finn basically means editing his half-book. If that isn't bad enough, it's awful. I mean *really* awful."

Someone laughed in the background on Uma's side. She smiled. "Sorry, Zack and a bunch of his friends are downstairs. They're watching a baseball game and raiding what little food's left in the fridge."

"Zack's there?" A little trickle of sadness ran through Pippa. Once upon a time, she'd liked Zack, a lot. But it never went anywhere, and he'd clearly liked Uma. That was part of the reason Pippa never mentioned her feelings to her best friend. "Something going on between you two?"

"Maybe." Uma grinned. "How's everything going? Are you getting good feedback on your story?"

A knock sounded. "Pippa." Finn's voice reached her through the door leading to their shared workspace underground. Tingles trailed over her skin at the sound of his voice.

"Hold on one second, Uma." She jumped to her feet and then opened the door.

Finn stood there, shirtless, a blue towel hanging around his neck. She tried not to look at his chest, the ripple of muscle, the happy trail . . .

Oh. My. God.

"Well, hello there," Uma said. Pippa glanced back at the laptop and realized Uma had a perfect view of the doorway and a shirtless Finn.

Pippa sputtered. "I'm FaceTiming my best friend." The words sounded pathetic coming out of her mouth.

"You are? Grand." A smile split his face, transforming him.

Bye-bye, Mr. Grouchy. Hello Hot Finn and his towel. A knot twisted itself inside Pippa's stomach.

"Finn, Uma. Uma, Finn." She gestured back and forth from the computer to Finn with a limp wave of her hand. Then she forced herself to meet his eyes, versus the alternative, which was looking at his hot, bare chest.

"Nice to meet you, Uma." Finn waved, almost seeming normal, instead of like the unpredictable hermit he usually was.

"You too, Finn." Uma waved, her eyebrows shooting toward the ceiling as she did so. "Do you usually write without a shirt on?"

Finn's face flushed, and he glanced down, as though he'd just remembered he wasn't wearing a shirt. That sounded about right. Finn forgot things. A lot. His car keys . . . various writing utensils . . . what day of the week it was.

"*Bollocks*. Sorry. I was working down at the keep. Anyway, I'm going to take a shower. Can you meet me downstairs in ten, with your comments?"

Pippa blinked. "Okay." Another switch. He'd asked, not demanded. Was that for Uma's benefit? Or Pippa's?

"I'll leave you to it." He turned away from her before she could say anything more, and then headed downstairs.

After Pippa had shut the door behind Finn, she returned to her laptop and Uma's Cheshire Cat grin. Pippa positioned herself on the bed, in front of the keyboard. The laundry lay forgotten.

"He was yummy. You didn't mention he was yummy." Uma's smile had widened to the point that Pippa feared it would crack her face.

"He's my boss. I can't look at him that way." There, if Pippa said that enough times, she might actually believe it herself.

"Of course you can. There's nothing wrong with window shopping. Besides, you won't be his intern forever and he . . ." She moved closer to the screen, as if fixating on Pippa's face. "There's something you aren't telling me."

Yeah, there was. Like how Finn had kissed her on her first day. And suddenly, Pippa needed to tell someone, or she'd explode. "He kissed me." To avoid meeting Uma's eye, Pippa continued putting the rest of the laundry away.

"Oh my God." Uma slammed her hands onto the arms of her chair. If the screen hadn't been separating them, along with over four thousand miles, Pippa had no doubt Uma would have launched herself through it. "Really?"

"It's not what you think. I fixed his manuscript. He thought he'd lost it." Quickly, she launched into the story about saving Finn's work. "And then he . . . planted one on me."

"You still didn't answer the most important question." Uma rocked back and forth with excitement. "How was it?"

Heat rushed into Pippa's face. As if she could adequately describe the way she felt when Finn's mouth had moved over hers. "It was amazing. I've never been kissed like that before."

Uma clapped. "Yay! Maybe you've found your person. You know, your one and only."

"He's my boss, Uma." She ran her fingers through her damp hair, trying to tame it into place. "If he didn't hate me for destroying his laptop, it would be so much better here."

Uma caught her bottom lip between her teeth, then freed it. "Mm. I don't think he hates you."

Pippa stood, and then rested the empty laundry basket by the door to her room, where Zoe had told her to put it. "Yes, he does. He's always glaring at me and giving me these huge assignments." She pulled a face as she stared at the previous night's enormous stack by the bed, decorated in her own red pen. "The stuff from yesterday kept me up until two a.m."

"I don't know about that, but I do know that guys never kiss gals they hate. Maybe, just maybe, Finn doesn't hate you at all," Uma said.

Her words ignited a whirlwind of thoughts in Pippa's brain. Could Uma be right? Finn didn't hate her? Pippa couldn't say how she felt about that.

Finn was a good kisser. And there was the way the skin around his eyes crinkled when he smiled, like he was putting everything he had into the expression. She couldn't forget the energy and enthusiasm of his lips.

Oh.

"Promise you'll tell me what happens, and that you won't be afraid to take a chance," Uma said.

Pippa wished she could hug her. Just for a second. "Yeah. I promise. I love you."

"I love you, too."

Uma leaned forward, and the video froze for a moment, before only Pippa's face remained on the screen. Yet, Uma's words kept replaying in her head.

Was there a chance Finn really did like her? She definitely liked him, and more than she should. Maybe she should try being nice to him? On a whim, she skimmed through the manuscript until she got to the one part of his pages from the night before that she liked. She added a smiley face to the margin in red pen.

There, that was being nice.

14

FINN

"Women are the devil. It's best to avoid them."
—Finn Burke, *Lost*

*J*aysus. What could he have been thinking? Knocking on Pippa's door like she wasn't his intern. And then she just had to answer the door the way she had—all messed up and sexy, looking like she'd stepped straight out of a dream. One of those dreams that had been keeping him awake for a week. Plus, he'd interrupted her video call with her friend.

When Pippa Darling first arrived, he'd thought she'd be nothing more than a nuisance. But somehow, whether he liked it or not, he'd come to rely on her.

That, right there, was dangerous. Women were trouble. He'd learned that when he'd given his heart to Amélie. Things hadn't ended well.

He'd trusted her, and she'd walked, leaving behind a bunch of baggage and a book nobody wanted.

Pippa wasn't Amélie. Despite the asinine way he'd

kissed her on her first day, there was nothing between them. Still, it was Amélie's behavior that made it so difficult to trust Pippa.

Which was why the pages he'd emailed to Phillip that morning had included almost none of Pippa's suggestions. He was so anti-trust at the moment, he wasn't willing to risk trying something new.

A nagging voice at the back of his mind shouted. Why had he bothered with an intern if he wasn't going to let her do her job? He quelled it. The email had been sent. The deed done. All he had to do was wait to see what Phillip had to say.

His phone rang, and Finn grunted. As a rule, he avoided the phone. He owned a mobile for when he was on the road, but he never used it at home. For that, he had a regular, plain phone, thank you very much. He swiped up the handset, prepared to deal with some other fool selling something. "Burke."

"Is that any way to speak to your Ma? Now really, Finnegan." Lila Burke's voice filtered over the line, calm and intelligent, just as it had always sounded.

"Hello, Ma." Finn smiled, despite himself, as he looped a towel around his neck and unfolded onto the futon in the corner of his bedroom. Zoe would have spilled to Ma by then, which meant it would not be a brief chat. He'd better settle in for whatever she had planned. "How's Florida?"

"How's Florida, my *arse*. You know the answer to that. A sunshine dream, as always." Despite her dismissal, happiness bubbled up in her voice. She'd struggled in Ireland for years. The damp and the cold had aggravated her arthritis. It had only taken one visit to Florida when Finn moved into Morris to convince her it was time to relocate.

"Good. Now, if you don't mind, I'm about to go to work." There was little chance of him brushing Ma off.

"It's your work that I'm calling about. I've been on the phone with Zoe." There she went. "You're taking up with that intern of yours? Pippa, is it?"

Finn rested his head in his hand. "I haven't taken up with her. She's my employee."

"Zoe isn't very happy about it. She said she walked in on you two *snogging* like a couple of teenagers. If Pippa's an employee, she's one with benefits." Ma's snappy words would have made Finn smile, if he himself hadn't been the target.

"It was an accident. My computer crashed, and she saved my work. I would have lost everything." In terms of articulating how his behavior had crossed the line, he didn't know where to start. "I was so relieved, I kissed her. I didn't mean to and it won't happen again."

"*Bollocks.* You don't just go around kissing women who help you. As far as I know, you haven't been with anyone since . . ."

Ma never spoke her name. She'd become the Voldemort of Finn's love life. "It's okay, Ma. You can say it. Amélie."

"Right." There was a slight pause on the other end of the line before she continued. "You haven't looked at a woman since Amélie. So why this woman?"

"It was a moment of weakness. That's all." Finn ground his teeth together, back and forth. "I'm not involved with her. It was one time and it won't happen again."

Ma sucked in a breath. "Why the bloody hell not? Zoe said you live like a monk."

Finn rolled his eyes. "As I recall, I pay Zoe well, so she'll respect my privacy." *Good luck with that, Burke.*

"Then what's the harm in taking the girl out, maybe to a nice dinner. She's of age, isn't she? She's not a minor?"

"Ma, really? She's not a minor. We're almost the same age." There was no way he could end the call without raising her suspicions. He opted for a lie as close to the truth as he could get. "I have to get back to work."

"I'm sorry for prying." Ma's enthusiasm dimmed, her voice softening. "I've been worried for so long. I just want you to be happy."

Guilt plagued Finn. She only wanted him to have what she'd had with Da. He couldn't help wondering how she was. If she was still as lonely, or if Florida had filled that void. For the thousandth time, he wished she'd come home.

"I will be happy, Ma. *Someday.* For now, I'm on the way to happy, so that'll have to do." He surprised himself with that admission. Mostly because he never considered his own happiness. His Ma's, sure. Those around him, like Zoe's and Bob's? Absolutely. "Today, you'll have to make due with content."

Ma sighed, but it was clear the harping had ended. "All right, then. I love you."

"I love you, too." He grinned at the empty room, as though she could see his smile.

They rung off, but her words danced around in his

mind like a story idea demanding to be written. Being with Pippa was an alternate plot he hadn't even considered, and one he'd have been better off forgetting.

Finn showered and dressed. Even though it was June in Ireland, rain fell in steady sheets outside, chasing him away from the roar of the gazebo and the consistent crashing pattern of the sea. Since he'd already met his own word count for the day, he'd decided to focus on another project.

By the time Pippa jogged down the steps with a marked up stack of pages, Finn had spread out boxes of books. In the past, it was a task he assigned to his intern, but he'd noted the dark hollows beneath Pippa's eyes when he'd gone to her room and figured he'd better take it on. She'd most likely been up way too late. Perhaps he'd been working her too hard?

"What's all this?" she asked, climbing over boxes of books to the printer, which had started humming as it spit out dozens of pages. She peered at one of the labels on the box closest to her.

Finn shrugged. "Just a little thing I call The Book Project. Every summer, I send books to all the libraries in Ireland. Well, not all of them, but as many as I can."

Pippa lifted the flap on one box and then another. She glanced up. "These aren't your book."

"Why would I want to send them my book? These are books *I've* enjoyed reading. If I like a book, I share it." He grabbed some packing tape and began sealing the box closest to him. He'd have to drop them off in town later.

Maybe he'd ask Pippa to go for a pint. No, a coffee. Or nothing at all—that would be more appropriate.

"That's a really nice thing to do." Pippa frowned as she said it, somehow managing to make the compliment sound like an accusation.

Finn shrugged. "I'm a nice guy."

"I wouldn't go that far," she said, but her lips quirked. She was teasing.

He grinned. "Nice one, Darling."

"You're not gonna fire me for that?" she asked, biting her bottom lip in that adorable way of hers. Hold on. Adorable? What was happening to him? It was like being around Pippa was unearthing the romantic side he thought was long dead and buried.

Pippa still waited in silence, she'd settled two fingers over her plump lips, as if to force her mouth closed. She likely expected a termination at any moment.

"Not today." He plopped down onto the couch. "Ya know, you look like hell. Why don't you have a lie down for a little while? I'll read through these." He gestured to the red-streaked stack she'd brought. Lord only knew how many changes she'd suggested in there.

"No. I'm here to work, not nap." But she sank to the couch anyway. A yawn slipped out, despite her efforts to stifle it.

His eyebrows shot up. "Okay. Then take the new pages with that little red pen of yours." He picked up her red Bic and tugged off the cap, offering it to her end first. "Go on, then."

"Fine." But she yawned again at the beginning of the word, distorting the "i" sound. She leaned against the pillows, rested the pages against her knees, and her eyes drooped. Infinitesimally, they closed until Pippa's dark lashes rested against her pale cheekbones.

He stared at her, memorizing the way her compact, petite body lay on the sofa. She wore the type of pants the women in the village had been all the rage about. Yoga pants. He'd never seen Pippa do yoga once. Why someone would buy pants for something they didn't even do was beyond him. Still, he believed, sitting there watching the way the dark material clung to Pippa's form, that the designers had had the right of it.

God, she was a puzzle, that Pippa Darling. She could, in equal parts, infuriate him and arouse him, though it was wrong for certain to be thinking the latter. Still, there was no denying he was glad she stayed. He took the pages from her knees, set them aside, and then snagged the throw that rested along the back of one armchair, spreading it out over her.

"That's enough now," he whispered, his fingers closing over hers as he freed the pen from her grasp. Finn drew the blanket up and over her arms, and tucked her in. "Sleep, fair Pippa. Sleep," he whispered.

With all of his resolve, he forced himself to his feet, abandoning the books and a sleeping Pippa.

"The whirlwind of life does nothing to quell my uneasy thoughts. Nor does it quench my desire for the touch of her hand."
—James Black, *To the Ends of the Earth*

*D*ean Montgomery had failed to mention Pippa would be working seven days a week, following the insane Finn Burke schedule for writing a novel. By the time July rolled around, Pippa had gotten to understand Finn's work schedule. If she'd had broken things out into an agenda format, it would have looked something like this:

- *4:45 am Get up and suck down as much coffee as possible.*
- *5:00 am Meet Finn either in the gazebo or workroom (weather depending).*
- *5:01 am Get Finn's new pages to read for the day.*

> *He asks questions about her edits from the previous*
> *day, which ends up more like shouting.*

- *5:45 am Write while Finn sleeps.*
- *12:30 pm Finn reads what Pippa has written that*
  morning and tears it to shreds.
- *1:00 pm Pippa takes three ibuprofens to prepare for*
  the afternoon.
- *1:30 pm Finn sends Pippa off to read his work, a.k.a.*
  Depressing Hole Manuscript, *for the rest of*
  the day.
- *5:00 pm Dinner, which usually involves Finn*
  complaining about Pippa's edits.

Of course, the schedule didn't account for the days when Finn decided to throw out whole chapters or rewrite them altogether. The schedule, like the man himself, was consistently *inconsistent*.

Fortunately, Finn at least paid on time. Every other Friday brought a nice direct deposit into her bank account. Which was why she didn't tell him to shove his commentary up his rear end.

Pippa was required to write at least 500 words per day. She normally hit quadruple that amount daily, but Finn had so many pages for her to read, she couldn't always get through everything. She usually followed that agenda by working until she face-planted on the table—frequently on a copy of Finn's manuscript. That morning, she'd avoided checking her reflection in a mirror for fear the bags had migrated to the top of her eyelids and not only beneath them.

Pippa had finally managed to piece Finn's manuscript

together. His biggest problems were that he never used consistent naming, never saved his work in the same place twice, and had been saving each chapter in separate documents.

She'd found all the separate chapter files, sorted them out, and tagged the most recent versions. She'd successfully recovered the content that had been on his old MacBook when it had taken The Great Plunge, as she'd come to think of it, over the stairwell. She'd also combined the single chapters into one file, which he'd begun working from. If Finn didn't start saving using that scatterbrained method of his again, they'd be good.

That day, it had stopped raining and they'd decided to work outside. Pippa had missed the gazebo. She'd learned to enjoy working outdoors. After being cooped up, she'd begun to grow antsy.

She could ask Finn to borrow his car, so she could get out of the house for a while, but she couldn't imagine driving in Ireland. Some of the roads she'd seen had appeared to be half the necessary size to hold two passing vehicles. Besides, the last thing she needed was to hit something in Finn's truck—even if it had seen better days.

Finn had brought a notebook and pen to their "lesson." Pippa planned to explain how the new writing software he'd bought worked. She also figured it wouldn't hurt to run through the old cloud storage process one more time. Hopefully, she'd ensure Finn never lost any work again. "Okay so do you see this folder here?" Pippa asked, gesturing to the one she'd opened on Finn's laptop.

Finn scowled, staring at the screen as though the

folder itself were a longtime enemy. "The one that says *Cloud Storage?*"

"Yeah, that's the one. That's where I want you to save all of your work from now on." Pippa highlighted the folder with the panache of a game show hostess. All she was missing was an evening gown.

"So, instead of the desktop . . ." Finn jabbed a finger at his laptop screen. "Save it there."

"Yeah. I set this up as your default saving location. Every day, just save a new version of your manuscript here with the date in the title. Your work will always be backed up." She slid her fingers from the touchpad. "You can get to it from any computer with an internet connection."

"Cheers for that." Finn grinned. "I wish I would have gotten around to it before. I'm not exactly what you'd call a technical expert."

"And why is that?" Pippa asked. "I mean, you're young enough to have learned computers in school. I guess I don't get why they cause you this much pain."

He opened his mouth, as though to say something snarky, and then closed it, his brow wrinkling. "I first started writing on my Da's old typewriter. It was one that his grandfather before him had used. I can still remember the sensation of the keys beneath my fingertips, the clacking sound that came with putting ink on paper.

"There's just something about it. When you write a book on a typewriter, it's almost like there's a physical connection to the keys."

Pippa gestured to the laptop in front of her. "There are keys in front of me now. I'm typing on those. I guess you could say I have a physical connection with a lot less work on the backend."

"*Bollocks*." Finn waved her away. But from the far-off look in his eyes, it was clear that it did. To him. "You don't understand."

"Then try me." No one was more surprised than Pippa that she *wanted* to know.

"When you type on a computer, you don't have anything to show for it. Just an intangible file that you have to print to really see. When you type on the type-writer, you're getting output onto the page—your work's right there in front of you."

Finn's eyes lit. There was more animation in his expression than Pippa had seen, perhaps *ever*. "If you're so enamored with writing on a typewriter, what made you stop? What made you turn to this expensive MacBook?"

"My agent, Phillip, started having a fit, saying things like I wasn't a professional writer. He told me I needed to learn to use the right *kinds* of tools. The next thing I knew, he sent me the MacBook. The next month, he sent me the bill."

Pippa couldn't believe it. Why stay with the man if he treated his clients that way? "He sounds like an ass. I mean, the guy is supposed to be helping you. Not only does he criticize your process, but he charges you for it."

"He does at that." Finn smiled, ruefully.

"Then why stay with him? You could probably have your pick of agents right now." Pippa did her best not to scowl as she said it. The guy could get representation from anyone, anywhere. Pippa wouldn't be able to say the same once she finished her own novel. Publishing was a cutthroat business, with some agents getting upwards of ten thousand submissions per year.

"Sometimes it's better to leave things as they are, rather than rush to change them." Finn sighed. "The writing came so easily to me on the old typewriter. It made me think about the words more. To only put down the ones that mattered. I was superstitious about writing on anything else."

Right at that moment, Finn seemed uncertain and maybe even a bit afraid. The Finn she'd known those past couple months did what he wanted—wrote with fearlessness. What had happened to him to make him feel he had no alternative except to put up with this agent? And what kind of agent wanted to kill a client's creativity?

"Why don't you just keep typing on your typewriter? You can always ask someone to type it up for you on your laptop later."

Great idea, Pippa. Volunteer to spend more time with the novel than you already have.

But Finn's face brightened so much, her regrets faded. Since she'd arrived, she'd learned more about Finn Burke than she would've thought possible before—like what a decent guy he truly was. Volunteering help didn't seem like a hardship.

"You'd do that for me, Darling?" A chill skated down her spine that had nothing to do with the weather and everything to do with Finn's smile. He should smile more. It made him seem like less of a crab-ass.

"Yeah, I would. Now back to your files." She cleared her throat, pointing to the screen, but she could feel

Finn's eyes on her, watching, considering. "What?" She faced him, her eyes narrowing.

"You're not what I expected, is all."

Of course. Another one of those comments that could be a compliment or an insult. Finn Burke sure did know how to talk to a woman.

16

FINN

"She wanted a piece of my soul. I told her I didn't have one."
—Finn Burke, *Lost*

Finn stared at the bolded email in his inbox. He had no doubt what it was about. His second book, which he still didn't have a title for. He'd sent in the first ten chapters at Phillip's urging. It was more of a peace offering than anything. Something to shut him up while Finn got down to the business of writing the rest of the book.

But the email awaited him, and he couldn't help wondering if he should have stalled more. The book had been enough of a bear to write without Phillip's comments. Steeling himself, Finn double-clicked on the email and began to read.

Finn,

These pages aren't even close to what they need to be. This is your second book, the follow-up to Lost, for Chrissakes. These pages are full of one-dimensional characters and zero emotion. Your heart clearly isn't in this project. Take another stab and send them back.

September 1st—I'm not delaying again.

Phillip

Jaysus, that was harsh. Phillip hadn't liked any of it? He skimmed the attached document and noted that he'd added a great deal of changes. The most interesting part was that Phillip's feedback strongly resembled Pippa's.

And Finn hadn't listened to her.

"I'll be damned." He ran a hand through his hair.

Pippa had been right. She'd sworn his characters didn't have any depth.

But he hadn't listened. He hadn't applied any of her feedback to the first ten chapters. Apparently, that had been a mistake. One that he already regretted. The weight of Phillip's criticism bore down on him.

Finn couldn't imagine opening those chapters again and digging in. He needed a break. They both did.

Lately, he'd noticed she hadn't been writing anything new. Her only focus had been on his work during the past week. That had to change. The internship was about helping her, too.

Leaving his office behind, he strode out into the gazebo. Pippa had a bit more color to her cheeks that day. He'd deliberately given her less to read the night before.

He'd wanted her to get some sleep, and that had obviously been a good decision. "Why don't we get out of here, Darling?"

Her face flushed in that way it always did when he said her last name. Like she viewed it as an endearment instead of as a simple form of address.

"And not work?" She stared at him as though she was incapable of processing such a thing. "What about your insane workaholic schedule?" Pippa raised her hand to her mouth. "Oops."

Finn's lips quirked. Ah, so that was what she thought of the way he worked. "I think we should take the afternoon off. You've been in Ireland four months and you haven't seen any of it. Don't tell me you're not just a wee bit curious."

She seemed to consider his words before saying, "Maybe." A sly grin filled her face, making him think of a pixie again, or a temptress. "Give me a few minutes to get ready?" She stood, and Finn got a good look at Pippa's smooth legs, exposed by her cutoff shorts, and her bare arms, left uncovered by her tank top. He forced himself to turn away.

"What you have on is fine." Though it would be the death of him if he had to look at her in those clothes much longer. Perhaps he'd have been better off if she wore a shroud.

"Okay. Let me stash my laptop and we can go," she said.

He forced himself to make a noncommittal sound as she walked back to her rooms. He wasn't sure whether he should be disappointed or relieved when she returned a few minutes later, having switched her cutoffs for jeans. She kept her sandals, though.

They took the ramp that led away from the gazebo and over to the garage. He passed the door that led to Da's old, beat-up truck. It was the vehicle he always used to take Pippa on trips to the village. In the bay over, however, he'd parked his classic 1967 Triumph Herald. Today wasn't the day for riding around in a clunker.

Pippa's eyes lit when she stepped inside the garage and touched the hood. "You own a Triumph? Seriously?"

"You know cars?" Finn froze, staring as Pippa popped the bonnet and surveyed the engine.

Pippa shrugged. "Yep. It's got a Honda engine, right?"

How was it possible that one woman could be such an enigma? She knew cars? That was *fecking* hot. *Jaysus*, she'd be the death of him. "It's a 1.3."

"Sweet." She shut the bonnet and walked around to the passenger door. "Ready to go?"

"I am. Hop in." Finn gritted his teeth as he climbed in beside her and started up the car. She rumbled to life with a turn of the ignition.

Within minutes, they'd pulled out of Finn's obscure driveway and onto the N56. Cars flew by them on either side. Finn didn't care. The sun was out, sending its rays scattering over the green hills. He cranked his window down just a bit. Pippa mirrored his actions and soon the wind whipped her short hair so that the tresses lashed her face.

"Where are we going?" Pippa asked.

"You'll just have to see when we get there." He grinned, knowing it would bother her. Pippa, with all of her schedules and plans. Pippa, with her carefully organized notes. He, himself, was far more easy-going.

"Who taught you about cars?" he asked, keeping his eyes on the road and his hand steady on the vibrating wheel.

Pippa straightened in the seat beside him—checked her seat belt and then her bag. Only when she was done fidgeting did she face him. "My grandpap. He was a mechanic. I stayed with my grandparents every weekend when I was a kid. We'd spend Saturdays taking car engines apart." She worried at her bottom lip. "He gave me this."

She pointed to a bracelet around her ankle. He glanced to the side, trying not to focus on her leg, and realized that attached to the bracelet was a tiny crescent wrench charm. It was a perfectly whimsical gift for a granda to give his granddaughter. Perfectly Pippa.

"Is he still with you?" Finn asked. He tried to conjure an image of his own granda in his mind and failed. It'd been too long since he'd passed for a clear recollection.

"No." She shook her head. "He just got up one morning, sat down again, and . . . died. We never even saw it coming. He was ninety-two."

Finn patted her hand, where it rested against the edge of her seat. "I'm sorry." He was. Family was everything—the beginnings and endings, and all the messy middles in between that.

"Don't be," Pippa said. "I can't imagine a better way to die. A full life. Friends and family all around me. Plus, he was a gentleman. Because of him, I hold out hope that I'll meet a gentleman of my own someday." She kept her focus straight ahead, from what Finn could tell, but he could make out her flaming face even in his peripheral.

"Did you leave behind some amazing car in the States?" Finn asked, skirting a truck that dominated the right lane.

Pippa grinned. "No. It's a Rabbit. I named him Jethro. He's very moody."

Finn chuckled. "Does Jethro like to rest on the side of the road?"

"Occasionally." She grinned. "My dad still tinkers with him. Jethro wouldn't have made it to Florida." She kicked off her shoes and brought her knees up to her chest. "What about your parents, your grandparents? You haven't mentioned anyone."

"That's kind of a personal question."

"I didn't mean it to be." She shook her head and stared out the window.

It was in Finn's nature to evade the question. Still, to close himself off then would have been hypocrisy. "Ma and Da ran the village pub where I'm from."

"And that is?" she asked.

"Tipperary. It's about four hours south of here." He tapped an inconsistent rhythm on the wheel. "It'd been in the family for, *Jaysus*, I don't know how long. I was supposed to take it over."

"Let me guess. You wanted to be a writer and they didn't understand." A wry smile tugged at her lips.

"Not quite. Da had a heart attack. Ma and I tried to save the pub. But my own heart wasn't in it." Finn shook his head. He was being kind. The truth was, he'd hated every moment of running the pub.

"What about your dad? Was he—*is* he okay?" Pippa asked.

"He passed on. It's just Ma and me now." Finn gripped the wheel tighter. He still had a hard time accepting Jack Burke's death. He'd been larger than life. A bear of a man with a quick smile and a mile-long fuse. He'd had to be that way to live with Ma.

"I wanted a change. I applied to several schools in the US. Morris had the best writing program, so that sold it for me." It had just as much to do with Amélie and the constant reminders Ireland had tossed at him." I enrolled at Morris. I needed a change.

"Ma moved to Florida when I started graduate school. She has a bit of arthritis in her hands, and the weather was kinder to her there. Ma sold the pub and moved to the States. She's running an antique business off eBay now and loving every minute of it."

"But you don't like that she's gone." There was little hesitation to be had in that statement. Pippa had seen straight through him and gotten to the heart of the matter. Too much. Too quickly.

"To tell the truth, I was so ready to leave Ireland and start my life. And now . . . nothing's the same." Damn it all. Now why had he gone and blurted that out? Pippa would want to talk about his feelings on things. He was setting a precedent for *conversation* when he'd much rather have had a pint.

"And you're back here, hours away from where you grew up." She toyed with the frayed edges of a hole in her jeans. Finn had to fight to keep his eyes from gluing to the spot where her fingers touched the fabric.

He cleared his throat and faced the road again. "I spent a weekend backpacking around Donegal. The place inspired me. It felt like home. The castle and the grounds were up for auction. I got the land for less than you'd think and made it my own."

"And did you buy your house or build it?"

"God, woman. You didn't read my 'official bio'?" He used air quotes for the term *official bio*.

She laughed. "Actually, I had a hard time finding information on you. Your picture's nowhere to be found, you barely have any social media presence at all. All your tweets seem to be written by somebody else. I sort of gave up researching you."

"Of course they're written by someone else. I pay a virtual assistant." He glared at her as though she'd offended him. "I didn't want any part of that. I just wanted to write. That's all there's ever been. All of that social media stuff's just noise to distract us from seeing what's right in front of us." He cleared his throat. Why had he told her all that? Finn had never been one for sharing, and he'd gone and dumped all his private life on Pippa's lap.

Not all of it. He still hadn't confessed to being James Black. It wasn't that he'd intended to let things go that far without telling her, but it had more to do with Finn not wanting anyone to know. He'd shared his soul and it had been rejected. He wouldn't share it twice.

But there were some things to be said. He cleared his throat. "I've been looking at your last round of feedback. It's . . . pretty good."

"Pretty good? Really?" she asked, her voice as wry as the smile he knew she'd have plastered all over her face.

"What?"

"Pretty good? That just means not lame—barely." She pulled a face.

"That's not what I meant. Your feedback is *good*. I've had a think on it, and you're right. Mia's one-dimensional."

"Huh. Why this sudden change of heart?"

He snuck a glance at her. She was staring at him, twirling a short lock of hair around one slender finger. "My agent, ah, may have agreed with you."

"Oh, he did? Then my feedback sounds better than 'pretty good'."

"Don't be getting cocky. I'm thanking you because you did a good job, Darling." He straightened behind the wheel. "But I think we should rework the first ten chapters."

Pippa groaned. "I have to read those again?"

"I was under the impression I pay you a fair bob to work as my intern."

"I'm assuming by bob, you mean money. Is this going to earn me another lecture on entitled Americans?"

Finn grinned. "Those Americans. They are all *so* goddamn entitled." *Jaysus*, he was flirting with her and she was giving it right back. What had changed between them? Something.

Pippa picked up *To the Ends of the Earth* and held it up. All traces of Finn's humor vanished. She'd brought *that* thing along? "This author—"

"Oh, not that bloody book again. That's a dreamer's book."

"I was going to say James Black lets you see into the

souls of the characters. Not just the flaws, but the good, too. People aren't one-sided. Maybe if you tried writing some happier characters, you'd be less miserable." She pulled a face. "I'm sorry."

But he couldn't argue with her—couldn't even consider it when every word she'd said was true. He'd been able to write characters with heart once, but that was before Amélie. Before *To the Ends of the Earth* flopped. Ever since then, he'd written black-and-white characters because those were the only ones he'd understood. The only ones he could stand.

He should have told her the truth right then. Explained who he really was and shared why he'd stopped writing as James Black.

He couldn't. Not when he'd worked so hard to bury those memories.

So he said nothing at all.

They traveled in silence for the last ten minutes of their journey. Pippa seemed so lost in thought that she didn't react when they approached Old Church Dunlewey, standing like a reminder of the past on the hill overlooking the lough. He pulled to a stop along the narrow road and killed the engine. "Are you ready for your sightseeing tour to begin, then?"

Pippa jerked her head up, those warm, brown eyes landing on his, seeing through him. "Definitely."

But as Pippa climbed from the car, she let out a yelp. Finn didn't hesitate. He flew from his seat, not even bothering to shut the door. Pippa needed him.

17

PIPPA

"The soft hush of the countryside holds secrets even the bold will not find. It is only when we aren't searching that the truth reveals itself."
—James Black, *To the Ends of the Earth*

*P*ippa had barely set foot outside the car when a blast of cold air pummeled her. It had been a warm day in July when they'd stood in Finn's gazebo, but it seemed as though the temperature had dropped twenty degrees. What had Finn been thinking telling her what she'd had on was fine? She needed a parka.

Finn flew around to her side of the car so quickly, it was almost as if he cared. His eyes had widened like they were about to pop out of his head. "What's the matter? Are you hurt?"

"Not hurt, just cold! It's freezing. It's like winter. How can it be winter in July?" She hugged her breasts with her arms, doing all she could to avoid showing Finn how cold she really was.

"Is that all?" He rolled his eyes halfway, seeming annoyed that she would even complain about such a thing. Stalking around to the trunk, he unlocked it and extracted a wrinkled fleece, which he tossed in Pippa's direction before shutting the trunk once more. "Put this on."

She didn't argue. Finn's pine scent assaulted her the moment the fabric looped over her head. Something about wearing another person's clothes had always seemed oddly intimate to Pippa. The fleece was so long that it fell to her knees. She didn't bother rolling up the sleeves. It wasn't a perfect solution, but she was much better off than before. With the scent of Finn wrapped around her, it was almost like a hug.

She forgot all about the cold when she turned around.

Ahead of them lay the ruins of an old stone church. She couldn't tell if it had once been black and white was taking over, or if it was the other way around. The building stood, intact, though damaged, a silent sentinel keeping watch over a blue lake. A low stone wall surrounded the church and its small plot of land, but it was obvious from where she stood that it did little good. The place had been gutted and abandoned, as evidenced by the missing front door and windows.

Wind whipped into the valley, sending more chills over Pippa's skin.

"What is this place?" she asked, as Finn swung open the gate leading from the parking lot to the church grounds and waved her in. Pippa fell into step beside Finn as they approached the sacred building.

"So the story goes, Old Church Dunlewey was built by

a wife as a memorial to her late husband. It's made from white marble. It was consecrated in 1853."

"What happened to all the people? It's so sad seeing this place abandoned like this." They'd reached the building itself, and Pippa ran her hand reverently over the marble.

"No one really knows. I think the congregation drifted away. The church was forgotten." He walked toward the opening in the wall and Pippa fell into step beside him. "It happens."

"I can't imagine anyone wanting to leave this place." She spun around, taking in the panoramic view—the church, the lake, the glen. "This is heaven."

Finn offered his hand for her to climb inside the church. She took it, and sparks seemed to shoot up her arms and down her spine at the contact. He dropped her fingers once she passed the threshold. Pippa stared up into the moody open sky where the church's roof should have been.

Finn chuckled. "Funny you should mention that. It's called Poisoned Glen."

"That's a terrible name." Pippa couldn't imagine any land closer to perfection. "Who chose that?"

"Some daft Englishman. The Old Irish name for 'heaven' is the same as 'poison.'"

"Lemme guess. He didn't have his Old Irish-English dictionary handy?"

Finn moved to what remained of the weathered door-frame and leaned against it. "So it would seem."

Pippa stared out into the churning sky and the lake, before leaving the view behind to investigate. She took several steps toward the rear of the church. It was wide open; all the pews and the roof had been removed—probably decades ago. Pippa didn't know what to look at first. The glen or Finn. It was a toss-up.

"This is where I come when I get stuck and I need to think. I've always felt this place must have inspired millions of stories." Finn didn't take his eyes from the view. "It's always worked to unblock my mind. Maybe it will help you."

The way he admitted that info made the trip sound like an intervention. "But my mind isn't blocked?" It's not like she had that problem. On the contrary, she wrote every day. She just hadn't written anything new for a while.

"Isn't it? Haven't you shown me the same chapter every day for the past week?" Finn picked up a rock and tossed it in the direction of the water, though it didn't come close.

Pippa stared at the tidy houses that filled the valley, and the imposing mountain that rose up around them, its rock craggy, like a battered warrior. The image of that place would be forever stamped on her brain. People had loved and lost there. There'd been baptisms, weddings, and funerals. Dreams were built and ended beyond the same threshold where she stood. There could be no place like it in the world.

The setting alone had probably inspired thousands of stories. Why wasn't one already percolating in her head? She'd never had a problem writing before.

It began a couple of weeks ago. That's when your story started giving you trouble.

For a moment, Pippa's mind abandoned the glen and Finn as that internal revelation took over. She *hadn't* written anything new. Hadn't even missed it. So that was what they called Writer's Block? She'd always sworn she'd never have it.

Funny how the "nevers" always came back to haunt her. It was even odder that Finn had noticed when she didn't. "Huh. I guess you're right."

"Of course I'm right." He winked as he picked up another stone. "That's why I've brought you to the place that's always worked for me."

"I can see why. A spot like this can get in your brain and haunt you."

Finn grinned. "Well, there's a ghost here. Some say the green lady runs this place. If you believe in that sort of thing."

"I'm not sure I want to hang around after dark to find out." Maybe it was the view that distracted her, or Finn himself. It didn't matter. Her heel caught on an uneven stone and Pippa sailed headfirst toward the rough surface. Inches before she struck the ground, Finn's arms latched around her from behind, just beneath her breasts. With care, he set her back on her feet, though he didn't release her.

"I've got you," he said, his breath hot, his voice rough against her ear.

She let herself lean into him, absorbing his touch. Warmth radiated from his hands on her waist. If she closed her eyes, she could almost pretend he'd held her because he wanted to. Not because she was a clumsy ass.

Something brushed against the top of her head. His

lips? Heat rushed through her even as she forced down the shudder that threatened to wrack her body. If only Finn would keep holding her. If only he wouldn't let go.

But that moment, like the single kiss they'd shared, was one Finn would most likely classify as a mistake. It was better if she didn't linger.

She stood, steadying herself, taking a step away. Maybe distance would help her breathe again.

Finn's light green eyes, the color of the grass that rustled across the Poisoned Glen, burned into her. As if he knew her emotions.

"Let's get you back in the car. You're cold." His voice dropped, as though that were a private message only for her.

He offered his hand, and she took it, letting him lead her over the cobblestones and back to the car. With his other hand, he began fumbling in his pants pockets for something. He scowled again, and Pippa already missed his smile. She couldn't help wishing he'd use it more often.

"What are you looking for?" Pippa asked.

"My damn car keys. You know I just had them here." He patted his front pockets.

"Back pocket, left side." Pippa didn't need to look to know they were still there. She remembered him stashing the keys after he'd leant her his fleece.

Finn reached into his pocket and retrieved the keys. "Thanks." He squeezed her hand, and it was oddly intimate, a special message just for her.

Once they'd climbed inside, Finn turned the key in the

ignition. A blast of warmth hit Pippa's hands and she sighed, her muscles relaxing in the heat.

She stared out the window, at the church, at the odd patterns of light the sun made as it tried to peek through the clouds. Something about the church and its grounds sucked her in. When they'd stood on the stone remains, they could have been anywhere and in any time. A quiet desperation began to build in Pippa's stomach. She wasn't sure her memories would do the place justice once she'd left. She wanted them to. She didn't want to forget.

"Check the glove compartment." Finn pointed to the space in front of Pippa's knees with one of his long, slim fingers.

Tugging on the handle, Pippa popped open the box. Inside lay roughly ten journals in various colors, and an assortment of pens. She met his eyes, and a small smile tugged at his lips. Of course he'd have known what was in her head. Pippa selected a teal notebook and a pen, then shut the box.

"That feeling you have right now—the one gnawing at you like it'll never let go. Write it down, before you forget. Make your writing *real*." His voice didn't have his usual authoritative tone. Instead, it brimmed with understanding. She'd come to Ireland not expecting to have anything in common with the international best sellout, Finn Burke. Again, he'd surprised her.

Gripping the pen between her still-frigid fingers, she began to write.

18

FINN

*"Dreaming? What's the point? Dreams don't make money. They
don't get you laid."*
—Finn Burke, *Lost*

*W*hat on Earth could he have been thinking,
taking her to Dunlewey? It was atmos-
pheric, but also inherently romantic. A place like the
Poisoned Glen got under your skin and stuck there. Of
course, he'd had to take Pippa. He'd just had to catch her
when she fell.

When he'd invited her to tour some of the sights, he'd
been looking for a distraction, nothing more. What he got
was proof. Inarguable proof that Pippa Darling had
become a problem. It was one thing to think about her
occasionally, but back in the old church, when he'd caught
her . . . he'd almost forgotten himself.

How could he possibly help her and release her, when
his mind had filled with thoughts of her? When he could
envision, all too clearly, what it would be like to taste her

again, as he had on her first day in Ireland. To take her body with his and pleasure them both past the point of lucidity.

He was about to pull out of the parking lot, when his phone vibrated in his pocket.

Putting the car back in park, he retrieved the phone and flipped it open. There was a text waiting from Zoe. *Are we still on for dinner tonight?*

Shite. He'd forgotten he'd invited Zoe over for dinner last week to celebrate Pippa's arrival. He'd meant to do it months ago, when Pippa had first come to Ireland, but he'd grown so wrapped up in the book that he'd forgotten. He could cancel. Nope. Better to get it done before he became absorbed in his characters again. Time was slipping away from him.

Besides, preparing for the dinner would be the distraction he needed to keep from asking Pippa back to his place for other reasons. Damn, if he didn't want to.

"Wait a minute. You have a cell phone? A *flip* phone? Those are ancient." Laughter filled her eyes and he'd half a mind to do more than kiss that smirk off her face.

"Some things don't need to be improved upon." He jabbed his finger in the center of the journal. "You're meant to be writing."

"Yes, Sir." Suppressing a grin, Pippa turned back to the notebook. After several moments of silence, she began to move pen over paper.

At least she was writing. Pippa's prose had been off. Maybe the glen would have the same impact on her that it had always had on him. From how fast she scribbled into that journal he'd given her, he had to assume so.

A half hour later, he pulled the Triumph into the gravel parking lot of Green Earth Farmer's Market. Rows and rows of vendor stalls lined an adjoining field. Even though it was late afternoon, the space was packed. Finn eased his baby between an old pickup truck in faded red and white, and a flashy red BMW.

Pippa rested the journal she'd been filling with words on her lap. "Where are we?"

Finn unbuckled his seat belt and then climbed out of the car. A moment later, Pippa followed suit, closing her door almost reverently, and then sliding her palm along the roof. Reaching into the back seat, Finn withdrew a handful of canvas bags. "Farmers' market. Do they have those in . . . where did you say you were from again?" He shut the door.

"Pennsylvania." Pippa joined him at the front of the car and accepted the bags he offered. "And yes, we have farmers' markets."

"This one's my favorite."

A half smile quirked her lips. "I can't say I pictured you as a farmers' market type of guy."

"I work all night, so when I'm awake, I like to do normal things." Finn couldn't say why he felt the need to explain himself. He just wanted her to know him. Another troubling realization. "One of those things is to cook—on occasion. We're having Zoe and her family for dinner tonight, and you . . ." He touched the tip of her nose with his finger, doing his best to ignore the heat that seared his skin at the contact. "You're going to help me cook dinner."

"Me, cook? I can't." Her eyes widened in protest, as though he'd suggested the most ludicrous thing imaginable. "I'm a terrible cook. There's no way you want my help with anything in the kitchen."

He grinned. "Thanks for the warning. I'm sure you can help with some things. I'll give you all of the disgusting jobs."

She jerked her chin up in mock offense. "No way. I'm much too special and important for that."

"You are." He blurted the profession.

Damn it, Burke. You can't be doing that.

He shouldn't flirt with his intern. He'd never had a problem in previous years. Of course, his other interns had both been men, but that wasn't the point. What he'd been feeling was *all* down to Pippa. It was as if he'd been destined to desire her.

Destiny. He had to be careful there. That almost sounded like something his alter ego, James Black, would have written.

Pippa had stilled, curiosity lit within her warm, brown eyes. He'd have been a fool not to notice the heat in them. He may've been the one initiating things, but Pippa wasn't arguing. Back at the church when she'd stumbled, he'd caught her. He'd barely held her after that, but she'd lingered, as though she'd wanted him to.

Wherever Finn might find his resolve, it wouldn't be in Pippa.

He shoved a ball cap onto his head and donned a pair of sunglasses. "Let's go." Finn took her hand, knowing it was wrong, trying not to focus on how right her small hand felt in his own large one. Of course, he'd only done it so she wouldn't trip in those practically non-existent sandals of hers. There was no other reason at all.

Keep telling yourself that, Burke.

She let him lead her. Soon, the atmosphere of the market allowed him to push thoughts of Pippa away to a comfortable distance. No matter what stall they entered, he was greeted with shouts of *Hey, Finn!, Burke!,* or even once, *Oh, look, it's that famous author!*

Each time, he shrugged, smiled, and then moved on, buying up what he needed. Still, it pleased him that he'd found a fit in the community. He wanted Pippa to see that —to see him as something other than she did, though he couldn't pinpoint what that was or why it mattered.

"They love you," Pippa said, trailing in his wake.

"They're neighbors, friends. We all live here, and I like to help them."

They visited each stall, and soon, their shopping bags were loaded down with grass-fed beef, chicken, vegetables, fresh bread, and something Finn hadn't tried but Pippa had to have—toffee and chocolate cheesecake. Finn packed their purchases in the boot, and they climbed back into his car. Immediately, the soft scent of her shampoo assaulted him.

Jaysus, that woman had him stirred up on the inside. Stuffing the key into the ignition, he twisted it. The car sparked to life. In fast, jerky movements, Finn used the crank to roll down his window. Hopefully, the chill air would clear his head.

They pulled back onto the highway. Finn needed to say something that would stop him from thinking and calm his mind. "How are you liking your accommodations, then? You never said."

Pippa stretched her legs, as if she, too, were antsy.

"Good. It's very nice. Your house. It makes me think of a movie I saw once, a long time ago."

"*Swiss Family Robinson*," he said, deadpan.

"What? No way! You know that movie?"

"Don't laugh." He grinned, waiting for her to start in on him anyway. "When I was a boy, I wanted my house to be like the Swiss Family Robinson's—minus the heights. I don't like heights."

She laughed anyway, but he didn't care. It pleased him that she understood. When he'd dreamed up his house on the back of a napkin, Amélie had told him it looked stupid.

"*Swiss Family Robinson*? The Disney movie?" A grin had transformed Pippa's face.

He nodded. "The very one. I had a fascination with their whole tree house system, only not some of the more primitive aspects of it. I came up with my own version, but closer to the ground."

"That's great." But then she frowned, as though she couldn't puzzle him out any more than he could her.

Finn wasn't one for drama. He preferred to lay out his thoughts when it suited him. It did then. "You don't like me very much, do you, Pippa Darling?"

A shiver passed over her skin. Had he done that? Or had it been the cool wind sailing through his open window that made Pippa wrap her arms tight around herself? Perhaps she was thinking up a suitable lie. People often lied about what they felt and thought. They hid their beliefs inside them, closely guarded secrets.

Finn didn't have time for such *shite*.

"I don't know." Her answer came out slow and quiet.

Still, he hadn't expected the truth. "I guess I'm wondering the same about you. But I'm grateful for your help fixing my files and . . . there's something about you." *Stop. That's enough, Burke.*

Relief swamped him as he pulled onto his drive. They'd made it home. He flicked the button on his visor and the garage door rolled up. Once he'd pulled the car inside, the door closed behind them, plunging them into dim light.

That shampoo scent of hers swarmed him. He swallowed. "I guess what I'm trying to say is, I'm glad you're here."

A ghost of a smile lit her face. "I am, too."

Forcing himself to reach for the handle, he stepped out and into the quiet of the garage. His head cleared a bit as he unloaded the boot. It had been too long since he'd been with a woman. That was it. He was just wound up.

When his book was done, he'd be able to think again. Then maybe he'd stop considering the pixie beside him so much.

Or maybe she'd get his undivided attention.

19

PIPPA

"We work in silence, work as one while the sun sets on the harshest of days."
—James Black, *To the Ends of the Earth*

First, Finn had taken her to that amazing old church. Arguably, one of the most romantic spots ever. Then they'd gone to the farmers' market, where he'd bought way more food than he needed to from the local farmers.

And then there was what he'd said in the car. *There's something about you.* Except Finn's accent made it even better.

There's some'ting about ya.

Her heart had slammed in her chest, waiting for the rest of the sentence that hadn't come. She'd tried to keep her focus on the road, but it'd been tuned in to the man beside her.

When they got back, Finn invited her into his cottage

to help prepare dinner. Pippa would probably end up setting fire to his entire complex.

There'd been too many close calls in her culinary past. Like the time that chicken had actually started smoking, and a guest at the B&B had called the fire department. Dad had not appreciated the unplanned building evacuation, either.

Pippa had a past filled with at least five blackened teakettles and even more burnt cookies. Hopefully Finn knew what he was doing in the kitchen. Of course, if he did, that would make him even hotter, and that was the last thing Pippa needed. He already dominated her thoughts. No need to make things worse.

The moment she stepped inside Finn's house, she realized she'd gotten the raw part of the bargain with her tiny cottage. The size of Finn's personal space wasn't obvious from the gazebo area, but it was five times the that of Pippa's cottage.

Wow. She trailed a finger over the gleaming countertops —a mixture of gray stone and something sparkly. Quartz, maybe? Definitely high-end. Countertops ran along one wall in an L-shape, with two massive islands in the center. Pippa could've taken a bath in the farmhouse sink. The sleek pine cabinetry probably hid built-in, professional-grade appliances, too. Dad would've killed for a kitchen like Finn's. How was it possible that Finn Burke, creator of depressing, cookie-cutter novels, owned a home like his?

Then she spotted Finn, leaning against an island, hands shoved in his pockets. He clenched and unclenched his jaw as his eyes seemed to track her every move.

She'd ticked him off again. "I'm sorry. I didn't mean to start giving myself a tour. It's just so cool."

He shook his head from side to side, fast, as if to clear it. "Please, tour the house. I *want* you to feel comfortable here, Pippa."

God. The way he said her name, like she was some fairytale creature. She could take a thousand years to describe it and never reach the mark. And he wanted her to feel comfortable. Right then, in that moment, she was anything but comfortable. Hot mess was a better descriptor.

He turned his back to her as he stashed groceries into the already overloaded fridge. She couldn't imagine a dinner for five requiring so much food. But maybe that was it. Finn hadn't needed all that. He was trying to help the local economy. From the pleasure written in his smile at the market and when he packed the library books for donation, it was obvious he enjoyed giving back.

And somehow, she liked him more. Again.

"Why don't you go and take that tour? I'll get things started here." Finn was in the process of loading his stovetop with pans of all shapes and sizes.

Since she didn't know what to make of the thoughts in her head, it was as good a suggestion as any. "Okay."

Forcing her feet forward, she moved through the kitchen. The walls throughout the house were wood, but they'd been manipulated, shaped somehow, to resemble twisted tree limbs. Random branches extended from the walls near the ceiling to form artful, sweeping support beams. Her own room had beams like that, but she hadn't made the connection with the trees until Finn shared the

Swiss Family Robinson inspiration for his home's design. The floor, like the rest of the open area, was a dark hardwood, with rich overtones of honey that matched the shades in the kitchen cabinetry and walls.

The full effect was magical.

She followed the three steps that led down to the glass-walled dining room. Her heart stuttered when she reached the bottom. The entire room appeared perched on the cliffs overlooking the ocean. She'd never leave that spot if she lived there.

A battered farmhouse table that could've easily seated twelve commanded the area. Rustic wooden beams, streaked in the same honeyed palette, made up its uneven top. No piece of wood on the table seemed alike—each was shaded differently, with varying degrees of dullness. Benches constructed with identical material had been positioned on each side. Fluffy flowered cushions covered the tops, inviting anyone to sit, to enjoy the view. These were a far cry from Finn's minimalist style. Whoever had put them there, it certainly wasn't Finn.

"What's the story with the table?" Pippa trailed her finger over the tabletop, noting the rough patches that sanding and finishing couldn't hide, and not caring.

"You like it?" Finn asked, an unmistakable note of pride in his voice.

"Love it." She faced him. "It's perfect. This whole place is the type of thing I'd want if I had the money."

He grinned as he trimmed small amounts of fat from the beef. "The wood came from this old barn in Belfast. They were tearing it down. It reminded me of home. I don't know why, really. Anyway, I tried to pay the owner for it, but he didn't want anything—just asked me to haul away what I could. Look underneath it."

She knelt and examined the underside of the table. Intricate scrollwork ran along the legs, culminating in a flower at each of the supports. "It's so cool. Can you imagine the memories embedded in this wood?"

"For sure. It's a history this has. It's also how I found this land. Zoe and her husband Bob are friends of my Ma and Da. I came to visit them because Bob owns a wood-working business. He built the table, and he told me about this property being for sale." Again, his face lit with boyish enthusiasm.

"Bob's very talented." Pippa moved away, but her mind stayed with the table. "And the cushions?"

"Ma made 'em. *Fecking* ugly, aren't they?" He grinned, obvious affection for his mother lighting his face.

"They're sweet." But it was Finn that was sweet. Using cushions his mother had made—because it had been a gift. Most people would have shoved them into a closet and only taken them out for visits. If they remembered at all.

Pictures of Finn with, she presumed, his family, lined the walls. A large photo of Finn with an older couple took center stage. He seemed about fourteen, all gangly limbs and an easy smile then. There seemed to Pippa to be very little of twenty-five-year-old Finn in that pic. Another of an older Finn hung beside that one. He was standing in a rowboat, balancing on the sides with apparent ease. "Did your family live on the water where you grew up?"

"Not on it. There was a *lough* within driving distance. We were right in the middle, so about two hours' drive to either the west coast or the east." There was a wistful note in his voice.

"Do you miss home?" she asked. Pippa scanned the pictures. Nature scenes filled the backdrop of almost every picture. There were blue lakes, stunning mountains, and crumbling castles. In one photo, Finn kissed the older woman (his mom?) on the cheek. They both beamed. Why couldn't Finn ever be that happy when Pippa was around? Instead, he always seemed angsty.

She didn't expect friendship, but it would have been nice if they could get along. Her attempts with Uma at FaceTime over the past couple weeks hadn't been successful. Dad was tucked away in Gettysburg, across the ocean, in the house with her flowered bedspread.

The truth was, she could use a friend.

"I do." Finn swept through her thoughts with his answer. "But you never really leave Tipperary. Like Ireland herself, she reaches inside of you and becomes part of your soul. But I do love the sea." He tossed the remains of the trimmings in the trash. "Enough with the questions. You're meant to be taking a tour. *Tour.*" He waved her away.

"Okay, okay." Pippa moved on to some sort of sitting area that was walled in windows. There were several chairs and a sofa with wooden legs—all covered in red damask. It was too formal for Finn. Probably another gift from Ma. From that room, she had a view of the castle keep Finn had been restoring.

French doors barred the entrance to the next room. She pushed them open and stepped inside. The room was smaller, with a less spectacular view. Plants encroached on the windows, caging in the area, filtering the sunlight. Judging by the framed book cover on the wall, it was Finn's office. She'd never seen a less uninspiring space.

As a testament to her own thoughts, a thin layer of dust covered the abandoned typewriter that sat on the polished desk's top. No wonder Finn preferred the gazebo over that dismal cave. She couldn't blame him. Pippa always chose to work in the light.

Shutting the doors again, she moved down the hall, following the sculpted wood walls. Two guest rooms over-looked a tranquil clearing, though it was obvious they, too, didn't get a ton of use. The beds had been made up like hotel beds, complete with hospital corners and smooth coverlets. The wood walls continued inside the two rooms, reinforcing the impression Finn lived inside a tree.

The final room had French doors similar to those in the office. It must've been Finn's bedroom. It was an invasion of privacy to go inside, but she opened the doors before she could stop herself.

Light spilled through the windows, sending patches of sun onto a massive four-poster bed. The sheets on the unmade bed were a shiny, dark navy—silk, maybe? *Sexy sheets*, Uma would've called them. A small pile of laundry had been stacked on the bureau in a neat mini-tower. A pair of gray briefs rested on top. A blush heated Pippa's cheeks as she envisioned Finn wearing them.

Moving through the room, she checked out the master bath. Wide windows at hip-level let in more light. She took a step toward the windows and realized those, too, had an ocean view. He probably wasn't worried about the neighbors peeking in. Not when his nearest neighbor was the Atlantic.

Her own bathroom was similar, except it didn't have Finn. God, what was happening to her? Turning on the spot, she swiftly exited Finn's bedroom, pulling the doors shut behind her with a soft click.

"Are you okay?"

She jumped as Finn's voice slashed through her thoughts. Doing her best not to cringe, she spun around. Pippa's entire face was on fire. *Hell.* Her entire *body* was burning.

"You have a beautiful home. It's . . ."

"What?" He frowned when her voice trailed off.

"It's magical."

"Magical, really? Good thing you write children's books." Finn smirked. Did he have any idea how sexy he looked when he did that? Of course, he did. He was a man. A sexy *Irish* man. He'd probably been born knowing the effect he'd have on women.

"You're the one who picked me based on my work, so you've only got yourself to blame."

His gaze seemed to zero in on her bottom lip for several moments before he blinked. "A minor drawback." Fortunately for Pippa's pale face and raging hormones, he turned away.

That's when she processed his words. "Why is my writing young adult books a minor drawback?" She lodged her hands onto her hips, waiting for his response. Sometimes he had the manners of a caveman, and the social skills to match.

Finn spun around, his proximity leaving her practically flush against the wall.

He was so close that she could read every detail in his eyes. Before, she'd thought they were light green, but at that proximity, she noticed they were rimmed in a gold so light, most people probably never noticed. And then there were his lips again, inches away. Those lips she'd dreamed about, both waking and sleeping. His gaze searched hers, pinning her in place, sending all her conscious thoughts into a panic room in the back of her mind.

"Here's why it's a drawback," he said, his voice as light and as soft as a caress, as though they were talking about something else entirely. "I like sex."

Oh, Holy Mother.

"Writing about it, of course." He grinned. "And—"

Pippa had no chance of regaining her normal complexion. Her face burned. She had to resemble a tomato. She'd have to make a point of avoiding mirrors for the rest of the evening. "I don't need to hear the gory details." She held up a hand, her palm inches from his lips. "Besides, there are *those kinds of scenes* in young adult books. I write them."

"Do you?" he asked, his voice soft, hushed in the hall. "Do you write sex scenes that take you over, Pippa?"

"Sure." It had grown too hot, and Finn's nearness sent her head spinning. God, she wanted to kiss him again, to lose herself in him.

"What do you feel when you write them? Do they make you come alive?" he asked.

That single question had frozen—no, *glued* her to the wall, its uneven, tree-like texture digging into her back.

"Isn't it that way for everyone?" She'd gotten lost in his eyes. When he leaned in and grazed her cheek with his lips, electricity sparked along her skin and shot through her body.

God, she ached to taste him again. If only. She didn't move as she waited for him to head back to the kitchen, to act as though the weird tension between them didn't exist. But it did. It was as though a string connecting her to Finn had been drawn taut. Pippa found herself overly attuned to his every movement, no matter how small.

"Do you think about me when you write those scenes, Pippa?" He held his breath.

Finn was her boss, but to push him away. to lie about her feelings, would have meant denying the slow, burning ache building within her. "Sometimes." *All the time.*

He exhaled, slow and steady, as though he were pushing through an invisible barrier. "I think about you all the time." He framed her face in his hands, guiding her to him, until their lips were a whisper apart.

Please. Yes, *please.*

Still, Pippa's logic had to get a word in. "I thought you said our kiss was a mistake?"

"It *is* wrong, this thing between us." His voice sent a thrill across her skin—the timbre almost as powerful as his words.

"There isn't anything between us." Pippa forced her voice steady and leveled her gaze on his.

He cocked an eyebrow. "You're not that naïve."

She forced herself to keep from shaking, but her resolve wouldn't last. It was his eyes. Those eyes did things to her. They could see into her soul. "No. but you said our kiss shouldn't have happened."

"That's because you're working for me. I'd never want you to think you had to be with me to keep your job. You don't." He trailed the pad of his thumb along her jawline, until he reached her bottom lip. He swiped his thumb once across the sensitive flesh.

"Finn." Pippa couldn't move. Couldn't even consider it. She'd been waiting for this, *needing* this. "That's the only reason you haven't kissed me again?"

He nodded, one slow, heat-filled nod that sent her heart racing and left her feeling bolder than before.

She tipped her chin, hoping she wouldn't regret her next words. "Then I quit."

20

FINN

"The bastard—I could have killed him right then. Shot him right between the eyes to keep them from seeing what was meant to be mine."
—Finn Burke, *Lost*

Finn's mouth was an inch from Pippa's. Like earlier that day, at the church, he knew what he was doing was wrong. He should have been keeping his distance, sending Pippa away on different sight-seeing trips to put distance between them.

He'd done the opposite. Her gaze locked onto his, burning him, branding him. He couldn't forget her.

Even the night before, he'd stayed up thinking about her. Imagining her wrapped around him, squeezing, hugging his flesh as he stroked into her. He'd finally taken care of the business on his own, until the ache subsided enough for sleep. Even then, it hadn't been enough.

Then her words sank into his clouded brain. "You quit? You can't quit. I need a bloody intern."

"Maybe if I just quit . . . *temporarily?*" That little divot formed in her brow again, generating an immediate response in Finn's body.

So, she did want him, too. "*Jaysus*, woman, you'll be the death of me."

"Well?" She bit her lip, sending heat plummeting to his loins.

Her mouth was an inch from his. She was so close he couldn't bring her into focus. Damn it all.

"Resignation accepted." He barely ground out the words before he bent down and captured her mouth in a soft kiss, brushing his lips over hers, reintroducing himself to her taste and touch. He wanted to be gentle. He did. He'd already crossed a line and that move couldn't be undone.

Pippa's mouth was a sin-packed present, even more tempting than he remembered. He'd meant to unwrap it slowly, but except for Pippa, he hadn't so much as looked at a woman in years, let alone kissed one. The plan to take his time went out the window the moment—no, the *instant* their lips touched.

Their mouths moved over each other's, exploring, memorizing. Pippa's lips seared Finn's. Each point of contact burned him, tripling the tension inside him until he traced his tongue along the seam of her lips, coaxing them apart.

On a sigh, she opened her mouth against his, allowing him to taste her. Their tongues met, and he swept his own around Pippa's, before moving back and forth along the sensitive spot on the roof of her mouth in a sort of dance.

He had no doubt she wanted this, too, for Pippa wasn't

one to get in line and just agree. She spoke her mind, no matter how awkward. She was the truth and the light, a ball of fire that had somehow reignited his soul.

Pippa's short nails dug into his forearms. Finn dragged her against him, pressing Pippa against the wall, if only to still the sensation of the room spinning. Her back was lean and muscled beneath his fingers, and he ached to guide her fully against him. To know her as a man knows a woman. He couldn't get close enough.

But then the sound of the front door opening sent them springing apart. They stood on opposite sides of the narrow hall as Zoe's *fecking* son, Caden, walked around the corner and came to a halt, the bastard.

"Finn," he said, but he wasn't looking at Finn.

The *arse* had focused all his attention on Pippa, his eyes roaming her body, taking in her every feature. The dog winked and flashed his pearly whites as he finished his inspection. "Hiya, I'm Caden. You'll be Pippa?"

"Yep." Pippa gave Caden a weak smile. It pleased Finn to note that Pippa seemed more than a little dazed. If Finn hadn't just been in the process of getting to know Pippa better, he would have assumed she was falling for Caden's bleached teeth and blond highlights. The *bollocks* looked like he was two steps away from starting a boy band. Some women were into that. But Finn, not Caden, had been the one to put Pippa in such a state. He couldn't help being proud of that.

He could kick the boy out, tell him dinner was off. He couldn't do that to Zoe and Bob, though. They'd both been good to him. It wasn't their fault Caden was a *fecking wanker* and had strolled in as if he owned the place.

"Your folks coming down?" Finn asked.

"Ma wants to know what kind of wine to bring," Caden said, as he shoved his hands into his pockets, eyeing Pippa again.

Finn ran a hand through his hair. What had he been cooking again? Right. Steaks. He was meant to be cooking steaks. "Red, maybe a Cab?"

Caden nodded. "Right, then." He turned and left, shutting the door behind him.

The moment they were alone again, Finn caught Pippa's hand in his. "Pippa."

"Please don't say that was a mistake." She gnawed on her bottom lip. Had she no idea how crazy that one action made him?

"It wasn't." He took her hand and brought it to his mouth, grazing her knuckles with his lips before releasing her. It would've been easy, too easy, to carry her to his room, to fulfill every one of the dreams that had been keeping him up at night for weeks. He didn't stand a chance at staying away from her.

He wanted Pippa Darling, make no mistake, but when they enjoyed each other, it wouldn't be something he did in a rush. He'd take his time.

Finn couldn't think of the right words to say. He knew he'd already taken things too far. He'd had a plan and he should have stuck to it, but somehow, plans went by the wayside when Pippa was around. "They'll be back soon. We have to get dinner started."

"Sure." Pippa nodded and followed, letting him guide her with loose fingers linked between her own. He liked the feel of her hand in his. Like he could be himself with her.

Guilt slammed into him. Finn had to tell her. He needed to confess his alter ego right then, but he couldn't. Later. Another time. A *better* time.

When they returned to the kitchen, he poured them both a glass of the red he'd already had on hand. God, if he'd ever needed a drink, it was right then. He'd been close to losing control. How could he possibly be expected to keep away from her? Especially when her body had vibrated from his touch. He had to keep it light. Still, he couldn't resist poking a bit of fun at Pippa, for it was in his nature.

"So, about these sex scenes you write. I bet they're really tame. Something like . . . 'He pets her boob'." He laughed as he set his glass on the counter and turned to seasoning the beef. There was no time for marinating. A few improvised spices would have to do.

Pippa jerked her head, as though she was fighting not to spit out her wine, but then she righted herself, arching one eyebrow. "At least it's better than 'I want to fuck you'."

Finn's eyes rounded. *Jaysus*, but it was something of a turn-on hearing her say his words aloud. Especially *those* words. He grinned like a schoolboy.

"Which I don't, by the way. That was j-just an example." Pippa blushed again, the red blending with her creamy skin, turning it a most becoming shade of pink. She tossed back the rest of her wine as though she held nothing more than a shot glass. "Actually, I think it's . . . *crass*."

"But you're an adult. With adult needs and wants." He

swallowed, unable to fight the million and one images of what he and Pippa could be to each other from sweeping across his brain.

"I'm also a romantic. I want to be loved and adored and everything else that goes with it." That sounded like her. Of course Pippa would want the romance of it all.

Had he botched things by kissing her? At least he hadn't pulled on her hair like that fool character of hers had been doing.

He'd been about to say so, about to make her see, when she averted her eyes.

"When my characters . . . *do it* . . . they love each other. The sex *matters*. It's not meaningless."

Finn frowned as he turned to slide the steaks into the broiler. He fussed and fiddled with the oven as he did so. Her jibe went so deep that he almost didn't realize it for what it was. When his brain had a moment of processing, he snapped his head up.

"I don't write *meaningless* sex. Sex can never be meaningless anyway. There are only fools who pretend it is. Then they spend half their time trying to forget what they did. Make as if it meant nothing." He leveled his gaze to hers, remembering the press of her body against his when they kissed. "It always means something."

Pippa set her glass aside, seeming transfixed by the empty wine goblet. "If it means something, then why don't you write it that way? I mean, *Lost* is such a was—"

But she dropped off, covering her lips. Her fierce brown eyes locked onto his, something undefinable brewing behind her irises.

Pippa turned away from him, grabbing a knife and a

pile of green beans from the colander. She began butchering the ends of the beans, cutting each one individually and badly. Every time she finished with one, she set it aside and lined them up. Perfectly aligned vegetables were the least of Finn's concerns.

He shouldn't ask the obvious question, shouldn't push any more than he had. Yet, he had to know. "What's the rest of that sentence, Pippa? Finish it. That *Lost* is a waste? Do you even *like* my writing?"

A firm knock on the door broke through the silence as he waited for her answer. Pippa swallowed. "That'll be Zoe. I'm gonna go say hello."

"Pippa," Finn said, not bothering to keep the warning note from his voice.

"We can't keep Zoe waiting." Pippa spun around and jogged from the room.

"We're not done talking about this!" he shouted as she left.

But he'd been given his answer. And for that, he had only himself to blame.

21

PIPPA

*"The greatest enemy is one who lies in wait, striking only when
we've found safe harbor."*
—James Black, *To the Ends of the Earth*

Despite the tension between Pippa and Finn,
Pippa enjoyed every moment of the evening
that followed. At least when she wasn't obsessing over
how she'd left things with Finn. Finn's steak dinner could
only have been described as a culinary orgasm. Every
carrot melted in her mouth. Each bean tasted light, but
had been infused with a buttery flavor. The meat burst
with juiciness—some sort of mesquite seasoning.

Dad was a pretty decent cook. He had to be, running a
B&B and all. Regardless, Jim Darling had some stiff
competition in Finn. Pippa stole a glance at Finn and then
quickly looked away. Every time she'd even hinted at
turning in his direction, his attention seemed wholly
fixated on her. Those eyes of his threatening to see
through her, like they knew all her secrets.

Still, the evening with Zoe's family was far more enjoyable than Pippa had ever imagined. The Hannigans were easy people to be around. Bob was a pleasant, large, round-faced man, with cheeks almost as red as Pippa's. Their son, Caden, was young, blond, handsome, and he'd kept shooting flirtatious looks her way all night long.

Finn seemed to have noticed. When he wasn't hyper-focused on Pippa, he'd spent most of the evening glaring at Caden. At one point, she was convinced that Finn would refuse to pass the rolls Caden's way.

"The lad came to me asking for help with his dining room table. To make matters worse, he actually wanted to help me build it. I've never seen anyone less handy with a set of tools than our Finn." Bob slapped his hand on the table, making Pippa jump.

"There's truth in that." Finn grinned. "But you sure changed things for me, didn't you?"

"You bet your *arse* I did." Bob gave Finn a high five. "You've been learning ever since, and now you're not afraid of hard work."

"How's the rebuilding of the keep coming?" Zoe asked. "I haven't made it over there in a while."

Finn shrugged. "A little day by day. Still lots of stone to stack, though. Perhaps your Caden could put in an appearance now and again. Help us out with it."

"Pippa." Caden flashed his baby blues her way. "It would be far easier to get out of this painful task if you'd go on a date with me. Let me show you the sights and sounds of our fair country."

"I'd say she's seen plenty of the sights and sounds,"

Finn said, his voice taking on a sharp edge. "Haven't you, Pippa?"

"Oh, I haven't seen nearly enough," Pippa said. Finn's stare turned murderous before her eyes. He was definitely jealous. It was nice to know that, despite the confusing feelings that had been circling around in the pit of her stomach ever since their kiss, Finn seemed to be experiencing the same. "But I do have a ton of work to do. I'm sorry."

"No matter. I'll just deal with my own broken heart, then." Caden sighed, but he grinned and winked at her, softening the blow.

Pippa glanced away, not wanting to encourage him. Caden was hot—all long limbs and a shock of brown hair with blond highlights. But there was no attraction there— at least not for Pippa. Not the way there was with—

Finn rested his arm across the back of Pippa's chair. His thumb grazed the exposed skin at the base of her neck, sending a wave of tingles across her skin.

Zoe cocked an eyebrow. Nothing was getting by that one.

"You've got plenty of experience with busted hearts, Caden. Especially, your own." Finn dropped the insult casually— a master move. Some of the light went out of Caden's eyes. "But let me worry about Pippa's education."

Oh snap.

Wait. Oh, shit. Pippa reddened at Finn's double entendre. She focused on her steak, but with Finn's wandering fingers of torture, it was hard to remember to chew her food. Especially when her face still tingled from where his whiskers had scratched her skin.

"To a summer of learning new things." Bob winked as he raised his glass in a toast.

She sat up straighter, trying to put herself out of Finn's reach, but his fingers stayed where they were. It was like they'd been designed to strip moisture from her throat and steal thoughts from her head.

And man, did Finn know it. Apparently, Caden did, too.

"Well, I'm off." Caden balled up his napkin and tossed it at Finn, hitting him square in the forehead. "That is, if it's all right with you, Ma and Da? Some lads are headed down to the pub. We're going to sit in."

"Go on then," Zoe said, grinning. "Don't leave your guitar at Dono's again. *And* don't drink so much I'll have to pick you up at one in the morning."

"You've a deal, Ma." He kissed her cheek as he stood and saluted Finn. Then he turned to Pippa. "Finn, thank you for dinner. Pippa, it was a real pleasure. Let me know if you find time for that tour."

"She won't," Finn said, gritting his teeth.

Pippa suppressed the thrill that ran through her at Finn's words.

With a nod, Caden strode to the door, cell phone in hand. It was only after he left that Pippa experienced being on the receiving end of one of Zoe's near-psychic, inquisitive stares.

"You're quiet tonight, Pippa," Zoe said.

"I'm sorry. I don't mean to be. It's just . . . this dinner is unbelievable. Thanks, Finn." She finally allowed herself to turn fully in his direction.

His eyes glittered as he poured another round of wine.

"*Sláinte*. To your health." He raised his glass. "I'm only sorry it's taken me far too long to make this dinner a reality. It's been a very stimulating summer."

"That it has." Zoe sipped from her wineglass.

"Are any of you up for dessert, by chance? Pippa picked out a cheesecake that she swears will put your heart in a state." Finn downed the rest of his wine.

"I'd love some. Come on, Pippa. Let's give Finn a break. Help me in the kitchen." Zoe stood, so Pippa had little choice but to do the same.

She practically dragged Pippa into the kitchen and didn't stop until they were standing close to the fridge. The dining room was still within view, and Pippa could see Finn's flannel-clad elbow out of the corner of her eye.

"What's going on between the pair of you?" Zoe's face was a picture of concern.

"I don't know what you mean." Pippa did her best to give Zoe an open and honest smile, but she'd never been much of a liar.

"That's bullshit, that is. I've been watching you two all evening. I thought he'd rip poor Caden's head off, just for trying to be neighborly."

Oh, so that's what Caden had been doing. "I'm sure Finn's just being protective. I am his intern."

"And that's what's concerning me. You're working for Mr. Burke, after all. Do you really think it's such a good idea to get involved as you are?" Zoe asked, pulling a stack of small plates from a shelf above the stove.

"We're not involved, Zoe. I don't know what we are." Since Pippa didn't understand what had been brewing between Finn and herself, she certainly couldn't explain it to Zoe. Opening the fridge, Pippa pulled out the cheese-cake and set it on the counter beside a long, thin knife. She removed the cheesecake from its container and then began to slice into the dessert.

"That's what I'm afraid of." Zoe transferred pieces to the plates.

"I'm not gonna lie to you." Pippa craned her neck. She still had a clear shot of Finn's elbow. "I like him. In a way I didn't think was possible, but I guess you picked up on that."

"Of course I did. I'm mother to a boy, after all." But Zoe's face formed its characteristic smile. "I'm just worried. Burke can be a moody sort."

"No, really?" Pippa asked. "I didn't pick up on that." She put her tongue in her cheek.

Zoe roared with laughter, but it didn't last. Her grin softened, and something close to a twinkle lit her eye as she plated the desserts. "You're something, Pippa. I can see why you would pique his interest."

Pippa poured tea into cups, deliberately keeping her voice level as she asked, "Have there been many women who've piqued his interest?"

Zoe added forks to the plates. "I told you I thought he'd turned celibate. That should tell you right enough what I thought. What we *all* thought."

Pippa fought a smile as she poured the final cup of tea. So there really hadn't been anyone else for Finn. Suddenly, relief overwhelmed her. Pippa threw her arms around Zoe and hugged her. "Thank you for looking out for me."

"Of course. Your people aren't here to help. Seems like

you need somebody on your side. Just promise me you won't go breaking his heart. He's like a son to me."

Pippa jerked her head in Zoe's direction. "I think it's the other way around that you need to be concerned about." She scooped up the teacups.

"Is it? Things aren't always as they seem, Pippa. Remember that." Plates in hand, Zoe turned and headed back to the dining room, leaving Pippa to her thoughts.

She'd believed the toughest thing she'd have to do was finish her novel. As it stood, her biggest challenge seemed to be cracking the case of Finn Burke.

FINN

*"She wanted me, and I her. What was the point in
conversation?"*
—Finn Burke, *Lost*

*A*round ten or so, Zoe and Bob said they'd best be
going. It was a good thing, too, as Pippa's eyes
had begun to droop. Finn contemplated carrying her to
bed, so she could spend the night in one of his unused
guest rooms. Or, much more in line with what he wanted
himself, he could take her to *his* bed.

Images of his mouth on Pippa's tumbled into Finn's
head. She hadn't backed down. She'd welcomed his kiss.
She'd even quit her job, as he recalled, so she could kiss
him. His traitorous body wasted no time reminding him
that it'd been too long since he'd been with anyone.

But wants and needs aside, there were things to say. It
had been strange, her reaction to the question about his
writing. He planned to get to the bottom of things.

Pippa rested her head against the front door as Zoe

and Bob walked down Finn's driveway, their choruses of "Thank you!" trailing behind them.

"'Night!" Finn called.

Pippa righted herself and stepped down onto the front porch. Clearly, she planned to follow in Zoe and Bob's footsteps. "Thank you so much for din—"

"Where do you think you're going?" He took her hand, leading her back into the house.

Her eyes locked onto his, but not before she stifled a yawn. "I was going to go to bed." Her face reddened. "I mean. Not with you, or anything. With myself. To sleep. To sleep by myself." She slapped her palm against her forehead.

Christ, that had been awkward. Finn would have felt bad—if it weren't damn funny. But right then wasn't the time to focus on Pippa's quirks. He needed to know what was going on in that head of hers. It would drive him *barmy* otherwise. "Come on, you. Those who don't cook, clean up."

"Okay." Pippa walked down to the dining room and began clearing the table.

Finn positioned himself in front of the sink, dropped some of the pots he'd used to cook with into the bubbles, and then buried his arms elbow-deep in soapy water. Little swirls of steam drifted into the air from its depths as he tackled the pots and pans he'd left out on the counter.

A moment later, Pippa returned, setting a stack of cutlery on the counter nearest to Finn. He added this to the dishwasher while Pippa retrieved the plates. She returned and set to scraping the plates one by one, loading them into the dishwasher as she cleared them. Finn finished washing the pots and pans, resting each on a towel beside the sink.

He went through the motions of adding soap to the dishwasher, shutting the door, and pressing Start, but his mind wasn't all there. Grabbing the towel, he took to drying some of the pots he'd washed, trying to figure out what he really wanted to ask her. It was tough getting to the heart of the matter if he didn't know which questions to ask.

"Why don't you make the dining room your office?"

He blinked, focusing on Pippa, who'd rested both her elbows on the counter.

Not what he'd expected. He dried his hands on the towel. "Because it's the dining room. People eat there, or haven't you heard of that?"

"Yeah, but the dining room is special. It's got this great view and you have pictures of your family in there. It's clearly where your heart is. Your office is so boring. It's so unlike you." Her eyes widened, and she covered her mouth. She'd said something else she'd meant to filter out.

"You think I'm *not* boring. That's something, at least." His eyes locked onto Pippa's as he scrubbed another pot, the sound of water rushing and the clink of plates in the dishwasher their only soundtrack. "But . . . you still don't like my writing, do you?"

He did his best to pretend the pot was worth more of his attention than Pippa. That he didn't care what she thought. He was doing a piss-poor job of it, if he did say so himself.

"It's not really the genre I read."

But he knew that wasn't true. She'd read James Black, after all. He'd been her favorite author for years. Technically, both iterations of his work fell into the same genre.

What was wrong with him? Pippa was his intern, a paid employee. It shouldn't matter what she thought of him and his work. His past two interns could have taken the job for the same reason she did. He never would have known. Still . . .

"So you don't like my work and you don't care for my writing advice." He whipped the towel out and began re-drying one of the pots he'd been about to put away. "I'm wondering why it is that you're here?"

"Because it's a great opportunity and because you picked me." Pippa moved out of the kitchen, returning several moments later with napkins, assorted cutlery, and an empty bottle of wine.

"That's all?" he asked, but he knew it wasn't, because at some point he'd started to understand her. There had to be more to the story. Pippa always had a reason for everything she did.

She pressed the heels of her hands against the countertop. "I want my name on the list. You can help me get there." Her voice was quiet. Almost so quiet that he didn't hear her.

Finn frowned. "What list?"

"NYT. The New York Times Best Sellers list. I guess I was hoping I could—"

"Use my name to get there? Use *me*?" His words barely masked the growing anger raging inside him. She'd come for one reason and one reason only: to get her name on some Goddamn list.

Then it hit him all at once. "And I played right into your hands and kissed you."

Her eyes narrowed. "What are you talking about?"

Finn tossed the pot aside with a bang as the full brunt of Pippa's secret hit him square in the jaw. "What better way to get attention than some sensational story about how I used you and got you into my bed?" Thank the Lord he hadn't confessed to being James Black. Then she'd have the opportunity to ruin two of his names.

"How can you even insinuate something like that, you jackass?" Pippa sputtered, her entire face burning. "I don't use people."

Gritting his teeth, he tossed the towel onto the counter. "That's not what it sounds like to me." He wanted her out of his sight. He'd begun to let someone in, to trust her. Look where that had gotten him. "It's a good thing you already quit." He forced his voice to even out and his eyes to their coldest setting. "Now all you have to do is get out."

Pippa's bottom lip trembled, though her eyes managed to flash fire at him at the same time. Turning, she left the room, hands fisted at her sides. Moments later, the door slammed.

And Finn was alone. *Again.*

23

PIPPA

"She held his heart in her hand, and it might have been the whole world for the way she cared for it—tender and achingly thoughtful."
—James Black, *To the Ends of the Earth*

Last night had been the worst. She hadn't slept. She couldn't get the look on Finn's face out of her mind. He'd worn the strangest expression. A mixture of hurt and knowledge—as though he'd been waiting to find out that information about her.

She'd done everything to prove him right.

"You sound awful." Dad's voice boomed over the line. Despite the warmth in his tone, Pippa knew Jim Darling would pound Finn's head into the ground if she asked him to. He'd do it with a smile on his face, too, because he always smiled. When it came to his only daughter, he'd be on her side—every time. She had to be extremely careful with anything she said. Otherwise, Dad would be on the first flight to Ireland.

"What's going on there? Is Burke still overloading you?" There it was again, that warning note. Pippa might as well start planning Dad's itinerary.

"I told him I didn't like his work." Pippa cringed as she recounted the tale of the previous night, leaving out the part where she and Finn had kissed. "The thing is, I thought he was a jerk when I arrived, but he's a good guy. I think I might have hurt his feelings."

Just promise me you won't go breaking his heart. That's what Zoe had asked of her.

Clearly, no one had passed on the same request to Finn on *Pippa's* behalf. Her chest still ached from the accusations he'd made. How could he even think she'd stood for something so base as seducing him for fame? After all those weeks together?

But the last thing she could do was tell that to Dad.

"If you really did hurt the guy, you know what to do. It's the same thing I taught you when you were eight and you stole Becky Salucci's jump rope." Several small sounds filtered over the line from Dad's side of the call. He was probably handing out maps or making change. "Apologize to him."

The idea of apologizing to Finn turned her stomach, though she couldn't say why. But there was no denying Dad was right.

"How did you get to be so smart?" she asked.

"I think it was from my incredibly smart daughter, who is also an excellent apologizer, by the way." Dad laughed. "Watcha gonna do, Pip?"

"I'm going to say I'm sorry. Call you later?"

"I'll be here!" Dad said, his cheerfulness bolstering her,

even though he was thousands of miles away. It didn't last, however. Her anger at Finn crept back into her thoughts the instant she ended the call.

She was pissed at Finn, but he needed to know the truth. Pippa wasn't going to just run off and let him believe the worst. It wasn't in her nature to get physical with a guy she didn't care about. Damn if she didn't care about that crab-ass.

Gathering her courage, she left her cottage and headed outside and up the walkway. She had a pretty good idea where Finn was. It was where he always was when they weren't writing. The keep.

Taking a breath to steel herself, Pippa began to climb the rocky hillside. In all her time at Finn's, she'd never once gone to visit on her own. Whenever Finn had left her with free time, it had always been late at night or raining.

The embankment grew steeper as she climbed over the rocks jutting out of the grass. It wasn't an impossible climb. She only had a couple more feet before she reached the flat land on which the keep stood. Throwing her arms out for balance, she continued upward. Finn really needed a good set of stairs.

Once the trees on her left cleared, Pippa took in the view. Cliffs spread out beneath her, impossibly stark and flirting with the wild Atlantic Ocean. Waves crashed against rock, their sound heavy and hypnotic, reminding her that she played only one small part in the world. Gray clouds rolled in over the water, painting drama into the sky.

The way grew steeper and steeper. She slipped and caught herself just as she reached the crest of the hill. The *chink* of stone meeting stone competed with the roar of the sea.

When she reached the top of the hill, the keep came into view. It was nothing more than a large, wide, conical tower surrounded by a crumbling wall. The gray stone rose into the sky, a picture of the past, but also the future.

She stepped through the only break in the wall and froze. Finn stood, shirtless, adding blocks to the remains of the castle's keep.

He stopped, his head darting back and forth as he turned from a pile of stone to the wall and back. She caught on to the problem right away. None of the stones seemed like a good fit for the wall. He was staggering them so that they weren't lined up exactly. Each one was too long.

That's when Pippa noticed a stone at her feet. The perfect size. Just a little shorter than the rest, like Pippa herself. Gripping the stone, she stepped up to the wall and added her find.

When she righted herself, she paused. Finn's eyes had locked onto hers. She couldn't keep her eyes from raking over his body. The memory of their kiss tore through her mind. Her throat parched.

Finn seemed just as taken with her. He swallowed, his Adam's apple bobbing along the fine column of his throat.

"I'm surprised you've come looking for me, since you're after hating every word which comes out of my mouth." He crossed his arms, somehow managing to make himself look even sexier. Before that moment, Pippa wouldn't have thought it possible. "Or is it media coverage you're after? Are you filming me right now? 'Seducing you?'" He used air quotes for the words.

"Okay, let's get something straight. I didn't come here to seduce you. And I don't hate all your words. Just *some* of them." She slapped her hand over her mouth. "I didn't mean that."

"You did." He said it without apology, but he wasn't the one who needed to give one.

"I'm sorry." She forced her eyes to meet his. "I didn't like your work when I took this internship. But I also didn't know you. You were just a name on a spine, and I didn't even have a picture to go on to help me form an impression. Only your name."

Finn nodded. "But don't you think it was inappropriate to take on this internship knowing how you felt about my book?"

He wasn't going to budge on things, was he? "I should've probably given the spot to a fan, but I was desperate."

Finn's face seemed to solidify, so that his expression became as impassive as the stone around him. "Desperate to work for me? You're not making one bit of sense."

"I was desperate not to go home."

That time, his frown lightened, and he leaned back against the low stone wall. "You don't like your parents."

Where only a bit of a breeze had shuffled through the tree branches before, it had picked up, tossing Pippa's hair this way and that. Even the temperature seemed to have dropped a degree or two. She crossed her arms over her chest.

"It's just Dad. Mom died when I was eleven. Lupus." She swallowed, forcing aside the familiar blockage that turned up when she spoke of Mom. "And we do get along, it's just . . . he wants me to take over his bed and breakfast so he can retire."

Finn nodded. "And you hate the idea." The understanding smile that lit Finn's face transformed it, sending heat through her entire body, even to the soles of Pippa's feet.

"Yes. I don't know how to tell him. Coming here has given me the chance to write, to really see what I'm made of without the interruption of guests. Getting on the list— I think it would prove to Dad that I'm a real writer. It's a tangible thing."

"So's finishing your book." He cocked an eyebrow.

"I know. But Dad worries. If I showed him I was successful enough that I didn't need the B&B, he'd take my writing seriously. Then I considered what this internship could offer me and . . ."

"And I'm the only downside," he said. But despite his casual posture, he sounded hurt. It still surprised her that a crab-ass like Finn Burke could be hurt by her words. Why did he care what she thought? "So sorry my words make your ears bleed."

"They don't." She sucked in a breath, trying to form an apology in her mind. Failing that, she opted for her patented verbal-vomit method instead. "I didn't come here to take advantage of you. I didn't come here to get anything. I want to learn, to be a better writer. It's . . . your books are . . ." She swallowed, tears stinging her eyes. "They're coarse, they're . . . edgy . . . they make me uncomfortable. But you're a brilliant writer when you let yourself be."

His hands fisted at his sides. "But I'm no James Black, right?" Just like that, they were back to the same stalemate they'd gotten stuck on before.

"I've read many versions of this book while trying to piece it all together. In your early drafts, your words were wonderful. But then you changed them into what you think people want to read. They could've stood on their own." Pippa moved closer, until she stood directly in front of Finn. "And anyway, I'm sorry. I never meant to hurt you."

Finn's face, his entire posture, relaxed, his shoulders softening. "I'm sorry, too. The things I said . . . they were unforgivable." Pippa wasn't sure he'd share any more, until he locked onto her eyes with his own intense green ones. "I have trust issues, I guess you could say."

"Don't we all." She forced a swallow and wished she'd stockpiled more courage. His apology didn't erase the hurt his earlier words had caused, but it was a start. "I forgive you."

"Pippa, about last night. I'm sorry. That shouldn't have happened." His voice was rough, husky. His thoughts just as impenetrable as before.

He couldn't have meant that. She perused his bare chest, the fine column of his throat, his locked jaw, and finally his face and those eyes. "I'm pretty sure it's been waiting to happen since the first time you kissed me."

Great. Would she ever learn how to stop unwanted things from leaving her mouth?

But it didn't seem to anger him. Instead, he nodded, as though that was the first sensible thing she'd said. "Maybe, but it still shouldn't have happened. I'm supposed to be your mentor, your teacher. Kissing you is . . ."

Incredible? Sinful? The best ever in his life?

"*Wrong.*" Finn cringed.

It shouldn't have hurt so much, hearing what Finn thought about their kiss. Shouldn't have, but somehow, the pain wheedled its way inside of her, leaving the smallest of holes in her heart.

"And the truth is," he said, "that I've been able to think of little else since. I don't know how to leave you alone."

"Does this mean I can have my job back?"

A myriad of emotions crossed Finn's face, ending in one Pippa knew well: the look of yearning that had flooded him the night before, right before he'd kissed her. "Not just yet."

She bit her bottom lip, waiting, listening. The chill air blew in from the sea, ruffling Finn's hair, making her want to run her fingers through it.

His eyes widened. "It's not— I just don't— If you *want* to leave . . . if you want to go because I've overstepped my bounds, I'd be more than understanding of that." He shoved his hands into his jeans pockets, reminding her of a little boy. "Of course, I hope you don't, what with the deadline and all, but I would understand."

The grip on Pippa's heart released and she took a step back. "So that's all you care about, is the deadline." She didn't buy it even as she said it, but she had to know where he stood. What was in that padlocked brain of his? The one that never let any thoughts escape.

His hands clenched at his sides. He wasn't going to answer. He'd walk away, leaving her there because she'd pushed him too far.

But he didn't. He strode forward, only to stop inches from Pippa, framing her face in his callused palms.

"I spend every night dreaming of you, imagining what it would be like to make love to you." His face looked stricken, as though he never should have mentioned it. "That's nothing to do with a damn deadline."

Her throat had gone dry, but she forced out the words she needed him to hear. She had to put him out of his misery, at least partially. "I want you, too."

Finn groaned then, as though all his resolve had evaporated. Trapping her face in his hands, he dipped down, his lips meeting hers. Not as gentle as the previous night, but more demanding, his desire evident in the intensity of his kiss. She reached up, placing her palms on his shoulders as the first drop of rain splattered, cold and sharp against her forehead.

They fought to get closer, their kisses deepening. Pippa clung to him, their mouths meeting again and again. He was the only real thing in her world.

Raindrops slapped the backs of her thighs and calves, but she didn't care. All that mattered was the pressure of Finn's mouth on hers and the hardness of him where their bodies came in contact.

He slid his hand up her side to cup her breast. With his thumb, he traced the outline of her nipple through her shirt with his deft fingers. Pippa's breath came out on a moan as he teased that same nipple under his thumb.

The rain soaked their clothes and made Pippa's fingers slide easily against the exposed skin of Finn's bare back. She clung to him as he worked her breast, her head spinning. If he had that effect on her when she was fully dressed, then without clothes . . .

Oh, God.

The rain picked up, transitioning from a few random splotches to a shower. It pelted Finn and Pippa until he broke the kiss once more. Yet, that time, *his* breathing had grown ragged. Releasing her, he dropped his hand and took a step back. Water ran from his soaked dark hair and funneled from his beard onto the muddy ground. "You can have your job back, but I signed a policy that I'd never get involved with a student during an internship. I have to keep my word.

"We're already crossing a line here. We can't, out of respect for the school, take things any further."

Did he mean to wait an entire month before he touched her again? If so, how the heck was she supposed to deal with that? "I'm officially done with the summer semester next month. What then?" she asked, doing her best not to sound desperate. *Epic fail there.*

His eyes lit, sending a wicked grin her way. "Then we'll see what we see."

"So if I want to kiss you again, I'll what—have to quit?"

"*Jaysus*, woman. You have a terrible employment record." But he grinned as he took her hand in his. "Let's go get into some dry clothes."

Relief coursed through her, but it was mixed with a

heady sort of anticipation. Finn had kissed her again. He still wanted her, and the man had the power to turn her to mush. How would Pippa be able to focus for the rest of her internship? She was already in trouble and she'd only just seen Finn with his shirt off.

24

FINN

"She marked the ground in a cold, red X. The perfect spot to slice off her victim's head."
—Finn Burke, *Lost*

inn gritted his teeth. He snatched the red pen from Pippa's slim fingers and then proceeded to mark each page of chapter forty-five with a large red X.

"What are you doing?" Pippa sat up straighter, reaching for the pen. Her lips quirked as he raised it higher and then higher still above her head. There was enough of a height difference between them that he could get away with that sort of thing.

"I'm borrowing your pen for a bit." She opened her mouth as though to argue, but Finn held up a hand. "It's not a permanent loan. Don't trouble yourself." Finn winked at her and turned back to butchering her work in fine point ink.

"I'm not worried about the pen. It's all of those pages

you're annihilating." She sat, cross-legged, regarding him through hooded eyes.

"It's *shite*, to be honest." He shook his head.

"Why, thank you, Finn. That's what every writer wants to hear—that their writing's shit." She scowled.

"That's why you're here, isn't it? For my expertise." Christ, was he ever flirting.

"Oh, by all means." She waved her hand in his direction as though he were bloody royalty.

Finn stared at the pages before him. "You're moving too fast. There are more holes in this plot than at a Swiss cheese factory."

"I think it's good. I've worked through some of the bumps. It feels right to me. Why go through it again?"

Spreading the printed pages of chapter forty-five across the table in front of him, he began highlighting the sections of the chapter arc he found to be the weakest. "If you rework this and this, you'll get there. Take the time and do it right."

Pippa rolled her eyes. "Says the man who would happily revise his manuscript to death."

He took the pages in hand once more, but put them down just as quickly. The problem wasn't her writing. Not really. She had all the promise of turning into an amazing writer. It was just that she hadn't found her voice. At least to the extent that it flowed through all her projects.

Finn had gotten a hint of it when he'd read the award-winning short story that had prompted him to choose her for the internship. But her novel could have been written by someone different. He wasn't the only one trying to write the way he thought he should. Pippa was just as guilty.

"Let's put this on pause for a moment." He tossed the stack of her pages aside, setting the red pen atop them. "We're going to have a little pop quiz, if you will."

"A pop quiz? What is this, eighth grade math?"

"Don't you be mocking my methods." Finn reached for his laptop and printed several pages. When he was done, he hopped up to grab them from his printer. They'd decided to work in his cottage that day, close to coffee for Pippa and tea for him. Plus, it kept them out of the rain.

The warm pages were waiting when he reached his office. Finn picked them up and then returned to Pippa. "I want you to read these pages. Shouldn't take long."

Pippa grumbled under her breath as she took the pages. He supposed it was no less than he'd done when she'd given him feedback. Still, she propped them up against her knees and began to read.

Finn picked up her pages, immersing himself in Jake and Cassidy. Again, the bones were there, but the voice, Pippa's personal stamp, was absent. If he could just get her to let go, eliminate whatever held her back.

Nearly a half an hour passed before Pippa announced, "Done." A grin transformed her face from ear to ear. "Can I just say—"

"No. Don't give me anything except the answers to my questions." He wanted those pages fresh in her mind. She needed to get this in her head. If he let her start asking questions, they'd be detour-bound. "Were you able to identify any of the authors?"

She bit her bottom lip, working it between her teeth as

she simultaneously fought a smile and contemplated her answer. Pippa must *really* like reading. "J.K. Rowling, Judy Blume . . . I think Lois Lowry . . . Suzanne Collins, and John Green . . . Thank you for picking some YA authors, by the way."

"Don't mention it." Excellent. The teacher in him was thrilled she knew them. "What else did you notice?"

"They've all got very different approaches. Each one is beyond talented. Each story had a strong hook." She stared at the pages, rifling through them as she answered.

Finn nodded. "What else did you notice?" *The voice, Pippa, pick up on the voice.* He locked his fingers together to keep himself from giving her the answer.

"Well, the last one was my favorite, obviously." She grinned, her eyes lighting. "I mean, how did you get it?"

"Whaddaya mean?" he asked, the confused one that time. He couldn't remember which one had been the last. Grabbing the stack, he flipped through the pages as curiosity got the better of him. When he got to the last page, he froze. He'd accidentally included one of the pages he'd written the night before. One he hadn't shown to Pippa. Just a new idea he'd been toying with.

"This is unpublished work by James Black! Do you know him? Did you have to call in a special favor?" she asked.

Shite. Had he really written that much like his old self? That wasn't the way he'd wanted to tell her the truth. "I just searched the internet."

"You didn't. I've scoured the internet, hundreds of times. There's nothing."

Huh. She had? He fought to keep his chest from

puffing out. "Let's not miss the point of the lesson. What I wanted you to take away is that every successful author has found his or her voice. If they've done it well, you can pick up one of their books and you know it's theirs."

Pippa's smile slipped an inch as she seemed to take in his words. "And I haven't found mine, have I?"

"You have. I'm just not seeing it here. The short story you wrote—the one about grief. That really came alive for me. You embraced your voice in that piece." He could still recall several lines of Pippa's gut-wrenching take on losing someone you loved. That was, in part, why he'd selected her to work with him.

"That piece. It was about Mom. About how I felt after she'd gone." She fisted her hands on her lap. "I don't know if I can write another story like that."

"You don't have to. You just have to write what matters to you. Put yourself in your characters' shoes and then try writing again." He jabbed his index finger at the pages in question. "Do you want to show me any of what you wrote at the church?"

Pippa moved to sit at the edge of the sofa, where she'd left her bag. The journal Finn had given her peeked out from one of the pockets, much like *To the Ends of the Earth* did the first day she arrived. Tugging the small notebook from the bag, she offered it to him.

Finn flipped to the first page. He noted how the printing was slanted and crammed onto the paper, as if she'd been writing as fast as she could. The opposite of Pippa's usually tidy penmanship.

But more surprising was the scene she'd written. It leapt off the page. It was as if someone else had written the story. Only Jake and Cassidy's names tied the writing to Pippa.

"Well done, Pippa." He handed the journal back to her. "Now I want you to read that the way a *reader* would."

"Okay." Taking the little book, Pippa opened it to page one. Finn stretched his long legs out in front of him so that his bare feet reached the table. He locked his arms behind his head as he waited.

"Wow. You're right." Her mouth dropped open as she met his eyes. "This is so much better. More vivid. More *me*."

"Don't you be sounding so surprised, Darling. We've established myself as the expert, after all." He winked. "But do you see what I'm getting at?"

"I do. I'm starting to see it now. Also, you were right. Cassidy isn't real enough." She picked up the pages he'd discarded, leafing through them as though they held answers. "She had no motivation to leave home in the first place. You said it yourself. If someone is going to leave a place they love, they need to have a damn good reason. Just like you."

It was Finn's turn to be puzzled. "I'm not following."

"Really? Cause that's what you did."

Finn stared hard at Pippa. That *was* what he'd done. Because of Amélie. Because of everything. But he couldn't say it. Because then he'd end up telling her about James Black, and he hadn't worked out how to do that yet. "I guess you're right."

Pippa regarded him, her over-observant brown eyes seeming to scan the inside of his mind. For just a moment, her eyes dimmed, as if she knew. As if she'd turned the inside of his brain out and read the book on his past. She took his hand in hers. Finn tried to ignore the rush of heat and the awareness that crept over him at her touch.

His heart thudded in his chest, as though someone had given his ticker a jump and it had begun to beat again. Concentrating with her hand in his took effort. It was easier when he wasn't touching her in some way, but having her nearby had proved a challenge, too.

The problem with Pippa Darling was that she didn't just sit and hang out. The woman was a *fecking* ray of light. And damn it if he wasn't drawn to her the way a moth would be to a flame. He noted she'd left the top three buttons on her shirt undone. That choice alone sent him into an invisible battle to fight for his own control.

When Finn had kissed Pippa the previous day he'd understood things would change between them. What he hadn't realized was how quickly his desire for Pippa would escalate. He'd dreamed of her for weeks, and those nighttime moments, when he'd awakened hard with his mind full of Pippa, had been difficult enough. Still, he'd been able to push those images to the far recesses of his mind during the day before.

"I can quit again." Pippa's eyes lit, and the mirth in them reminded him again of the fairies. Whenever mortals tangled themselves with the Good People, they always ended up *banjaxed*.

"How about we change things up. You're fired." He brought his mouth over hers, and she twined her arms around his neck on a sigh, drawing him closer. Rain pelted the windows of the dining room, leaving trails on the glass. The rest of the house was silent. It was Saturday, which meant it was Zoe's day off. No surprise visitors.

Their mouths moved over each other's, exploring, memorizing. Something inside Finn relaxed, as though he'd been holding every muscle taut since their last kiss, waiting for more. Just another taste and he'd be able to get back to his work.

But the calm didn't last. The tension began to build in him again as she straddled him. *Jaysus.*

He knew she could feel him, but if she was intent on tormenting him, Finn reasoned there was little point in hiding the end result. He slid his hand to her waist, gripping her hip.

Pippa tugged his bottom lip with her teeth, her lips demanding. Finn grew dizzy, the room spinning with each nip and suck. He opened his mouth over hers, caught her tongue between his teeth, and sucked gently.

What is she doing to me?

Finn released her tongue, ready to end things, to break apart, but Pippa deepened the kiss. She sought the farthest recesses of his mouth, aligned her lithe body against his own, wiggling closer, making things worse.

He nipped lightly at her bottom lip, then moved downward, tracing her collarbone with his tongue. Pippa gasped, gripping a fistful of Finn's shirt, her fingers grazing his chest with the action, leaving a path of fire behind them.

Finn broke away, moving to place a hand on her chest before thinking the better of it and settling for her shoulder instead. "You're going to bloody kill me. Now,

I'm on a deadline, if you don't mind. Give a man a chance to think."

She saluted him. "Of course, esteemed mentor." But she winked as she picked up the pages he'd printed for her. Reading them, studying them. "Back to work."

Finn didn't have any such luck focusing. All he could think about was Pippa's mouth on his, the feel of her against him. Any chance of concentrating fled from his head.

"Damn it, then." He launched himself to his feet and thrust his hands through his hair. He was losing his mind.

Her brow furrowed, just a touch. "Maybe you need some time alone."

"What I need, *Darling*, is you. Every bit of you wrapped around me." Her eyes widened at his words. Finn shook his head. "But because I'm an honorable man, I'll be keeping my distance." He picked up his laptop and pile of marked-up papers, slowing only to squeeze Pippa's shoulder as he passed. He couldn't even meet her eye.

ONCE HE'D PUT distance between them, the air and his head, began to clear. Finn could think again. He'd been acting like a schoolboy. Maybe it had just been too long since he'd wanted anyone. Amélie was the last. And she'd left him with so much baggage, he might as well have booked an international flight.

Pippa left Finn with the sensation that he was walking a tightrope. That any moment he could teeter to one side and lose his balance altogether, falling to the depths below.

He needed the clink of stone against stone and the constancy of the sea to soothe him. He needed to breathe.

He needed a pint.

Finn climbed the hill that led to the keep and found Bob there, hard at work. "Hey, boyo, whaddaya up to?" Bob grinned as he lodged a stone into place. He wore his tool belt and had brought a toolbox besides. "This is a little early for you to be joining me."

"Just needed a break from it all." Finn got to work, avoiding Bob's eye as he reached for the first stone.

"That's a line if I ever heard one." Bob grinned, as jovial as Father Christmas and somehow just as intuitive as a master psychic. Or Zoe. Come to think of it, Zoe could beat out a master psychic any day. His eyes narrowed a fraction. "It's Pippa you're getting away from."

"It's nothing. I'm knackered." Finn turned away, focusing on the next block he'd need to stagger the layout.

"What's happened between you and Pippa? I thought you were getting acquainted." Bob winked as he reached for another stone, placing it next to Finn's.

Finn contemplated denying it. Bob wasn't someone Finn would have been after contacting if he wanted to discuss women. Of course, Bob wouldn't bring it up with Zoe, which meant whatever Finn said would stay confidential. "How did you know there's something between Pippa and me?"

Bob rolled his eyes, slathering mortar atop the level of stones. "The whole *fecking* world knows. You might as well plaster a billboard on the N56." Bob leaned over and added another stone block to the fresh mortar.

It was better to focus things on his writing instead of Pippa . . . or easier, anyway. "What's wrong is I'm not sure I know what to write anymore. Phillip keeps telling me my characters aren't *real*."

"Phillip, that *bollocks* of an agent of yours?" Bob shook his head. "You should never listen to that one."

Finn shrugged, grabbing another block. "Maybe so, but he is my agent. I'm not certain how to get the book where it needs to be."

"And what does Pippa think?" Bob asked, eyeing up the dwindling selection of stone blocks.

"Pippa keeps saying the same. Only, she also says it's crass. Particularly, the sex scenes." The last thing Finn ever imagined was that he'd be discussing sex scenes with Bob Hannigan.

"I'd have to agree with her there. Those were a little rough for me, too, boyo." Bob shrugged and moved stone onto stone with another *chink*.

Finn's eyebrows shot toward the sky. "I didn't know you read my work, Bob."

"I did at that. It's not my cup of tea. I'm a little more of a romantic at heart." He winked.

Bob Hannigan, the romantic. Finn tended to assume Bob, who'd been his father's best friend, was just like his father. Bob was a whole other animal altogether.

"Still, I enjoy a good story, and you tell one." Bob shrugged and added another stone to the keep wall. "You have to remember that everybody's dream is to meet somebody they can *connect with*. That's what I was looking for when I met Zoe."

Finn had never considered Bob and Zoe Hannigan having a great romance, but since Bob had voiced his thoughts, Finn might be forced to think differently.

"You think I should just change everything I've been doing? Write it in a different way?" The very idea had Finn's frustration building. He would never be finished with that book.

"I'll never suggest you change who you are. You write what you want to write. But maybe, well, you might consider putting a little more romance into things. Write it the way you think Pippa would want to hear it. Your first book . . . now that was romantic. I know you have it in you."

There he went with *fecking* James Black again.

Bob stopped, jerked, and then looked at his watch. "Uh oh. I'm meant to be picking up Caden. I'll be back, though."

"Sure. I've got this." Finn waved him off, but as the older man walked away, his mind stayed stuck on Bob's words. On his suggestion that Finn might try writing a part of the book the way Pippa would want to read it. It wasn't that he had to change who he was, but maybe he needed to change how he presented the same information.

Of course, if he was honest with himself, he'd admit that the way he'd been writing wasn't really who he was. Not deep down. Once, he'd been the dreamer, James Black. He'd turned into Finn Burke, the cynic. But maybe Finn Burke, the writer, rested somewhere in between both men. That was something he needed to figure out. He had to find his own voice.

He reached inside the keep opening and snagged the outdoor chair he'd stashed there. Setting it up among the rocks, Finn took a seat and then stared out at the sea.

But instead of turbulent waves crashing against the rocks, all he saw was Pippa. Everything was Pippa.

That was dangerous thinking. Or was it?

Pippa wasn't Amélie. Finn wasn't a green boy of eighteen who'd fallen hopelessly in love with a woman four years his senior. He'd changed, become a man in his own right.

He forced his attention to the novel and the sex scene he'd written before. Would he speak that way to Pippa once he got her in his bed? It was likely he wouldn't be able to speak at all.

Pippa would want the romance of it, because she was more like a fairy creature than anyone he'd known. What *if* Finn wrote the romance instead of just sex?

"Always did like a good dare," he said out loud, as if issuing a cosmic challenge to the universe. With a grin, Finn reached back inside the keep wall and pulled out another journal and a pen, encased in a freezer bag. Choosing a spot on a wide, flat rock with jagged edges pointing out the sides, he sat and began to write.

25

PIPPA

"My words are yours, and yours alone. For I could write twenty-thousand and you'd bring out the heart and soul in everyone."
—James Black, *To the Ends of the Earth*

A stream of obscenities spewed from Finn's mouth at whisper level that muggy August morning. Some of them Pippa recognized. Others were new, unchartered verbiage she could add to her vocabulary.

"Cut all of page 310? Are you daft?" He pointed at the page like it was an accusation.

Pippa peered over his shoulder to refresh her memory as to the contents on the page. "Yes, because you said it better two pages ago."

A furrow formed in Finn's brow. "I did?" He flipped back through the pages. A grin spread across his face. "I did!"

Pippa's breath hitched. It would have been so easy to

kiss him. She gripped the fabric on the couch, holding herself back. Positioning his laptop on the table, she clicked her way to his cloud storage folder. The most recent copy of the manuscript was from the week before.

"This file isn't there. Where have you been saving your work?"

He scowled, jerking his head in her direction. His intense eyes seemed to scan the screen. He jabbed his finger at one of the folders. "There. Documents."

"That's not where you're supposed to save." Pippa slapped her palm against her forehead. "Right here. I even made the folder a happy green for you, so you'd remember."

He didn't spare her a glance as he returned to the pages in front of him, cross-checking her notes against his copy of the manuscript. "A *happy* green. Well, isn't that just lovely?"

"You really want to lose your work again, don't you?" Pippa flattened her lips into a straight line as she moved his copies into the cloud storage folder and labeled them correctly.

"Mm." Finn emitted a sound somewhere between disagreement and consent. After a moment, he reached into his bag and pulled out the journal he'd written in at the keep. He thrust it at her. He'd been holding onto it, debating as to whether he should show it to her.

"Would you read this? If you don't mind." That crease was back in his brow. Finn seemed nervous.

"Sure." She scanned the notebook. Man, not that scene again. It was the same love scene that Finn had revised five times previously. One that she'd read many times before. But although the characters were the same, the scene was wholly different.

She knew Lucas and Mia. They were the main characters in Finn's book. But somehow, he'd written them so that they came across as more exposed than ever. They'd become vulnerable. And they were about to kiss.

Lucas took Mia in his arms, brought his mouth to hers, and possessed her. The kiss took over the scene. And somehow, it was as if Pippa was there with them. Her entire body reacted to what she read. Her breathing hitched, and her skin tingled in places that hadn't tingled since Finn last kissed her. It was as if she, herself, was Mia.

Finn had never written anything like it before. Pippa somehow felt strung out. As though her emotions were being tested.

She clutched the journal. Line by line, she read the words before her, captivated. It was so different, so new, and so *unlike* Finn. She couldn't stop reading until she got to the very end. At which point, she rested the pages on her lap and regarded Finn. The whole chapter was way more exciting than anything he'd written in *Lost*—that was for sure.

Finn folded and unfolded his hands so many times in the seconds since she'd finished, she expected he'd have a panic attack if she didn't say something. Pippa wanted to hug him.

"You wrote this?" Disbelief rang through her voice whether she wanted it to or not.

"I did." He stopped pacing and shoved his hands into the pockets of his worn khaki shorts.

Pippa began fanning herself with the journal. Her white knuckles accented her grip.

A slow smile spread across Finn's face, breaking off just a little piece of Pippa's heart. Every time she'd said anything nice about his writing, it seemed to thrill him.

"It's just so hopeful. So . . ."

"Unlike me?" His eyebrows shot into the air, twin caterpillars on the rise.

"Exactly!" Pippa jabbed her finger against his chest. "Since when did you start writing hopeful things? I mean, this is so romantic and there's love and they're happy, too!" Then sanity set in, and she shook her head. "Sorry, I'm rambling."

"I don't mind the rambling, as long as you get there in the end." The strangest expression crossed his face. It was somewhere between confident and fearful. "But you still haven't told me what you think."

"It's wonderful." She kept her grip on the pages.

"So, you're saying I might've done well, then?" That cocky smile that made Pippa's heart throb had returned. She was falling for Finn, tumbling hard. The only problem with falling was that, eventually, she'd land on Earth.

But that day, she didn't want to think too hard on what motivated her. Seizing the moment, enjoying her time with Finn, seemed the only option. She'd been shy with the last guy she'd been interested in. Zack. She'd never spoken up, and it never went anywhere.

She wouldn't make that mistake with Finn. Though

shyness and Finn were definitely two quantities that didn't mix. She forced a swallow. "Definitely."

Pippa set the pages aside and rose to her feet. She took two slow steps in his direction, forcing herself to move, as though she waded through water. When their toes touched, she slid her arms around him, linking her hands behind his back.

"Something I'm still not clear on." She stood on tiptoe to press a kiss along his jawline. "Am I still unemployed? I can't remember." She graced his jaw and chin with feather-light kisses, one after the other, painstakingly slow, until she ran out of jaw to kiss and moved to his lips. His scratchy beard sent the blood pumping faster in her veins.

If she'd had to describe Finn's reaction, she would've said that it was like waking a monster, a beast, a dragon. For Finn growled somewhere deep in his throat. "I don't remember re-hiring you."

He pressed his fist against her back, drawing her more securely against him, and brought his mouth to hers. He coaxed her lips apart with no effort, his tongue meeting hers in a dance as timeless as the island on which they stood. She dug what little fingernails she had into Finn's shoulders, pressing into the worn cotton of his shirt, clinging to him, as though he were the only thing that mattered.

Pippa's lips tingled from the impact of Finn's against her own. Every inch of her body had caught on fire. A slow burn that had started as a tingling in her shoulders moved to a tight ball in her chest, to a queasiness in her stomach, and then on to an ache in all the places she'd neglected for many years.

It'd been way too long since she'd been with anyone. Pippa hadn't consciously given up on sex. Being with Finn, with his mouth roaming over hers as though *he* possessed *her*, was driving her mad.

"Pippa." Finn managed to speak, tugging her with him to the futon, so that she lay on top of him. He guided her head to his chest, the hardened length of him pressed against her belly. Though she ached to be closer, to touch him in other ways, she enjoyed the sensation of stillness.

She had no idea how long they'd been laying there, wrapped up in each other, when Finn finally broke the silence. "There's something I have to tell you. Something I should've told you ages ago." Finn scooted upward into a sitting position, taking Pippa with him.

"What is it?" Pippa bit her bottom lip. She didn't like the sound of whatever it was Finn was about to say.

"It's just that . . ." Finn ran a hand through his hair. "I . . . I'm really glad you're here."

Pippa smiled on instinct, though part of her knew that wasn't what Finn had meant to say. "I'm glad to be here. And you know you can tell me anything."

"We should get back to work. That deadline's close." All of Finn's concentration seemed to lock onto the book. She'd lost him—for the time being. He shifted away from her, retrieving his laptop, and moved to the edge of the futon.

"Okay, I'll keep reading. But I want you to go back and make some more changes like you did for Lucas and Mia."

A small smile tugged at Finn's lips. "As you wish, boss."

Pippa couldn't resist smiling back. But her mind was elsewhere, stuck on whatever it was that Finn had been about to share. Since he'd clammed up, however, she had no choice but to go to work.

After all, as Finn pointed out, they had a deadline.

26

FINN

"The end of the road is a descent into hell. Fuck."
—Finn Burke, *Lost*

Ten more days had passed. Finn "rehired" Pippa and had no choice but to keep her on the payroll as they moved into late August. His deadline grew closer with each passing day, so it was just common sense. Finn and Pippa had been working day and night to finish his book. Some of those nights had been damn hard, and mostly because of how soft and right Pippa felt sitting beside him.

It was getting more difficult to keep his hands off her. But it wouldn't matter soon, because once Finn turned in his pages, he'd consider Pippa's internship at an end. Then he'd have no reason to hold back. He was looking forward to learning all of Pippa's secrets.

Still, he was so close to finishing his manuscript that he couldn't afford for Pippa to distract him just then. He needed to wrap a few more things up. Then he'd send his manuscript to Phillip for feedback. That was a whole other monster waiting in the mist.

His own fear was to blame for that, and it *was* fear, plain and simple. Fear that had left him blocked for so long. *To the Ends of the Earth* was his ghost, the constant reminder that writing what was in his heart meant failure. Finn was a smart guy most of the time, and certainly smart enough to know that writing a book like that one was a practice best left avoided. But writing alongside Pippa had inspired him. His craft had grown stronger, his words fresher.

Guilt nagged at him for not telling Pippa he was James Black. It still galled him that she had no idea about his dual identity. She'd lauded his alter ego in front of him every chance she got, carrying his book around as though it were the bloody Bible. Yet, she had no clue about who he really was. He couldn't blame her. Truthfully, he'd done nothing to let the world know of the connection between Finn Burke and James Black because it was *personal*. His personal pain.

He and Pippa had gotten involved and he should tell her the truth. But it had never seemed like the right time to reveal to Pippa that he was James Black.

He was afraid of her reaction for certain. Afraid that Pippa would decide she didn't want to be with a liar. He didn't want to risk losing her when he hadn't even had a chance to take things further.

Pippa rifled through a stack of pages marked in red pen. She'd lodged the writing utensil in question behind her left ear. "Okay, so I got through the pages you rewrote last night. I like what you did with Sarah, but you need to change a few things." She held up the stack bathed in red.

Finn forced his mouth from dropping open in horror. "I may be a revision addict, but I'm not changing bloody else. You've asked me to rewrite that chapter three times. When do you expect me to get this book done? Christmas?"

"If you want it to suck, that's your choice. You asked for my help and I'm telling you, you can make it better. And you won't make it better with this wishy-washy scene."

"I don't write wishy-washy scenes," he spat, enjoying the verbal sparring match with Pippa, despite himself.

"You just did!" Pippa plopped back against the futon and glared in his direction. But her anger didn't last long, and a smirk took over her lips. In no time at all, she burst into laughter. It was a slow, small chuckle at first, but it quickly grew into a full-fledged guffaw.

"I'm just messing with you. These are old edits I did at the beginning of the summer. You don't need to change anything in that scene with Sarah." Pippa grinned.

His mouth did drop open that time. "Why, you little minx." Finn launched himself at Pippa, straddling her, trapping her in place. Sliding his hand under the hem of her top, he began to tickle her. She writhed against him, twisting beneath his fingertips.

"No! No! I hate being tickled." She giggled, scrunching up her face.

"Rewrite this scene, my *arse*." Finn grinned, intent on showing her no mercy. But the more he touched her, the gentler his fingers grew. Christ, her skin was soft.

Pippa howled with laughter despite herself. "I think I deserve a little fun after all the effort we put into this book. Uncle. Uncle."

"I don't know who this uncle person is you're calling for, but he's unlikely to help." But he propped his head up on his elbow and relented anyway. Tears streamed down Pippa's face. "But seriously, what else do I need to change? You read through the entire thing again last night and this morning. What else needs to be fixed?"

Pippa reached up and pressed a kiss against his cheek, laying back to rest on the pillows. "I think you're done. I didn't find anything."

Finn couldn't help but remember his observation that she was filled with sunshine. It practically spilled out of her eyes just then.

Then her words hit him. "You're joking."

"I'm not. I think it's ready to go to Phillip." Pippa grinned. "Finn, you did it."

A million emotions slammed into him. Before Pippa had come to help, he hadn't been certain he'd even get as far as a first draft. Since she'd arrived, he not only had a second draft, but a polished one. One he actually felt proud of. He knew, without a shadow of a doubt, that it was the best work he could possibly turn in. That was all down to Pippa.

"*We* did it." He leaned in and brought his lips to hers. Finn had kissed Pippa dozens of times, but there was nothing familiar about it. Every time he did, it brought something new, something different. He trailed his mouth against hers, and at the same time, he slid his palms up to cradle her breasts.

Finn couldn't imagine more perfect breasts. They were just the right size to fit in his hands, as though she'd been made for him to touch her. And though he hadn't yet seen them, he'd certainly *felt* them.

Her breath caught when his thumbs found her stiff nipples through the fabric of her shirt. He knew what she wanted. Lord knew it was exactly what *he* wanted.

But not yet.

She lit up the sky in a shower of light so bright he'd been star struck. Never again would he see anything but her.

What had that been about? Writing in his head again? That wasn't the way Finn Burke wrote . . . it was the way James Black wrote. Had he shifted back to his old voice and his old ways so easily because he was with Pippa? Had any of that voice slipped into his new manuscript? Phillip wouldn't like it.

Finn froze, letting his hands slide to his lap. He kissed the tip of Pippa's nose as he moved off Pippa to sit beside her.

Pippa remained in place, her breath as heavy as Finn's. He could read the desire in her eyes, but he couldn't give her what she wanted. Finn pulled away, shifting to hide his reaction from Pippa. He reached for his laptop, concealing the evidence.

"Let's get this thing shipped off to Phillip. He may have a heart attack when I meet my deadline early. I still don't have a title, but . . ."

"There's time for that." Pippa closed her laptop and walked the pile of old edits to the shredder. "Make it fast, Burke." She grinned in challenge.

"I promise." He did just that. In a series of clicks and

keystrokes, he sent the current version of his manuscript to Phillip. It was only after he pressed the send button that he turned to Pippa. "Done."

"You sent it off?" Pippa glanced over her shoulder, the only indication of the moment they'd just shared was the faint hint of red in her cheeks.

"I did." Finn shut the laptop with the snap, a rush of relief coursing through his body. He'd done it. Not only did he finish the manuscript, but he'd submitted it. And not just on time, *early*. Phillip really would pass out when it showed up in his inbox.

Pippa leaned over the side of the futon and returned with a fat envelope. She offered it to Finn. "Here you go. My first draft." A grin bunched up her cheeks.

"You're joking." Finn reached for the envelope and accepted it, sliding out the stack of papers inside. "When did you have time to finish?"

"When you were sleeping, and whenever *I* was supposed to be sleeping. Your lesson about voice—it struck a chord with me. Once I went back to the book, I couldn't stop writing." She grinned.

"I'm sorry." Finn pressed a kiss to her cheek. "I should have given you more time."

"You gave me more than enough time." Pippa shrugged. "But, come to think of it, there's definitely a nap in my future."

He scanned the title page. *To the Edge of My Heart* by Pippa Darling. A ball of warmth grew in his gut at the sight of the title. It was an homage to her favorite author. Only she didn't realize her favorite author sat beside her.

He had to tell her.

But when he looked into her eyes, they were so excited and so full of emotion—for him. For the work she'd created. It wouldn't be right to taint her memories of finishing her novel with a fight.

He would tell her. Soon. After he let her have that day.

"So, what do we do now?" That faint tinge of pink took over Pippa's cheeks again.

He'd carry her to his bed and peel off those shorts of hers and . . . He cleared his throat, hoping to do the same for his head. "Pippa Darling. I think it's time you were wooed."

"Wooed? So that's a thing?" she asked.

"Not one I'm very good at, but there's a first time for everything." Yes, there was. "Make sure you dress warm and wear your boots."

"Where are we going?" Pippa closed her own laptop and slowly rose to standing.

"Somewhere magical. Somewhere perfect for a dreamer like you." With a wink, Finn leapt from the futon and took off to ready himself. Pippa's internship could be considered over. After all, she'd done everything he'd hired her to do.

Now, it was time to coach her in something besides writing.

27

PIPPA

"I never expected love. It grew without my knowledge until it
burst from my chest and I didn't stand a chance."
—James Black, *To the Ends of the Earth*

*P*ippa's heart raced as she walked toward her cottage, her laptop under one arm. Finn had opted to wait for her back at his place. Thank God for that. She'd known Finn's novel was ready to go to Phillip.

And not only was Finn's novel finished—so was hers. It was only a first draft, but it was as solid as she could get it. She could probably send it off to the dean that day and it would have been fine.

But then Finn's lessons filtered into her brain.

Take your time and do it right.

Find your own voice—make the reader know who's written the book.

Maybe there was something to that. When she'd written her short story, "Blue Room," it had been the anniversary of her mother's death. She'd holed up in the townhouse and reread the piece until her eyes bled. Not really, but almost.

Either way, that was the piece that had brought her to Ireland. The internship had been the best thing that had happened to her. Not just because she'd gotten to see the country, but because she'd gotten to see herself. She'd gotten to dig into her work in a way she never would have been able to at home.

Her stomach twisted. Home wasn't too far away in her future. She had a return flight booked for September 10th, though she hadn't yet reminded Finn of that. Pippa wasn't sure what her future held, but she knew one thing. She'd need to talk to Dad about the B&B. After she'd lived the way she had, with her writing as her priority, she couldn't imagine schlepping laundry around Yankee Hollow.

Not only that, but she couldn't help wondering what would happen between her and Finn. They'd never talked about it, and Pippa wasn't ready to ask. It was as if their relationship, or whatever it was, had been put on pause while they waited for her internship to be over.

What would happen now that it had ended? She'd been dying to talk about all that with Uma, but her friend hadn't been home.

"You're gonna have to figure this one out on your own, Pippa," she muttered to herself as she tugged on her favorite pair of yoga pants. Finn seemed to take her to some very windy places. As she'd learned, the weather in Ireland was as unpredictable as Finn himself. It was better to be prepared. Wearing layers never hurt.

He waited for her outside the cottage when she

opened the door. His eyes darkened as she stepped outside, closing and then locking the door behind her. His gaze could have burned a hole straight through her. "Ready?"

No. "Yep! Where are we headed?" she asked, falling into step beside him.

He grinned, twining his fingers with hers. God. How was it possible that all the man had to do was hold her hand and her legs melted?

"I thought it was time I took you to a castle." Finn grinned, as though already anticipating her response.

"A castle?" Pippa's eyes shot open, all traces of drowsiness gone. No way. Technically, she was living on castle grounds, but the keep wasn't anyone's idea of complete. "A real, honest-to-goodness castle? I've never seen one."

"I thought you might enjoy it."

There he went again, surprising her. "You know, I can't figure you out sometimes."

"What do you mean?"

"When I first got here, you acted like this miserable old man who wanted nothing to do with me. And then you go and do something like this. Something . . . thoughtful." The truth was, however, that Finn *had* changed. He had been miserable when they'd first met. He'd claimed he had trust issues, but he'd been opening up a little more, day by day.

"People aren't only one thing, Darling. Not everyone's just black or white. I'll have you know that I have many sides." Tugging on her hand, he led her toward the car and their destination for the day.

≈

FORTY-FIVE MINUTES LATER, Finn and Pippa tore down the highway in the Triumph. It had grown warmer that day, and they'd both wound their windows down halfway. The wind whipped through Pippa's short hair and tugged at Finn's shirt. She couldn't remember the last time she'd felt so lighthearted. Maybe in the early days when she'd first started grad school, but certainly not since. There'd been too many deadlines and too much pressure.

"What's the deal with the colors on the sheep's fur?" Pippa asked. Ever since she'd arrived, she'd noticed sheep everywhere. In the fields, along the sides of the roads, *in* the roads . . . and some had red dye on their backs.

"Those are the *naughty* sheep. The ones who went out into the night, had a bit of fun, and got pregnant. Poor ladies. They have the ultimate walk of shame." Finn roared with laughter at his own joke.

"Nice, Burke." She leaned back in her seat, gazing out at the fields and hills that rolled past on the other side of the Triumph's window.

"I'm only being partly serious. It's much more scientific than that. During mating season," Finn began, "the farmers, they attach a bag of dye to the ram's chest. When the ram mounts the ewe . . . the bag breaks."

Oh my God. "Okay, enough with the animal husbandry lesson. How far away is the castle?" Pippa perched as far forward as her seat belt would allow. She hadn't been doing touristy things nearly enough.

Finn tapped his fingers along the wheel as he steered.

"A little over an hour's drive now. North of here. If you wanted to sleep, you could."

"No way. I can't have you taking advantage of me when I'm taking a nap." Shit. She pressed two fingers against her lips. Why had Pippa been born with the inability to keep those thoughts inside her head?

"If I'm going to take advantage of you—and make no mistake, I will—I'll be after doing it when you're wide awake." It was his turn to share a sly smile that stretched slow and easy.

Restlessness raged through Pippa's body. What exactly did Finn have in store for her? Damn if she didn't want to find out.

28

FINN

"Life has made fucking liars of us all."
—Finn Burke, *Lost*

Finn and Pippa fell into easy conversation. They talked about books they loved to read, and about their favorite movies and TV shows. Pippa was well-read, and it pleased him. They had far more in common than he ever would've guessed. Pippa Darling was an enigma. One moment, she was analyzing classic books, and the next, talking about car engines. She was 217 different combinations of hot, and Finn had barely scratched the surface.

About an hour and a half later, they drove down a lone road. As was the norm in Ireland, they had to drive on a private road to reach the castle grounds. When they pulled up outside the gates of Doe Castle, there was no crowd, just a vendor trailer selling coffee and a few other cars. Finn parked and then ran around to open the door for Pippa. She'd beaten him to it. She stood outside the car, resting against the passenger side door and taking in the tall tower on the other side of the fence.

"This place is cool." She took several slow steps toward the gate.

"I can show you castles all day, if that's what you're after." Finn rested his hand against her lower back. Her answering glance told him she was after much more than castles. "Come on."

They bought a coffee for Pippa and a tepid tea for Finn from the vendor, and took their time perusing the grounds. A handful of people were there. A few families and a couple showed up and then left. The rest of the visitors trickled out, and Pippa and Finn soon had the place to themselves.

Finn marveled at the way Pippa inspected every inch of the castle. She wanted to investigate every single marker, read every historical note within the place. That suited Finn just fine, as he was keen to do the same. The interior castle grounds were small, with high walls blocking the view of everything except gray, cloudy sky.

Before long, however, guilt crept up on him. He and Pippa were involved. He wanted to make love to her. Still, he'd need to be honest about who he really was if they were going to move forward. He wanted to move forward. He only hoped she'd forgive him once she learned the truth.

He must have been brooding, for Pippa faced him, a small crease in her brow. "Is something wrong?"

"Pippa, there's something I've been meaning to tell you." He gnawed on his bottom lip a little. How to begin?

I'm James Black. I'm the bollocks who wrote the book you love, and I've been lying about who I am this entire time.

"What's wrong?" she asked, worry etched into her face. She linked her hands together, but they were white-knuckled, as though she was preparing for the worst.

"I am . . ." No, he couldn't tell her. Not then. Not there, inside the castle. Later, at home. That way, if she tried to kill him, there'd be fewer witnesses. *Feck-all.* "I've been wanting to show you the view." He offered his hand and she took it. "Come on."

They continued their walk along the outside wall. Like everything else in Ireland, Doe castle had been built in the middle of the breathtaking countryside. Green hills stretched as far as the eye could see, interspersed with water from the bay at low tide. Tidy farmhouses sat like white polka dots around the sea of green. Pippa downed the rest of her coffee, and Finn tugged the empty cup from her fingers, tossing the remains into a trash can.

"You keep taking me to these breathtaking places." Moving forward, she gripped the stone wall at intervals as she picked her way toward the water.

"It's all part of my master plan." He chuckled darkly. "What I have in mind is to get you alone. Because, you see, we turned in my manuscript. So, as we've established, you're no longer my intern."

Finn spun Pippa around to face him. She gripped the front of his shirt for balance, tugging, so that he was forced to step closer. It was no hardship. He reached up to take Pippa's cheeks in his hands. Bringing his mouth to hers, he claimed her parted lips with his own. He swept his tongue inside, coaxing her mouth to open farther, giving her a taste of what he'd wanted to give her since the first time they'd kissed.

Finn wrenched her body between himself and the hard surface of the castle wall, though his body felt even harder than stone. Finn had no qualms about showing Pippa exactly how much he wanted her. It seemed that she didn't have any of her own, either.

"Pippa, I want you." Finn pressed his lips along her jawline, moving up to her cheekbone, grazing her closed eyelids, before he worked his way down to her mouth, nipping at first her upper lip, and then her bottom lip.

"Maybe half as much as I want you. I'm just . . . It's been a while. I may be a little out of practice."

Finn ducked down to trail kisses along her jawline. Each kiss, each nip, brought with it the taste of Pippa's skin. "I'm sure you're not as rusty as I am. Or maybe I just need to get back in the practice of things? Can you help me with that?"

"Yes." Pippa's voice grew breathless.

"Good. There *are* a few things I have in mind." Slowly, he brought his knee up between her thighs, pressing against her heat and the stone behind her in equal measure. She ground against him in response, though he didn't ask her to. Her movements were instinctual, part of a dance as old as time. It seemed the most natural thing in the world for Finn to slide his hand between her thighs, to run his fingers against her.

Pippa gasped. Her eyes locked on his.

"Do you like that, now?" He glanced behind him, searching the area again for any signs of tourists. They were alone. When he brought his gaze back to Pippa's, she regarded him through heavy-lidded eyes, waiting.

She nodded. Christ, there was heat in those eyes. It'd burn him if he wasn't careful.

But he'd waited so long to be with her, it was as if his body was a brittle thing. They'd have that night to be together, but there was no harm in a preview. She arched against him, her hooded eyes silently pleading as he moved his fingers back and forth in slow movements. She clutched his forearms as he teased her, rocking her hips, showing him how things should be as he tortured her through her clothes.

Finn ran his lips over her neck, brushing the tender skin there, trailing his mouth along her collarbone. He reached up to cup her breast, his thumb finding her nipple through her T-shirt.

"Do you think we can . . . go now?" Pippa's voice was muffled against his chest.

"So soon? I'm wondering how far I can take this, this castle being a public place and all. It's kind of hot." What in hell was wrong with him? If he kept that up, he wasn't sure if he'd be able to end it.

"You are?" Her eyes widened with desire and a hint of curiosity.

Finn pressed his lips to her forehead as he drew his fingers away from her, dragging them to the waistband of her pants. He wanted to plunge his fingers into her heat, to feel her tighten around him. He pulled back, meeting her eyes. Waiting. He wouldn't take it any further if she didn't want him to.

Her slow nod of consent was all he needed.

"Mommy! Look at the water!"

The child's voice shocked him, having the same effect as a bucket of water being doused on his head. He dropped his hands, backing away from Pippa as a family of four came around the corner.

For several moments, they stared at each other, processing. Pippa was the first to burst into laughter. Finn followed, wondering how it was that Pippa always got him to smile.

"Maybe leaving would be a good idea."

"Mm hmm." Pippa nodded vigorously, but her face remained flushed. They had to get out of there.

Finn took her hand, and he helped her pick her way through the marshy grasses of the castle grounds. Breathless, they moved quickly back to the car. That time, Finn opened the door for her, and, using all his willpower, he slid behind the wheel. It had begun spitting rain, and fat drops splattered the windshield.

She met him halfway, bumping her nose against his as she guided him into position for a kiss. Her lips found his —teasing, tempting. The car might as well have spun in circles, for her kiss made him dizzy. "I think we'd better go."

She didn't move. If anything, she scooted closer. He could finish what he started at the castle. But no. He wanted more for her.

"Unless you want the first time I make love to you to be in a car."

Pippa bit her lip. *Shite.*

"No. I think we should go. It's raining anyway."

"So it is." Dragging in a breath, Finn started the car,

navigating back the way they'd come. No matter that he'd had more stops planned for the day. He needed Pippa. It was time they headed home.

≈

THE WEATHER HAD OTHER IDEAS. They'd only been traveling about twenty minutes when the rain transitioned from a healthy shower into a torrential downpour.

"It's a mess, this." He peered over the steering wheel, trying to see through the gloom in front of them.

"If we need to pull over, do it." Pippa rested her hand overtop his.

"I'll take it slow and we'll see what we see." Inch by inch, he guided the car forward, around the winding roads in the narrow lanes that were typical Irish. He rounded the next bend and eased the car up the hill. If he could just make it to one of the many small towns they'd passed on the way. "Okay if we stop for lunch and get a bite?"

"Fine with me. Anything to get out of this rain." Pippa wrapped her arms around herself and sat up straighter. Her whole body tensed. "We don't usually get rain like this in Florida. I mean, it rains for sixty seconds, and then clears up. But you know that."

"I do. That was something to get used to, along with the heat and the bloody alligators. You know, when I first moved in—" But Finn didn't get a chance to finish his sentence, because in the next instant, the Triumph hydroplaned. He eased his foot off the brake, steering into the skid as he did his best to regain control of the car.

Finn eased the car down a gear. Slowly, it came to a stop, but it wasn't in the best of places. They'd ended up in a muddy ditch on the side of the road, several feet above a raging river. A rickety fence and an embankment were all that separated the Triumph from the water below.

Once the car had come to a halt, he realized he'd flung his arm out in front of Pippa at some point. Finn turned to her, shaken. "You all right?"

"Yeah, you?"

"I am." He forced his breath to still. "Let's see if we can get ourselves out of this." Finn threw the car into reverse and pressed down on the gas. The tires spun. The side of the road was a muddy mess. At that rate, he'd only dig himself deeper.

"Grab your stuff, Darling. It looks like we're taking a walk."

29

PIPPA

"I search night's shadows, hoping to glimpse her, to spot the hem of her dress, the waft of a singular curl as the wind holds it in its embrace."
—James Black, *To the Ends of the Earth*

They climbed out of the car. The earth had transformed from something solid to a muddy mess. Finn, on the other hand, looked a lot like Pippa had when she'd first arrived at Finn's house. Mud ran up the front of his jeans, soaking his calves. He didn't seem to notice.

Finn gripped Pippa's shoulders. "Are you sure you're all right?" The level of concern in Finn's eyes was almost comical. Particularly when he had been in the same car accident that she had. But it was more than that; it was also endearing.

And the way he'd thrown his arm out to protect her . . .

Still, she wasn't sure where to go from there. Things

with Finn had been physical. She'd wanted and needed his kisses and more those past few weeks, but that had all focused on the physical. That day, she'd felt . . . *cared for*. He'd wanted her to rest, to take time for herself. He'd tried to protect her.

Finn didn't just want her body, though that was part of it. Uma had been right—he did care for her.

"I'm fine. They have these things called seat belts, you see."

At least the storm was ending. The rain slowed to a series of random sprinkles. Finn pulled her against him anyway, grinning. "This is no time to be a smartass. I'm just glad you're all right. We're in Letterkenny, and I know the area. There's a good pub about a five minutes' walk from here. We can call for help." He took her hand in his and squeezed it.

"Can't we just call someone now?" She asked, fishing for her cell phone.

Finn held up his phone in front of her. The words "No Signal" dominated the upper-right corner of the screen. "Nope."

"Then a walk and lunch it is." She shrugged.

"Good." Finn led her in the opposite direction from which they'd come.

"Finn, is that you?" The cry came from behind them, and as they turned around, an older gentleman walking a small, white-and-black terrier closed in on them. The terrier seemed out of breath, panting as it ambled on four squat legs. It wore a green and white kerchief and a pink leash.

The man's outfit clashed just as much. He wore red-and-green plaid shorts and a purple T-shirt. A red and white plaid cap sat atop his crop of white curls. "I thought I recognized you."

"Connor, what the devil?" But Finn's face broke into a broad smile and he thrust his hand out to shake the man's waiting one. "Still picking out your own clothes, I see."

"I'm a bit color blind." Connor shrugged. "The missus is on holiday. I thought I could handle it. Is it that bad?" He asked that of Pippa.

"Oh, it's fine." She waved his concern away. Connor's outfit was anything but fine. It was a fashion disaster, but they weren't on the runway, so he was safe. The dog had trotted forward and lay on the ground in front of Pippa, rolling on her back for a belly scratch. Pippa dropped to her knees and obliged. When the dog's leg began to thump on the asphalt, Pippa knew she'd found her preferred spot.

"That's Ginger. I think you have her loyalty for life. And who's this lovely bit of sunshine?" Connor grinned at Pippa, much in the same way Caden had. Was every man in Ireland that big of a flirt, or was it only Finn's friends?

Finn shook his head. "Connor O'Keefe, this is my summer intern, Pippa Darling."

Ouch. Just a summer intern? She supposed it *was* an accurate statement, despite the sting. It would've been weird to call her the girl he'd been making out with. And girlfriend seemed like too casual a term for Finn Burke to ever use. The woman in his life would be everything to him—all or nothing.

"Nice to meet you, Connor." Pippa waved.

"A pleasure to make your acquaintance, Pippa." Connor tipped his hat.

Ginger crept forward and leaned against her, resting her entire body on Pippa's foot. Finn lowered himself to the ground to rub Ginger's head. His fingers trailed up, twining with Pippa's.

"We ran into a spot of car trouble down the lane. There aren't any bars on this damn thing." Finn held up his cell. "Can you point us to The Deer? It's been a while."

"Aye. Down this lane a little further, take the first right, and then the first left. You can't miss it." Connor reached into his shorts pocket and dug out a large smartphone, far more modern than Finn's. "I can get you home when Bertie, my daughter, gets back from her shopping. I'm not sure when that will be, though. She's just left and she's out all hours, sometimes."

"Thanks, but I can get us a ride." Finn returned his attention to Ginger. The small dog rolled onto her back again, tongue lolling to one side.

"Nice to see you again, Finn. Don't be a stranger. I'd best be off. Pippa, it's been a pleasure," Connor said, with a wave.

"Nice to meet you, too." Pippa stood.

Connor snapped his fingers. Ginger jumped to her feet, but not before giving her owner a look of disdain, as if to say, *Really? We have to go now?*

When Ginger refused to move, Connor reached down and scooped her up from the pavement, positioning her under his arm. "Come on, you. No insubordination in the ranks, thank you."

"Take care of yourself." Finn gave Connor a mock salute, but the look also held something more. He was trying to make the goodbye casual, but it wasn't. There was something there.

"You, too," Connor said. With a wave, the other man turned away with his dog and headed back in the direction from which he'd come.

"He's nice. I like his dog," Pippa said as she and Finn began walking again.

"Ginger's great," Finn agreed. "And totally in love with you." He shot her a sideways glance.

"I'm a sucker for dogs. What can I say?" Together, they climbed a small hill. Once they reached the crest, the village came into view. Finn hadn't been wrong. Letterkenny was close, and it wasn't exactly a thriving metropolis. "How do you know Connor?"

"He helped me with my mortgage. He's a good guy." But he didn't offer any more information.

Instead, Finn kept walking, his strides long and constant, leaving Pippa to catch up. He seemed lost in thought. Probably the thing he kept wanting to tell her, but never had.

She could bring it up again, try to drag whatever it was out of him, but she knew Finn well enough to recognize pushing would have the opposite effect on him. He'd most likely clam up and that would be the end of it.

Still, the mystery of it all left Pippa with a nagging sensation in her gut, one that continued to bother her all the way to Letterkenny.

〜

THE MOMENT PIPPA stepped inside The Daft Deer, Finn went off to find a phone. She grabbed them an empty table in the back corner. By the time Finn returned with a pint to see what she wanted to drink, Pippa had herself a nice glass of wine.

"Bob and Zoe are out at the shops, but I got ahold of Caden. If we order quickly, we'll have time to have a nice lunch before he gets here." Finn scanned the chalkboard menu on the wall as he drank deeply. Pippa did the same, deciding on a hearty Irish stew with a side of soda bread. Finn placed their orders at the bar, and it wasn't long after that when a server arrived with two steaming plates of heavenly smelling food. Pippa dove for the carbs first, stifling a moan as she bit into the warm, raisin-filled bread.

"So, you sent your manuscript to Phillip. Your completed manuscript. We should toast to that."

Finn's face broke into a smile. "I did. *Sláinte.*" He raised his glass to Pippa's. "And thank you for all you did. I couldn't have written it without you."

"Thank you." Pippa mimicked his actions. But her mind wasn't on the toast, or on Finn's book, or even the food. It was on what would happen between them when they got back home. Wait—not her home. Finn's home. The memory of what he'd done with her at the castle, of what she wanted him to do to her, still raged in her mind.

Both of them ate in silence, lost to their own thoughts. It wasn't uncomfortable, but companionable. Still she jumped when Caden arrived.

"There you two are. If you're about finished with your lunch, there's another storm rolling in. We'd best be getting on the road." Caden stood at the end of their table, his arms crossed over his chest.

Finn rose from the table. "Sure and let me pay the bill." He snatched the paper receipt from the tabletop and moved off to the bar.

Caden plopped onto the bench across from Pippa. His blue eyes seemed to memorize her face. "You're with Finn, then?"

Even though he wasn't that much younger than Pippa, Caden wore the age difference in an obvious way. He acted too confident, as though he couldn't fail. She supposed he just needed the right woman to come along and kick his ass. That would be fun to watch.

Pippa almost felt guilty for brushing Caden off, but there was no point. She only had eyes for one Irishman, and Caden didn't come close. "Yes. I am with Finn." She tipped her chin in a challenge.

"That's a shame, that is." Caden winked at her and rose to his feet. "But no worries. I know when I've been beaten."

"You're presuming there was ever a competition." Finn had returned. His jaw already had that rigid set to it that he seemed to reserve for Caden. He reached over and took her hand. "I thought we'd have a look at the car's location first. Are you cool with driving over there before we head home?" Finn asked, turning to Caden.

"That depends. Is it far?" He'd led the way outside, under the darkened Irish sky. There was definitely another storm brewing, and Pippa understood Caden's hesitation about going back in the opposite direction.

"Not far." Finn squeezed her hand.

Pippa squeezed back and allowed herself to be led to Caden's car. It was a beat-up old thing that looked more ancient than Finn's Triumph. Pippa couldn't tell what the make was, because the manufacturer nameplate had been removed from the back.

Together, the three of them climbed in and then drove down the road. But when they got to the spot where they'd left Finn's car, there was no Triumph in sight. There were tire tracks, certainly, but the car itself was completely gone.

"What the *feck*? This is just where we left it." Finn launched himself from Caden's ride, rushed to the side of the road, and froze. A moment later, he placed his hand over his mouth and stood staring. All the blood had drained from his face. "No."

Pippa flew from the car to join him, but when she stood by his side, she wished she hadn't. For Finn's Triumph was in the river, courtesy of a mudslide. Half the embankment was missing.

"*Bollocks.*" Finn smacked his hand against his forehead.

"That'll be a pain getting out." Caden moved behind Finn, shoving his hands in his pockets.

"That it will. I hope you didn't leave anything behind in the car. There'll be no getting it out now." Finn patted her shoulder, as though she were the one who needed consoling.

"No, I think I've got everything." Pippa rifled through her bag, anyway. Everything seemed to be there—her wallet, her phone, all of it. She did her best to push her lingering doubt aside. "I'm good."

"Let's go," Finn said. He took her hand and led her back to the car.

Unfortunately, the feeling that Pippa had forgotten something didn't go away.

30

FINN

"The bastard wanted her, too. He'd never stood a chance."
—Finn Burke, *Lost*

*P*ippa fell asleep against his shoulder on the ride home. It would have been better manners to sit with Caden in the front seat, but Finn didn't want to be apart from Pippa just then. That knowledge rocked him to his core. Something had happened inside him that day, in between the moment when he'd (almost) pleasured Pippa at the castle and when his car had landed in the mud, and he'd thrown out his arm to protect her.

He was *feeling* things for Pippa that he hadn't expected to. Though he found it easier not to examine those emotions just yet, he still didn't want to be apart from her.

Caden drove, keeping his eyes on the road, though they did occasionally flicker back to meet Finn's in the rearview mirror. He chatted easily about university, answering questions Finn hadn't asked about his professors and his friends. Filling him in on the women Caden had dated.

Finn must have nodded off, too, because soon Caden eased his car to a stop. "We're here."

"Caden, thanks." Finn reached in his pocket and extracted twenty euro, which he thrust at Caden. "For petrol."

Caden waved him away and turned back to the steering wheel. "Don't worry about it. You would have done the same for me."

"I would not," Finn said, but he grinned. Caden shook his head, so he knew Finn was taking the piss out of him.

Gripping Pippa's shoulder, Finn gently shook her awake. "Pip-pa."

She awoke with a start, her mouth falling open as she realized she'd fallen asleep on his shoulder. "Did I drool?" she asked as she sat up. "Sometimes I drool, and I wouldn't want to do that on you. On anyone, really."

"That'll be something to look forward to tomorrow morning," Finn said. A blush colored her cheeks. He didn't feel the least bit guilty. Rather, Finn felt a strange sense of triumph. "Come on. See ya, Caden."

"Bye, Finn. Pippa." Caden winked at Pippa as Finn led her from the car.

Pippa must have been seriously knackered. She didn't have two words to say as they walked to his front porch.

"What were you and Caden talking about back in the pub?" He had a pretty good idea about that, and he wasn't overly bothered by it. That didn't stop him from asking.

"He was asking if we were together." They climbed the short steps, coming to a stop before the door.

"And what did you tell him?" Finn reached down to cup Pippa's cheek. He was baiting her, but she didn't take it.

Instead, she slid her arms around him. "You already know."

She rested her cheek against his chest, and somehow, it felt like home. Not because of the place, because of Pippa.

But all too soon, she dropped her hands and backed away from him, shaking her head. "Oh my God."

"We haven't gotten to that part of the evening yet. Give it time." Finn smirked.

But Pippa waved her hands in front of her face, as though cooling herself off. "You don't understand. I've lost my book."

Feck all. "What do you mean?" Finn's eyebrows shot to his hairline. "The James Black book?"

"The *only* book." Pippa took several steps back and slid to the porch swing. Dejection seemed to run over her like a river. "You don't understand. That book is out of print. I'll never get another copy. It was pure chance that I got that one in the first place. I picked it up at a library sale. When I tried to buy a newer version, I couldn't find one."

Guilt pummeled him. If he wanted to be with Pippa, really be with her, he had to tell her the truth.

Finn took her hand again, but that time, he unlocked the front door and led her inside. "We really do need to have that talk now."

31

PIPPA

"If I should bare my soul for her, she will know, with all certainty, that she's won every part of my being, has the power to claim me as her own."
—James Black, *To the Ends of the Earth*

*P*ippa's head spun. She'd lost her book. How could she have been so careless with it? And Finn wanted to talk to her right then? Why then, when something so important to her had probably been destroyed?

But Finn didn't seem to care. He hadn't even acted like it was a big deal. He'd just said they needed to talk and started leading her to the basement. As if the basement was going to make things any better.

They didn't speak until they reached the downstairs wall with the whiteboard. Gripping the eraser tray beneath a section of the board, Finn tugged on it. A portion of the wall swung back. He flicked the light switch, illuminating row after row of shelves, most of which contained boxes or unmarked storage containers.

Pippa gasped as Finn shut the door behind them, her lost book all but forgotten for the moment. "A secret door? I didn't know this was here." She resisted the urge to shield her eyes from the brightness of the overhead fluorescent lights.

"Of course you didn't. It's a secret room."

"Oh." Did that mean he hadn't trusted her with the room? Or was it just not that important to him that she know?

"Come on," he said, taking her hand. Together, they walked past rows of bookshelves until they reached the last one. There, in the very last aisle, were three large boxes. The front of every box was labeled, in Finn's dramatic, spiky script, *To the Ends of the Earth*.

Pippa sucked in a breath. Her mind reeled as Finn opened a box and withdrew a new copy of the book Pippa cherished more than any in the world. Where had he found so many copies of the same book?

She spurted out the first thing that came to mind. "I don't understand. You said nobody wants to read a book like this."

Finn didn't say anything as he reached into a jar of markers sitting on one of the shelves and chose a black Sharpie. He popped the cap. Whipping open the front cover of one of the book copies, he wrote something, his expression tense. After a moment, he blew on the text he'd written, and then waved the acrid stench of marker from the air before handing the book to Pippa.

She could only stare at him. "I don't understand."

Finn slid a hand over his face. "Read it, Pippa."

Dread, confusion, and something like fear mixed in her stomach, making Pippa shake. Opening the first page, she read the inscription.

To Pippa, for whom all dreams are spun. – James Black

Pippa's gaze shot to Finn, still unseeing. "I don't—"

"Pippa. I *am* James Black." Finn cringed.

"What?" Disbelief slammed through her, through every pore, through every part of her. "Why didn't you tell me? You made fun of your own book!"

Finn shrugged. "Maybe because I didn't want anyone to know?"

"Why?" Pippa stepped closer, clutching the book to her chest. "Why would you hide this from me? From the world?"

"Because no one wants it!" He shouted the words, shattering the quiet moment.

Although she'd complained about him shouting when he'd read her critiques, she realized then that he'd never raised his voice before. It had been intense, certainly, but not loud enough to cross a line. But at that moment, his words rang in her ears. His anger wasn't directed at her, but that didn't make it any less of a surprise.

"It's worthless, don't you see? All the months, *years* I spent on this book. I put my own heart and soul into *To the Ends of the Earth*—and no one wanted it!" He thrust his hands into his hair.

"How can you say that?" Pippa asked. "*I* want it."

"But you're the only one." The anguish in his eyes, the

obvious pain, took over his features. "I know I should've told you. I should've told you on the day you arrived. At first, I couldn't believe you didn't know who I was, but when I figured out that you didn't, I couldn't bring myself to say anything."

"Why? I don't understand. I thought we were getting closer. I thought there was something between us." It was as if someone had reached into Pippa's chest and squeezed her heart. She held her breath, everything she had resting on his answer.

"There *is* something between us." Finn reached out, but let his hands fall, as though he didn't dare touch her. "I didn't set out to deliberately deceive you. At first, it was too painful to talk about. Then I was afraid to tell you in case you decided to never speak to me again."

"The truth is, I wrote *To the Ends of the Earth* for a woman. I was young, eighteen, and I fell in love."

"Amélie." Pippa breathed the name from the dedication.

"The very same." He drew in a breath. "I wrote this book for her. I proposed to her, and then she left me." That admission seemed to exhaust Finn. He stood, ragged, leaning against the bookcase for support. "Then, to make matters worse, the book didn't sell. My publisher wasn't impressed. They let it run almost out of print. When I could, I bought up the rest and canceled my contract."

Pippa's breath had begun to slow. She was listening then, not panicking, because no matter how hurt she was from Finn's betrayal, he seemed to be going through something far worse.

"I started working on a different book. After Amélie

had gone, I couldn't stay at home. Then Da died. I went to school, and Ma came with me. I started writing *Lost*. I'd submitted *To the Ends of the Earth* to a publisher without an agent, but I thought having one might make a difference in my sales. I also decided to use my real name."

"And you got the deal of the century, all kinds of fame and fortune." Pippa was beginning to understand more than she'd expected to. "You even got your name on the best seller lists."

"I wanted to write something that would sell. Because what was worse than being left by Amélie was seeing my testament to our love sit on the shelves, unsold."

She pushed down the urge to cringe. Her favorite book had been a testament to Finn's love—for *someone else*. Even though only the pair of them stood in the room, the ghost of Amélie was right there.

"Besides, best seller lists are games the papers play. A book should never be about a number. About proving one book is better than another. They all have a place." He took her hands in his. "I'm so sorry. Truly."

All traces of anger began to evaporate from Pippa's heart. Finn Burke wasn't a liar, not really. But he was brokenhearted. "Do you have any idea how beautiful the book is?"

"People don't care about beauty." His voice was jagged, bitter. Cynic Finn was battling with Dreamer James. She wanted both sides of him to come back together, so she could find her way to the Finn she'd come to know.

"I care." She whispered the words, but it was almost as if he didn't hear her. As if he couldn't hear her.

"Poetry and grand adventures don't sell. That's not

what people read. They read about pain, sex, and everything miserable in the world." He stuffed his hands into his pockets, as if to restrain them from something she couldn't name.

"Who cares what people want to read? Write what you want to write. Someone out there will want to read it. Someone will care."

"You sound like my ma." He moved as if to brush past her, as if to close off the room, and walk away from *To the Ends of the Earth* once more.

Pippa stepped in front of him, effectively blocking him. "I thought my life was going to be all about the B&B. I'd take it over and stay in Gettysburg until I was old enough to retire. Then I read this book, and it made me feel like I could write, too. It made me feel like there was another way."

"I don't deserve the courtesy and understanding you're giving me just now. You should be throwing things." Finn stared at her, the last vestiges of the wall he'd built around himself seeming to crumble.

"Maybe"—Pippa squeezed the book close, wishing it were Finn—"you have to believe in yourself. Your words changed my life, Finn. Believe it."

"Pippa." Her name was a whisper on his lips, a promise and a curse all at once. Reaching up, he took the book from her and rested it on one of the boxes. "I don't know where I stand. I wasn't honest."

"I wasn't honest at first with you, either. You told the truth—just a little later than you should have." Her breath came out light, airy, as though she could barely force out the words. "I trust you won't make that mistake again."

"I won't." His green eyes were intense, holding her in place, making her want him closer. "Not ever. Only the real me, from now on."

"Then . . . yes. To us, to you, to *everything*." Whatever he wanted, *yes*.

Her answer had the effect of demolishing Finn's hesitation. He filled the space between them, sliding his hands up her back, drawing her to him.

His mouth covered hers, his lips invading her own in a slow torment, sending unspoken possibilities singing through her veins. "Ah, Pippa." And the way he said her name, like she was every wish he'd ever made on any star, sent heat spiraling through her.

Finn's hands drifted to her hips, and in one swift action, he tugged her against him. With their height difference, the hard length of him molded to her stomach. A heady rush of feminine power coursed through her. A dull ache persisted between her thighs as Finn's callused hands swept under her shirt.

There was no ceremony with Finn. No assurances—at least not those of the verbal variety. Though he was promising her something else with his hard body and those intense green eyes.

She rocked against him, wanting to feel him. Finn spun them around, so that she was backed against one of the monster industrial bookcases. She jumped up, wrapping her legs around him, the need to be as close to him as possible caging her in, sending her breath leaving in a burst.

It wasn't enough. It would never be enough with Finn. The room spun. How could she have gone so long without knowing what it meant to want someone this way?

"I need you in my bed, Pippa." Finn's voice grew husky, the timbre sending an arrow of electricity sparking through her, stoking the fire. "I want to look at you."

"Yes." She kissed him, drawing him as close as she could, want making her sluggish, overheated as he carried her toward his bedroom with the gray briefs and sexy sheets.

"We had each other, and then she begged for an encore."
—Finn Burke, *Lost*

Finn trailed invisible lines down Pippa's sides with his fingertips, sending her shivering in response. He'd barely touched her, and already he'd become a quivering mess. He needed her in a way that he'd never needed any woman. Not even Amélie.

There was no denying his attraction was physical. Yet, there was a part of him that was reacting to Pippa on an emotional level. He'd told her the truth. That he was James Black. She'd loved it. There was no denying *that* was a bit of a turn-on.

Maybe she would hate him in the morning for it. Maybe she wouldn't. All he knew was that he needed Pippa Darling with every breath in his body. And damn it, he would have her.

With unsteady hands, he tried to unzip her hoodie. The zipper stuck. *"Jaysus."* He grunted the word. Again and again, he tugged the zipper and it refused to give. Finally, he gripped the bottom around her waist. "Arms up."

She complied, and he tugged it over her head, taking her T-shirt with it. When Pippa stood before him in a pale blue lace bra, he forgot to breathe. His eyes locked onto hers. He couldn't remember ever wanting someone so much—as though she were some essential part of his soul that had to be reunited with his body. Without her, Finn would be only partly himself and mostly lost.

With care, he ran his fingers from her neck to her breastbone, and down to her navel. She tensed at his touch, arching toward him the way a flower seeks the sun. He knew what she wanted. They'd had enough moments like that one—moments where they had to decide how far they would take things—for him to know what she needed.

He reached behind her, flicking open her bra. He freed her arms from the straps and let the contraption fall to the floor. Finn tugged his T-shirt over his head. Instead of giving his attention to Pippa's breasts, he splayed his hands over her bare back and drew her flush against him. She gasped as her breasts met his solid chest. Her nipples hardened. Finn's body tightened in response.

Pippa stood on tiptoe to brush her lips over his, her erect nipples teasing his chest with her movements. He sat down on the edge of his bed and tugged her onto his lap, so that she straddled him. She thrust her knees against the sides of his hips. Her heat surrounded him, and he hardened even more despite the tiny problem of them both still wearing pants. That would have to be rectified. Soon.

He claimed her mouth, meshing his tongue with hers as he took back control of the kiss. She didn't fight him. Instead, her tongue welcomed his slow invasion, matching him stroke for stroke. Her breath had shortened, releasing and contracting. Finn moved his attention to her breasts, running his palms in circles over her nipples. She locked her hands together behind his neck, giving him access.

"What are you doing to me?" She whispered the question, her breath hitching.

"My plan is to drive us both *barmy.*" He leaned in, capturing the stiff peak of her nipple in his mouth. He sucked her, quick, brief, before releasing the sensitive flesh and moving his attention to its twin. Pippa cried out. "How am I doing so far?"

"I'd say you're succeeding." Pippa's voice came out light and breathy as she ran her hands over his chest. Finn's pulse slammed against her palm with the force of a racehorse. She had to feel it. She had to know what she was doing to him.

"My turn." She breathed the promise, though she'd driven him to the point of madness already. He'd be lucky to keep himself from exploding in his pants like a teenager, for Chrissakes.

Pippa trailed her fingers over the ridge of muscles on his abdomen. He watched as Pippa glided over his skin, turning him to stone beneath her fingertips.

Images of things he'd planned to do with Pippa tumbled through head, though he hadn't done them yet. Every thought made him grow harder.

Pippa reached for the button on his fly. He stopped

her, guiding her flush against his chest, trapping her hands between them. "Not yet," he said, his mouth imprinting hers with his kiss. "If you get in my pants, it'll be all over. Trust me."

Some part of his brain told him he should've laughed, but his wires had short-circuited the moment their skin came in contact with each other's. Her mouth took his again, and he was lost, all logic buried under a series of dizzying moments. She hooked her leg over his hip as his tongue slid over hers, forcing her mouth to open even more, deepening their kiss.

Finn guided Pippa from his lap, so that she stood before him. Gripping the waistband of Pippa's yoga pants, he tugged them down, taking her panties with them, until Pippa stood before him practically naked. Except for her socks. Socks with little white cats wearing pink bows.

Somehow, they were undeniably hot, and so Pippa.

She bent to remove them, but he rested his hand on her shoulder. "Keep the socks. I like 'em."

"You do?" she asked, straightening, more than a little breathless. "You like my Hello Kitty socks?"

Finn grinned. "I like all of you. Or haven't you figured that out yet?"

Without waiting for her reply, he slid his hand between her thighs, but that time she wore no clothes to hold him back. Finn coaxed her already-slick folds apart. Pippa gasped, arching her back, pressing herself into his hand as he teased her most sensitive spot with his middle finger.

"Come for me, Pippa." He ground out the request, even as he worked her with his finger. She gripped his shoulder, keeping him in place as her entire body tensed. "Come, *macushla*." *Macushla*. Darling. He couldn't think of a more fitting endearment as he coaxed her toward the edge.

Her hold on his shoulders tightened. On and on he stroked her, bringing her to where he needed her. She convulsed against his hand, crying out as he brought her to orgasm. On and on he teased, until her shaking subsided and she stood before him, her body limp, her breath heavy.

He could smell her everywhere. Her scent clung to the room and to his fingertips, which he brought to his lips for a taste. He licked them one by one, enjoying the musky flavor of her before he pulled her back onto his bed so that they lay side by side.

He ground his hips against hers. He knew she could feel him through his jeans. Hard. Wanting. Wanting *her*. His mind cried out that he couldn't wait anymore, that he had to have her. He forced those thoughts aside. He wanted to pleasure her, to savor every moment with Pippa in his bed.

He kissed her again, knowing she could taste herself on his tongue, wondering if she ever had before. That time, Finn did the seeking. He deepened their kiss, gliding his tongue around hers in a dance.

Finn growled low in his throat. "Do you know how much I want you?"

Pippa blushed. He couldn't help remembering her reaction to his feedback on her first day—when he'd analyzed Jake and Cassidy's love scene.

Ten points for irony.

33

PIPPA

"With open eyes and knowing smiles, we drink in each other;
remembering, holding onto this collection of moments for as
long as possible."
—James Black, *To the Ends of the Earth*

Pippa slid her leg over his hip, guiding him closer. God, she'd never felt like that before. Never wanted anyone that much. He traced her nipple with the pad of his thumb and someone moaned. She was pretty sure it was her.

"Finn, please." She wanted him, needed to feel him inside of her or she'd fall apart, shattering to pieces at his feet. "Please . . . I—"

"Not just yet." Again, he slipped his fingers between her thighs, that time working them inside of her, managing to tease her most sensitive place before exiting again. "Ah, Pippa. That's grand, that is."

She dropped her forehead to his shoulder, unable to concentrate with his hand on her. Again, he teased her, taking his fingers deeper and deeper, triggering a pendulum of sensation that had her writhing against him. "Finn."

She knew what she wanted from him—exactly where he needed to touch her. She let her head fall back, allowing Finn to hold her still as he pleasured her.

He found her nipple with his mouth, drawing the bud between his teeth, sucking, biting. Visions of him doing that in the same place where his fingers teased rushed through Pippa. Soon, she was spinning, a spiral of need coiling in her core, increasing, increasing, until she couldn't stand it. Until she was sure she'd die at his hands.

And then one more stroke . . .

"Finn!"

He took her over, his fingers furiously occupied as he drew out her release. His lips found hers, but she couldn't even kiss him. She was at his mercy. Heat burst through Pippa as she came, shaking, gasping for air. It was even better than before.

It was only after she'd collapsed against him that he raised his fingers to his lips and tasted again. "Next time, Darling . . . I'll savor you with my mouth."

Holy shit. Her knees knocked as his lips brushed over hers, and his tongue swept into her mouth, bringing with it her own unique flavor. She needed him more than air, but she was done waiting. Before he could protest, could draw things out even further, she unbuttoned his jeans and slipped her hand inside his briefs. She grasped Finn's hard shaft, craving him inside of her.

He groaned, thrusting against her palm, those searching green eyes locked onto hers. His cock was so hard, he seemed ready to burst. He confirmed it when he stood to shuck his jeans, shoving them onto the floor. His long, hard length sprang free. Moving to the nightstand, he opened the top drawer and grabbed something from inside. A condom. In a series of deft movements, he rolled it on, and then returned to the bed. Then he was beside her, his eyes taking over hers, soaking her up as though they'd devour her.

"I thought you hated me when I first came to work here." She blurted out the words before she could stop.

Finn shook his head. "I've wanted you since that first moment when we crashed into each other. Maybe even before then. Maybe always."

"Then have me." She barely managed the words. He must have heard her, though, because he moved over her, lowered himself onto his elbows, and buried himself inside of her, taking what she offered.

34

FINN

"I made her mine. Period. And the saucy wench liked it."
—Finn Burke, *Lost*

Sunlight hit Finn's face, a silent, unbidden alarm clock. He stretched, and his fingertips found soft, warm skin.

Pippa.

Finn opened his eyes, taking in the sight of her. Her brown hair was tousled from sleep and her plump lips even more swollen from his kisses. There was something about Pippa that was undeniably sexy. Perhaps it was the way she held herself—chin tipped, with a straight back, like a warrior. Or it could have been the way she'd blurt out something she hadn't intended to say, and then cover her mouth when she realized what she'd done.

It didn't matter. Snatches of memory, bits of passion from their night before, slammed into his brain. *Shite.* He doubted any other woman could hold a candle to Pippa.

He found he didn't want one to, either. He only wanted her.

He reached over and cupped Pippa's cheek. She stirred and popped open first one eyelid and then the other. Her eyes seemed to come together and focus on him all at once.

She instantly sat up farther on the pillow, that crease in her brow back with the fullest of forces. "Are you going to say last night was a mistake? That's usually what guys say. Not that I've had many nights like last night. I mean, I haven't had *any* nights like last night. I'm just saying, if that's what you have planned, just say it, because I'd rather—"

But Finn didn't let her get the rest of the words out, because he brought his mouth to hers, raining soft kisses over her lips. He cupped her breast through her T-shirt. *His* T-shirt, actually—one that he'd lent her the night before. He molded her breast, shaping it and tweaking her nipple. He scooted closer, aligning his body with hers.

He hadn't meant to do more than kiss her on the forehead, but things quickly moved out of his control. He rested his forehead against hers, breathless. "Does it seem like I think last night was a mistake?"

Pippa opened and closed her mouth.

Jaysus, he'd rendered her speechless *again*. He'd have to add that to his list of abilities.

"Last night was . . ." He locked eyes with Pippa. He wanted to give her something, so she would see. So she would truly understand what she meant to him. And then it was there. The right thing to say. The way to frame the words so Pippa would know. He cleared his throat. "And every dream I had exploded into brilliant fireworks, lighting the sky in a million singular, crystalline stars that illuminated a path through the universe . . ."

Her muscles went limp as he spoke, and she lay there, her ardent gaze seeming to seek the depths of his.

"That was from the new pages you let me read the other day." A small smile tugged at her lips. "You just quoted yourself to me, *James*."

When she put it that way, he felt like a daft *fecker*. "I had you on my mind when I wrote it. I just wanted you to know that I don't think last night was a mistake.

"And I am sorry. Again."

She held a finger to his lips. "I should probably be furious with you about this, but I just get it. We all have parts of us we want to lock away. You did, too. At least I found out from you."

He stared at her as though for the first time. "You don't just get what I did. You get *me*." Admitting that left him feeling vulnerable, exposed. He wasn't sure what to think about it. "Even if I've started today by quoting myself like an *arse*."

She shook her head. "I don't think you're an ass, and the quote was perfect." Pippa curled her leg over his hip. "I'm in bed with the great James Black."

"James Black I may be, but the great part's debatable." He grinned despite himself, however, burying his face in her neck.

"Why did you let it go out of print?" she asked, her breath warm against his shoulder.

He was tempted to take her again, just to avoid

answering the question. She was owed the truth, though. Especially after everything he'd kept from her.

"I was a fool. I bought every copy I could, and hid them." He slid his hand under his pillow and lay against the fluffy surface. "Like it was tarnished. I hated *To the Ends of the Earth*." He shook his head. "But then you came, Pippa . . ."

She touched his cheek and he sucked in an answering breath. He had to have her again, and soon. "You need to write the way you did in *To the Ends of the Earth* again."

If only. "People don't want to read fanciful escapes. They want pain and angst."

"Maybe some do. I just want a happy ending. I want adventure. I want lust. I want *love*." Her cheeks turned pink at the word love. "I mean, I don't mean love as in *you*, like I want *you* to love me, but maybe . . . I mean . . ." She slapped her palm against her own forehead.

"Just stop there. In fact, maybe it's time we stopped talking at all." He rolled onto his back, taking her with him, settling her on top of him.

Still, he couldn't halt his thoughts. Even later, when Pippa's mouth moved over his and their bodies had joined. A tiny, nagging voice cried out in his mind, warning him. Warning him about Pippa Darling . . . and what she might do to his heart.

*"Regrets are wasteful indulgences. Life is only real if it's gripped
firmly and embraced with abandon."*
—James Black, *To the Ends of the Earth*

*O*h. *My. God.* She'd slept with Finn. And he had
mad skills, so beyond anything she could have
imagined. In the light of day outside of Finn's bedroom, it
all seemed surreal.

By the time they'd finally made it out of bed it was
almost noon. At that moment, Finn was cooking Pippa
breakfast—in his UNDERWEAR. If that wasn't something, she didn't know what was. Holy shit. He was
gorgeous.

He grinned from his spot behind the stove. Had he
realized she'd been checking him out? She gulped. How
the holy heck had she ended up there? As recently as a few
months ago, she hadn't been sure she could stand the guy
enough to get through her internship. That morning, she

was hanging out with him in her pajamas. She dragged his T-shirt down over her knees.

"Earth to Pippa." Finn's voice was close, closer than she'd realized. He'd somehow ended up right in front of her. "I asked how much you'll eat. I guess I don't need to ask that in *inches*." He tossed her another one of his should-be-patented smirks.

"Oh my God!" She covered her face with her hands, but he caught and lowered them. She had to be blushing. Her skin was such a traitor.

"Don't be telling me you're embarrassed about last night. Or this morning." He moved toward her, parting her thighs with his knee. "Because I'm not." Finn leaned in, capturing her mouth with his. It was one of those kisses that blotted out everything from her mind. His hand slid up the nape of her neck. He leaned in, pressing her against the breakfast bar, his arousal insistent. Someone was making his intentions known. And they'd just—oh, heck.

His hand skated up her shirt and splayed against her bare stomach. Then he must have thought the better of it, because he gripped the hem of her T-shirt and tugged it off and over her head.

And then Pippa found herself sitting there, in Finn Burke's kitchen, wearing nothing but a pair of panties. He seemed to drink her in, his inspection intense as his eyes scrutinized all of her. His breath grew heavy, his eyes hooded as he hooked two fingers behind the damp crotch of her panties and tugged.

Pippa's heart raced as she raised herself off the stool to

help. Once her panties had reached her kneecaps, he pulled them down, over her feet and toward the floor.

What was he . . . *Oh.*

Finn slid his hands under her buttocks, lifting and guiding her forward. Instead of taking Pippa with that generous cock of his, he dropped to his knees and brought his mouth to her. For once, her home bikini wax seemed worth it.

Almost worth it, anyway.

Leaning in, Finn swiped his tongue up and over her sex, wasting no time finding the spot where she wanted him most, sending a wave of sensation coursing through her. He quickly switched from a slow lick to a passionate suck, teasing her, coaxing her, tasting her as though he wanted all of Pippa in his mouth and he couldn't get enough.

The wood of the breakfast bar rubbed against her bare back. Her nipples had hardened from exposure to the cool, air-conditioned room. Finn took her hands in his and guided them to her breasts. He positioned her nipples between her own thumbs and index fingers. "Touch yourself for me, Pippa. Show me what you might do if you were alone."

Her breath hitched in her chest. The aching between her thighs increased. Finn groaned as she complied, rolling her already hardened nipples with her fingers. Oh God. She'd never imagined that it would make everything better, but it did.

When he brought his mouth to her again it was as if she *felt* five times more than she had before. Finn applied his tongue with that speedy flicking action. That time, Pippa was the one to groan, arching her back. She kept her hands on her breasts as he'd asked, squeezing and toying with her own nipples, while she thrust herself harder against his mouth, letting him know what she wanted.

A spring of desire coiled inside her. She was close. So close. This was what she'd been missing and needing for so long. She planted the soles of her feet on his shoulders even as tiny whimpers escaped her lips. Finn continued to alternate between sucking and licking, winding the spring inside of Pippa tighter and tighter so that only his mouth on her mattered. With each stroke of his tongue, each suck, he drove her further toward the edge.

"Come for me, Darling." Finn's voice, the throaty male sound of it, undid her. She unraveled under him.

"Finn!" Pippa gripped the sides of the stool on which she sat as if it were her only link to sanity. He coaxed her through wave after wave of bliss. She thrust herself against his tongue as he worked his magic. Finally, she collapsed against the breakfast bar.

When she couldn't move another muscle, Finn stood. Pippa expected him to drop his briefs, to take her right then. Instead, he gathered her close, dragging her against his chest with those strong arms of his.

"Pippa." He pressed his lips to the crown of her head.

It was in that unexpected moment of tenderness that she knew she was glimpsing James Black, the dreamer, the romantic—the other side of Finn. Not the cynical mask he wore for the rest of the world. And right then, in his kitchen, Pippa was the one he'd chosen to share himself with.

He raised his head, and the emotion in his eyes almost knocked her from the stool. It was heated, deep. All for her. She nudged her nose against his as she pressed a kiss to his lips.

Then he had to go and open his mouth against hers, his tongue teasing, seeking, deepening the kiss. When he finally stepped back, his breath was heavy, his arousal pressing against her through his briefs. "Be right back," he said, dipping in for another quick kiss before he broke away and stalked from the room.

For a few moments, Pippa sat frozen, waiting, wondering if she should tug his T-shirt back over her head. She'd just picked it up when Finn returned with a condom in hand. "Don't you dare put that back on," he said.

"Fine by me." Pippa dropped the T and sat up straight enough to claim his lips as he dropped his briefs and slid the condom into place. Then she was gripping the length of him, guiding him closer, urging him inside her heat.

God, he was hard. The spring inside of her reset itself as he parted her sensitive flesh. Pippa gasped as he slipped inside of her, but he ended her breath on a kiss. The taste of her own arousal spurred her on, and she thrusted against him, bringing him deeper inside her each time. Their bodies moved in a dance, as if they'd always known each other and this was the reunion.

They rocked together, faster and faster. Her thoughts turned to mush as he tugged one of her nipples into his mouth, sucking. He moved his other hand between them, teasing her with his thumb. Pippa tensed, ready to splinter apart again. She blocked out everything around them, even pushed the pungent scent of something—she couldn't name what—aside.

"Again, Pippa. Come."

His accent caressed her name, making her body tighten from craving him. "Finn." Her own climax staggered her. She dug her nails into his forearms as she came. He continued the sensation, plunging himself inside of her. Slamming into her again and again, the rhythm between them fast, faster, until he tensed and shuddered. Only once he'd finished did he collapse against her shoulder.

They stayed like that for a collection of moments Pippa couldn't measure. When Finn finally raised his head, his eyes found hers and a thought exploded inside her mind.

I love you, Finn.

It was only a thought. She didn't speak it. She wouldn't be able to speak for a week. Or *walk*.

Beep! Beep! Beep! The shrill sound of the smoke alarm sliced through the moment as Finn's forgotten eggs burned.

36

FINN

"Love is for the weak."
—Finn Burke, *Lost*

inn scraped the burnt eggs from the pan, but he was just as tempted to toss the whole thing—pan and all—and start over. He should've been annoyed that his best pan had been destroyed, but he could hardly feel that way when the cause of the kitchen disaster was Pippa.

"I've never had sex in a kitchen before," she said as she walked back into the room, having changed into a pair of those damn pants for yoga and a close-fitting tee. She hopped up onto the counter beside him.

"I've never burnt eggs before." He stared at her, his voice half accusing.

"Maybe it's a day for firsts?"

"Maybe it's you who should be teaching me a thing or two about writing a love scene? As far as love scenes go, that was pretty damn good." He grinned, leaning in and kissing her eyelids, her cheeks, and the bridge of her nose.

"Really? That's quite a compliment coming from you." She shoved her tongue in her cheek.

"Sure, and don't you be getting used to it." He set the pan back in the sink and went to the pantry. "Bagels?" he called as he opened the door.

"Only if you have cream cheese." She somehow twisted that sentence into a question, managing to tack on her query at the last moment.

"I do have cream cheese." He opened the fridge and withdrew a small container. "This was my one vice from the States. This stuff's as expensive as *shite* over here and not quite the same." He set the small tub of cream cheese on the counter and popped a bagel in the toaster.

"No way. You can get Philly cream cheese here?"

"In Tesco's." He winked. "Ireland isn't that bad, now is it?"

"No." Pippa froze, an odd expression taking over her face. "I love it here."

"You do? Good." Pleased at her reaction, Finn rescued the first bagel from the toaster before adding a second for himself and pressing the lever. He dropped the hot bagel on a plate, just as it had begun to singe his fingertips. He grabbed a knife and used it to slather cream cheese onto the bagel, which he then offered to Pippa.

"Thanks." Pippa brought the bagel to her mouth, her pink tongue darting from between her lips to lick the cream cheese.

Finn's body hardened in reaction, but he forced

himself to focus on his breakfast instead. "What do you want to do today?"

"Do you mean to tell me that you're taking the day off *again*? That's two whole days. The world is going to go into shock." She smirked, but then bit her bottom lip.

He fought the urge to kiss the tip of her nose. *Feck it.* He leaned forward and did it anyway. When he pulled back, she'd blushed. He wanted to tell her that he loved the way the pink took over her pale skin. That he loved the way she crinkled her nose when she was uncertain about something.

Finn couldn't remember when he'd allowed himself to feel so relaxed. It was almost as if his life was beginning. Right there, in his kitchen, with Pippa.

"We could spend the day on the beach, or go find some more castles, or sleep. You didn't get much of that last night." He caught her hand in his. It was as if his body acted out of his control. Being with Pippa last night had changed him. He could practically *feel* the old sentimentality oozing back into him.

Pippa Darling had done more than help him get his novel where he needed it to be. She'd unearthed some of the parts of him that he'd shoved into a dark corner in his mind. She'd brought him to life again.

"Let's do nothing. Let's be lazy and read or watch movies and eat more bagels." She licked another spot of cream cheese from her lips.

Finn could name a few other things he'd like to do. "Or all three," he offered.

"Yes," Pippa said. "All three!"

A vaguely familiar ding sounded. His computer. Finn

didn't get very many emails. As a rule, he avoided most of them, but the ding on his laptop was unexpected. "I'll meet you on the couch. Go pick a book."

"On it," Pippa whirled around and headed down the hall.

Opening his laptop, he navigated to his email, feeling much more comfortable with it all since Pippa had begun tutoring him. There was one new email.

From Phillip.

It was probably just a quick line to let him know that he would read Finn's manuscript. He double-clicked the message.

Finn,

Thanks for sending your manuscript, and early no less. Though I'm not sure we can call it early since I've been asking for it for months.

Anyway, I stayed up all night reading your pages, and I have to say I'm disappointed. All the time we spent discussing the importance of writing to your market. You can't just write whatever you want. Readers expect punchy, hard-hitting fare from you. This is a fanciful romp that doesn't even resemble your voice.

I'm sorry, but if this is the direction you're going in, I feel I'm unable to represent you for future projects. Of course, the amendment you signed to your original contract states that if we terminate that, I manage Lost for the next five years. So, nothing will change there.

Phillip

Finn froze, staring at his laptop screen as though he'd never seen it before. His jaw grew rigid. A strange, detached numbness settled over him.

Was the new book really like that? How had that happened?

He couldn't publish books without Phillip. It was because of his agent that *Lost* had sold. What if he never sold another book again?

They'd all end up like *To the Ends of the Earth.*

He should never have listened to Pippa. Instead of thinking, he'd let his own *fecking* hormones play a part in it.

"Finn, are you okay?" Pippa asked as she returned to the room and wrapped her arms around his waist. "What is it?"

"Phillip's thoughts on my manuscript." Finn stayed rigid, detached, as though he'd turned to stone.

"I'm getting that much already, and you didn't even need to speak. Are you going to tell me what he had to say?" She pulled back and hopped onto one of the stools. The same stool he'd made love to her on not more than a half hour ago. Sliding the new copy of *To the Ends of the Earth* that he'd given her onto the counter, she faced him.

Finn turned on her. "I'll tell you what he had to say." He drew himself up, pushing memories of his night with Pippa out of his mind as best he could. "He said he hated the manuscript. That it was foolishness—a book that would never sell." Finn gritted his teeth.

Fire lit within Pippa's eyes. "You know that's not true.

And you *know* the version you just submitted is better—because the people are *real*."

"Yeah, so real he thinks there's no market for this book." Finn glared at her. He'd been split in two. On one side was the part of him that had been pondering a new life with Pippa. On the other, the part of him that Amélie had chewed up and spit out. The same part with a failed book. Except the lines were blurring, and with each passing moment, it grew harder to distinguish the two.

Pippa seemed to know exactly which camp she'd chosen. She'd crossed her arms over her chest. "Why are you even listening to Phillip anyway? We both know he's bad for you."

"He's my agent. The last time I checked, Phillip was the only game in town. The only one who wants to partner with me. Now he's not even that. He says that if I'm going to change the direction of my writing, we can't work together."

Pippa planted her palms on the breakfast bar. "Who cares? He's an asshole. You can query again."

"The only thing I wanted to do was come up with a book that would keep me writing. I'm not fit for anything else." He couldn't imagine getting a job in a bloody Tesco, bagging groceries. Not after he'd spent the last few years writing near the ocean. He'd have to sell his house. Maybe move to a flat somewhere. That way, he could prepare for the day his royalties ran out. Because with no other books to boost the sale of *Lost*, that was most definitely what would happen.

"You've already penned a runaway best seller. It's not like you don't think you can write."

Finn flinched. It was beyond foolish to feel the way he did. Still, there was a singsong refrain that played inside his head every day. It spoke of his failure to belong, his inability to write, his fear that he would be a one-hit wonder.

"That's it, isn't it? You don't think you can write." Pippa moved toward him, her hand outstretched as if to console him. But he couldn't let her. He couldn't trust or believe anything she said.

"Of course I can write. You don't know what you're talking about. And now you've not only wasted my time, but your own. Because after you ruined my book, you'll be lucky if I don't blacklist you."

He'd gone too far. He recognized it the moment the words left his mouth. But once they were free, he found them impossible to take back.

"What? You're blaming me for this?" Pippa shook her head. "How could you even think about doing that to me? After last night? After everything we've meant to each other?"

All the stress and insecurity and exhaustion from everything came crashing down around him. He couldn't think. He couldn't even envision his next move. It was as if his brain and body had separated from each other.

"What does it matter?" he asked, not bothering to keep the bitterness from his voice. "You never liked my writing anyway. You were only chasing the *List*."

Unable to bear the expression on her face any longer, Finn turned on his heel and stalked down the hall, right out the front door, letting it slam in his wake.

37

PIPPA

"She was stardust and magic combined."
—James Black, *To the Ends of the Earth*

*P*ippa stared at the door, the echo from its slamming still ringing for dozens of seconds after Finn had gone through it. The squeal of the Triumph's tires on the gravel drive followed. Had that really just happened? After last night, and everything they'd been to each other? After a whole summer of dancing around their mutual attraction, they'd finally come together. She'd fallen in love with him, and one email had blown it all.

She ran across the room, snatching up her purse and, out of habit, her book before running outside. The door banged closed behind her as she headed to her cottage. It had rained at some point and the walkway was wet again, a reminder of how it had looked when she'd first arrived.

She entered her cottage and went immediately to her closet to retrieve her luggage. Her body had gone numb.

She couldn't feel. Couldn't process anything. She could only act. Spreading her suitcase and carry-on bag on the floor, she opened both, tugging the mouth of the bag wide.

From there, she began shoving anything she could into the largest case. She opened her laptop and logged in once the screen lighted. A few clicks later and she'd initiated a FaceTime with Uma. "Please pick up. Please pick up."

After several too-long moments, Uma answered, and her face appeared on the screen. She yawned, rubbing her eyes. "Pippa, how are you doing? We haven't done a Face-Time in ages!" Uma grinned, but Pippa only felt guilt. She hadn't FaceTimed because she'd been so focused on finishing Finn's manuscript, as well as her own.

"I'm leaving . . ." But she didn't get any further than that, because hot tears burned Pippa's eyes. A sob stuck in her throat, and she fought to dislodge it, fought for air. She would not cry. Finn Burke didn't deserve her tears.

"What happened?"

Pippa swallowed hard. "Finn and I slept together."

"No way. You slept with Finn? Oh my God. How was it?" Uma inched closer to the screen. "Details."

Pippa scrunched up her face. How could Uma ask her to talk about that when it felt as though her chest had been scored open? But she had to talk to someone—it was the only way she'd survive the trip home.

"We sent in his manuscript yesterday and he took me to this castle to celebrate. And then, when we got back to his house, I realized I left my James Black book behind in his car."

"Okay." Uma's brow scrunched up.

"In Finn's car, in the river, underwater."

"Oh my, God. I'm sorry, Pippa. I know how hard it was to get a copy." Uma reached out as if to take Pippa's hand, but blinked and let her hand drop.

"Well." Pippa reached toward the dresser behind her and grabbed the new book. She held it up for Uma to inspect the cover. Then she opened the page to Finn's inscription.

"What? What the frig?" Uma gripped the desk in front of her and leaned in. "You met James Black?"

"Finn *is* James Black. The only reason he didn't tell me is because he wrote this book for an ex-girlfriend who dumped him and left him messed up."

"Oh my God. That is so . . . What did you do when you found out?" she asked.

Pippa bit her bottom lip. "I slept with him, and we had last night. We were together all morning." And she loved Finn. She wasn't quite ready to share that out loud yet, though. "It was so romantic. But then he got one email from his agent and he stormed out."

"An email from his agent? What did it say?" Uma rested her hands on her fists, which she'd balled beneath her chin.

"You know we've been working on his manuscript all summer, right?" Pippa paced as she talked, adding more things to her bags.

"Of course, it's the thing you've been complaining about from the moment you arrived."

Had she been complaining about the new book? That sounded like something she would have done. Not lately, though. "Yeah, well, Finn turned it in, and his agent hated it."

"But you don't like his writing either. That's the reason you didn't want to go to Ireland in the first place."

"I don't hate his writing. He *is* James Black. I just hated the way he wrote *Lost*." She shoved the rest of her clothes into her cases and began tearing posters from the walls. "It doesn't matter. He doesn't want me now. He blames me for what happened with his agent."

"You already know it's not your fault. He's the one who took your advice." Uma's sympathy printed itself on her face. "What are you going to do?"

Pippa picked up a pair of underwear and threw it into the case. Clean, dirty, who cared? She'd wash it all when she got home. "Come home. What else can I do? Screw him."

Uma frowned. "I've got to go now, I've got class. If you need to talk later . . ."

"You'll be there," Pippa replied. "Thank you for being my friend. For being there for me when I needed you."

"That's just how I roll." Uma's image winked out.

Pippa sank to the bed, closing the laptop lid. She felt so isolated, she could have been on another planet. Especially given the fact that she and Finn had been attached at the hip for weeks. Not only was she not with Finn, but he had gotten in his truck and taken off.

Little did he know that Pippa planned to do the same the first chance she got.

She grabbed her cell and scrolled through her contacts, searching through the list until she came to the one name she wanted. Pippa pressed Zoe's name and waited as the call began to ring through. "Please be home. Please be home"

"Pippa? Is that you?" Zoe's booming voice filled the line. The warmth in her tone sent Pippa tearing up again.

"Zoe, I have a huge favor to ask you." She fought to keep her voice from wobbling and failed. It was hitting her then—the realization that she wasn't only about to leave Finn behind, but Zoe, as well, who'd stepped in as a surrogate mom.

"Sure. You know you can ask me anything. Anything at all." And Zoe meant it. That was just who she was. Pippa could almost picture her grinning on the other end of the line.

"I need you to take me to Dublin airport." It was a pretty big favor. A three-hour drive—six both ways—was a lot to take in.

"I'll take you back later this month, of course, when your internship is over, but it's always good to plan ahead."

Not that far ahead. "No, Zoe. I need you to take me back right now. Preferably within the next ten minutes."

"I don't understand." Zoe grunted as she processed Pippa's request. "Oh, I see. The *fecker bolloxed* it up, did he?"

"Can I tell you all about it in the car? Right now, I just need to get out of here." All she knew was that she wanted to get far away from Finn, as quickly as possible.

Pippa's bottom lip began to tremble. She wouldn't lose her shit on the phone.

"Of course, I'm coming to get you. You asked."

"Zoe, you're a lifesaver. I'll wait by the entrance." Relief swamped her. So much so that Pippa's knees were seconds away from buckling.

She got all her things together, and in a fraction of the time it took her to unpack them in the first place. Once she had everything in a pile by the door, she spun around, indulging herself in one last look at the room that would no longer be hers.

"Goodbye Ireland. Goodbye Finn. I love you."

Shoring up her strength, Pippa laid her new copy of *To the Ends of the Earth* on the nightstand. With effort, she turned and grabbed her bags. Straightening her shoulders, Pippa drew a steadying breath and walked away.

38

FINN

"She bled me dry. Turned my pockets inside out."
—Finn Burke, *Lost*

Finn hiked through the uneven fields along the Donegal coast. It had been three days since he'd walked out on Pippa. Three days since he'd called in a favor and rented a cottage close to Shalvey.

He'd needed to get away. To clear his head of the noise, along with the words in his own brain, that infernal nagging, telling him what he should and shouldn't have been doing.

Finn had been so desperate for some space that he hadn't packed. He'd arrived under duress, with no change of clothes or even so much as a toothbrush to his name.

The little cottage had been just what he needed. A tiny, one room affair, along the Wild Atlantic way. Amélie had spent summers in the area as a child, and as Finn picked his way along the rocky coastline at low tide, he thought of her. Of how things hadn't been the same since she'd gone.

Even worse, it did nothing to lessen the ache in his soul, the hole in his heart, and the hardening of his body whenever he thought of Pippa. Right then, he might as well have had hundreds of pounds of weights resting on his shoulders.

His phone rang. Finn jerked the phone from his pocket and scanned the display. Ma. Though he was not even close to being in the mood for the call, he took it.

"Hello Ma," he said after he'd accepted the call.

"Finnegan. What in hell are you doing?" Lila's voice cut through the line, a direct connection to reality.

"I'm only answering to ensure you're still breathing. If you've called for a lecture, I'd like to reschedule." Finn kept his tone respectful, but with effort. He'd just taken three days to himself. The last thing he needed was to be thrust back into his real life by his ma, of all people.

"I have. What are you doing scaring the girl off like that?" Ma demanded.

"Am I to assume you've been gossiping with Zoe, then?" he asked. What a stupid question. Of course she'd been gossiping with Zoe.

"What a stupid question. *Of course* I've been gossiping."

Finn grinned at his mother's ability to end up on the same wavelength as him every time. "Have you now?"

"Sure, and I know all about how you were when you were around Pippa."

"And how might that be, exactly?" Finn climbed up on a large, flat rock to stare out at the sea. He'd never tire of living so close to the water.

"Different. Happy. The kind of happy you used to be all the time, before *Amélie* came along and bloody well ruined you for all others."

"Maybe." He began walking again, pressing onward across the rocky turf. There may have been something to that. He had been happy with Pippa, but telling that to Ma would be like giving a bone to a dog. She'd never let go.

"Zoe seems to think you were a bit hard on Pippa," Ma pushed. "Were you? Too hard on her?"

"I don't know," he admitted. It was just that so many things had happened at once. Finn and Pippa had gotten involved. Phillip hated the manuscript and dropped Finn as a client. . .

"Pippa would never do anything to intentionally sabotage my book."

He knew her so well. He'd watched the way she made friends easily, was eager to help others. She was a plotter and a planner, but also a daydreamer. He'd seen Pippa's face when she'd spoken of her dad. When Pippa loved, she loved with her whole heart.

"Who are you really mad at, then? Pippa? Or yourself?" Lila's question practically stood up and slapped him across the face.

"What do you mean?" he asked.

"You know, I've been watching that TV psychologist in the afternoons. I think your anger is stemming from your own insecurities."

Finn rolled his eyes to the heavens. For *feck's* sake.

Ma sighed. "I mean, you've never been sure of yourself and your writing. Come to think of it, you've never been sure of love. Lord knows why. You certainly got nothing but love from your da and me. But when you love someone, they pull out your insides and tie them into knots."

Pippa had certainly done that. Truth be told, she'd been tying him into knots since the first day they'd met. She'd never once let up.

"It's nothing Pippa did, but only your own failure to believe in your work. Pippa can't fix that, Finnegan. Only you can."

"What's this? Bloody therapy?"

"I've got to run. There's a seniors' triathlon competition coming up, and I'm going to grind those *feckers* into the ground on my way to first place. Call me later?" she asked.

He heard the jingle of car keys in the background. "I'll call ya."

"Finnegan, I'm no expert, but you need to find Pippa. Apologize. Tell her how you feel. Tell her you love her."

"Bye, Ma," he said, his voice gruff.

Even though he'd ended the call, he couldn't help pondering her words. Were they accurate? He couldn't say, but right then, they *felt* true. If Ma's call had been intended to make him feel better, it hadn't. If anything, it left Finn feeling more isolated than before.

The path ran through a series of farmers' lands. It wasn't uncommon to pass others along their way for a morning's walk. In truth, Finn was too tied up in what Ma had said to notice much else, until he heard his name.

"Finn. Twice in one week, eh?"

Finn jerked his head up as Connor picked his way

among the rocks. His clothes were even worse that day—
an orange polo paired with pink plaid pants. It was as if
his family wanted to torture him. Ginger daintily side-
stepped the stones. Once the land smoothed out, she
raced for Finn, rolling onto her back for a tummy rub.

"Hey, sweet girl," Finn said as he obliged Ginger,
running his palm over her soft fur. "What brings you
down here, Connor? This isn't your neck of the woods."
They were over an hour away from where the older man
lived.

Connor began walking and Finn followed. Though the
other man hadn't announced his direction, Finn knew
where they were headed. The one place Finn had avoided
the entire trip. As though if he didn't go, it wouldn't be
there.

He supposed Connor expected Finn to visit. For most
people, it would seem a natural stop.

Not for Finn.

Still, he followed, knowing the visit was long overdue.
Knowing it would help Connor.

The older man shrugged. "Just checking on a tenant.
The cottage working out for you?"

Finn nodded. "It is. Thanks for the last minute rental."

Connor's eyebrows shot up. "You haven't been over
this way in a while. I just wondered if it had anything to
do with the young lady I saw you walking with the other
day?"

"*Jaysus*. Is *everyone* after interfering in my life now?"
Finn shook his head.

"I'm not trying to interfere, Finn. It's just that I saw the way she looked at you. The way you both looked at each other." Connor cleared his throat as they picked their way down the hill a bit, coming to rest in front of a single gravestone. The engraving on the slab was familiar and still achingly painful.

Amélie O'Keefe

He'd only visited her gravesite twice before. Once for her funeral and once in the year following her death. Going to that spot, where the sea air battled the headstone of the woman he'd once loved more than life itself, had grown unbearable. The memories were what did him in, and no place brought them all snapping back like that one.

The knock on the door. Connor. Tears in his eyes. There'd been an accident. Amélie. Her car went over the cliffs. They were trying to recover the body.

It was an old pain, but that didn't make it any less real.

"She would be happy for you, you know. Amélie would." Connor patted Finn's shoulder, an action that had him reaching up. "Do you think . . . maybe it's time you moved on?"

"You're her da, Connor. You haven't moved on. You still come here whenever you can."

Connor nodded. "You're right. I do come, but it's out of respect for my daughter's memory. I have moved forward, but it's you who lives in the past."

Finn jammed his hands into his pockets. "Maybe I never had time to work through it." Amélie had been the one to end things between them, after all. They'd fought. She didn't want things to get so serious. He'd written a book for her? He wanted to marry her? It was all too much.

And then she'd gotten behind the wheel and he never saw her again.

"Then do that. With your girl, Pippa. My daughter was fickle and flighty. She wasn't ready for you. I spoiled her, so she wasn't ready to grow up. It's sad that she never got a chance." Connor glanced down at Ginger and squatted, giving her a pat on the head.

Finn kept quiet. There was a time when he would have beaten a man for saying such things about Amélie—even her da. That day, the truth of who she'd really been slammed into him.

She'd been careless with his heart, and even more so with her own. That was something Pippa would never have done, and yet he'd done it to her.

"If you love Pippa—"

"But I don't love her." Finn was quick to add that.

"You do. If you didn't, you wouldn't be in such a state," Connor said, oozing patience, the same way Finn's da might have.

Damn it.

Connor's statement was so simple that it knocked him back a few notches. Did he love Pippa? He remembered a million moments they'd spent together. Her smile. Her laughter ringing in his ears. The sliding of her skin against his own. Pippa. Everything Pippa.

He couldn't pinpoint when it had happened. But sometime between her first day on the job and the moment he'd lain with her in his bed, buried deep inside her, Finn had fallen in love with Pippa.

Dear God. Ma had been right, as usual.

But knowing didn't make things easier. Finn was no closer to knowing what to do about Pippa than before.

She'd become his world. He'd listened to her advice about his writing because he'd come to respect her opinion. He had overreacted. He'd blamed her for something neither of them could control.

He owed Pippa an apology and a great deal of groveling—something he wasn't schooled in.

"Connor, I think I need to be on my way," Finn said, giving Ginger another pat on the head.

"I thought you might." Connor tipped his hat. "I hope to see you again soon, Finn. Bring your girl."

"Me, as well. I will." Finn grinned and went back to the cottage. There was nothing of his there, but he checked it anyway before locking up. It was time to go home. He had things he needed to say to Pippa.

TWENTY MINUTES LATER, he was back in the driver's seat of his truck, motoring down the road. The cottage was only a half hour's drive from his house, but it might as well have been four and a half. He grabbed his phone and chose Pippa's name from his contact list.

Finn jammed the cell between his ear and shoulder as he searched out the entrance onto the highway he needed. He held his breath. Waiting.

She didn't pick up. The phone rang and finally went to

voicemail. It wasn't even Pippa's voicemail, but some generic message. So he was even to be denied the pleasure of hearing her recorded voice.

Finn gritted his teeth and dialed the number again. Same thing. Voicemail. No Pippa. Finn hung up again without leaving a message.

No matter, he'd tell her everything he wanted to say to her face.

By the time he finally arrived home, Finn was gripping the steering wheel white-knuckled. He parked the truck off to the side of the garage, then launched himself from the driver's seat.

"Pippa," he whispered, turning and jogging in the opposite direction from the garage, nearly losing his footing on one of the walkways. He raced to the gazebo first, but found it empty. Then Finn turned and ran to Pippa's cottage.

He knocked on the door. "Pippa. Pippa, it's me. I'm sorry."

But only silence answered him. Finn fished his keys from his pocket, slid the cottage one into the lock, and turned it.

Finn pushed the door open and stepped inside. He drew a breath. He was greeted by an empty room, its walls bare and its mattress stripped. The cottage was completely empty. There was no sign that Pippa had ever taken up residence there. Finn moved into the room, placing a hand on the bare walls—walls that had once held pictures of old cars and Pippa's motivational posters. There was nothing but white. He checked the drawers.

Empty. He moved into the bathroom and found not one towel out of place.

And then he spotted it, lying on the nightstand beside the bed. His book. The copy of *To the Ends of the Earth* he'd given her.

Pippa had truly gone.

39

PIPPA

"If it had been a dream, I could forget it. Move on from the pain. Yet, it was real. It was all real."
—James Black, *To the Ends of the Earth*

*P*ippa carried a load of laundry down the steps, forcing herself not to groan out loud. The guest laundry was her least favorite thing. It was only their sheets and towels—she didn't have to wash anyone's undies. Still, God only knew what they'd been up to with the B&B's set of sheets. She wasn't usually a germaphobe, but she could be when the occasion called for it.

She plastered a smile on her face as she passed through the guest common area, though she felt like doing anything but. She hadn't really smiled in days.

She yawned, still jet lagged, and made her way to the laundry room. Finn. That bastard. He'd pretended to care and then he'd just left. He'd acted like everything was *her* fault.

Pippa threw the wicker laundry basket with such force

that it bounced. Towels spilled across the cement floor. Shaking her head, she dropped to her knees and shoved them back into the basket.

"That was quite a show." Her dad stood by the door grinning. "I mean, not really. Things aren't super exciting around here."

Pippa resisted the urge to run forward and hug her dad. If she did that, then he'd only be suspicious. Even more suspicious than he'd been when she'd shown up at ten o'clock at night, unannounced, with red, puffy eyes.

Plus, there was a good chance she'd start crying. Dad had always been a sucker for her tears. So much so that she'd given up using them as a form of manipulation as a teen. She'd felt too bad for him.

"Why don't you leave this here, and we'll go for a walk?" Dad asked.

She frowned, kicking the laundry basket to the side before turning to face him. "You never leave the guests during the day."

"I've got John McCarthy watching the front desk. He can handle it. What I want is a walk with my daughter." Dad shrugged. "Is that too much to ask? I haven't seen you all summer."

It was a thousand times better than laundry, at any rate. "Sure." She followed Dad and grabbed her hoodie from beside the door. She shrugged into the material as she and Dad stepped outside.

Even though they were just hitting the beginning of September, there was already a slight chill in the air. A hint that a classic Pennsylvania winter was on the way. She zipped her hoodie, pulled the hood over her head, and fished a pair of sunglasses from the pocket. She thrust the latter on her face.

"What way do you want to go?" Pippa looked around. The area was so familiar she could have walked it blindfolded. Yet, it seemed as though things were so different. She'd been gone so long that she felt disconnected.

"I thought down by the old cemetery." Dad patted Pippa's shoulder.

"Which one?" Pippa smiled, for perhaps the first time since she'd arrived.

"Evergreen." Dad chuckled as he began walking in the direction he wanted. Pippa fell companionably into step beside him. Fall was a busy time of year in Gettysburg. Seniors were pulling in by the busloads. Dad probably couldn't afford to take time off for their walk, yet there they were.

"What's going on, Pip?" Dad locked his hands behind his neck. "I mean, you come back early, looking like your soul's been gutted, and with no explanation."

"I'm fine, Dad. Don't worry."

"I'm a father. Of course I'm gonna worry about you. It's in my fatherly DNA."

Pippa sighed. Normally, she would have laughed. She would have claimed that it was in her daughterly DNA to keep secrets. Right that moment, she didn't have the energy. She didn't want Dad to worry about her. He'd had enough on his shoulders ever since Mom had passed.

She could still lie to him, tell him nothing was wrong. But she needed to talk to someone and she didn't have the energy to keep on pretending.

"Finn Burke is James Black." She'd decided to start

with the easiest truth first. Though the moment she confessed it, she wasn't entirely certain it had been any easier. It reminded her that not only had she lost the man she loved, but she'd lost the author she loved. She was in double mourning. She could never *un-know* James Black's identity.

"What?" A myriad of emotions ran over Dad's face, from disbelief to confusion. "You didn't know this before, did you?"

Pippa shook her head. "No. Finn has gone to great lengths to keep James Black's identity secret. Then I had to show up with the book—one that held a lot of bad memories for him."

"Let me guess. You met Amélie." Dad nodded to two couples who passed them on the sidewalk.

Pippa turned to him in surprise. "You know about her?"

"I do. You were so into the book, I decided to give it a try. I borrowed your copy while you were at class one day. It's not my cup of tea—I like mysteries." He grinned. "But that one dedication stood out. What happened?"

She released Dad, knowing the rest of the confession would be harder. "Daddy, I fell in love with him—with Finn Burke." Pippa bit her bottom lip.

Dad had been there to talk to her about everything. From the moment she'd gotten her period, through her first kiss, and her first crush. Why was it harder to talk to him about this than any of those other things? Probably because Finn had somehow taken over her life and her heart.

"I see." Dad's face was unreadable. Not the norm for

him. "What happened, Pippa? And I want it to be clear that if you had sex, I don't need to know about it. Or at least no details. Maybe just tell me the bare minimum."

"Finn Burke kissed me." He'd also ravaged her body, though that definitely didn't fall within the "bare minimum" boundaries Dad had set. "Then his agent told him he hated his manuscript and was basically dropping him as a client. It was the manuscript I helped Finn rewrite."

"Okaaay." Dad drew out his syllables as his brain worked to figure things out. "That sounds harsh, but it doesn't explain why you're here and not in Ireland with the man you love." Warmth radiated from Dad's voice, but she knew it cost him. It couldn't be easy watching his daughter, one he'd practically had to raise alone, grow up and fall in love. But, that was exactly what Pippa had done.

"Finn blamed me for ruining his book." Pippa shook her head. "It's like he doesn't believe in his own work. It's as though he thinks Phillip is the only agent he could possibly get, and whatever Phillip says is law. Then he walked out on me." She bit her bottom lip. Tears stung the backs of her eyes. She couldn't cry anymore. She just couldn't—on principle.

Dad sighed, and Pippa waited for his outrage, his anger. Instead, he seemed his usual calm self. "Let me guess. You hurried and packed up all of your things before he got back so you didn't have to face him?" Dad kept up the steady pace beside her, occasionally nodding to tourists and various neighbors he knew.

"Yeah." There was no reason to dress it up. Pippa had

run. "Under the circumstances, I didn't think I needed to wait around to be humiliated again."

"Do you know how often your mother and I had arguments where one of us would storm out?" Dad skirted an uneven section of pavement, only to return to her side. "At least once a week. We were always fighting when we were first married. There was always someone storming out. Then the best part happened."

"What was that?" Pippa frowned, trying to anticipate his answer in her head.

"Making up." Dad winked at Pippa. "You, my daughter, just left before the makeup part."

Pippa shook her head. "You don't understand. He doesn't trust me. He followed my judgment and then blamed me when someone else didn't like it."

Dad patted her on the shoulder and then reached into his pocket. He extracted two butterscotch candies. They were the same kind he'd always had at the ready, after school. He offered one to Pippa. She accepted, unwrapping the candy and popping it into her mouth. It tasted of home and her older, simpler life. "It sounds to me like the man doesn't see his own worth. Something I think would be pretty easy to do in your line of work."

Pippa didn't bother to tell him about her own dark days after agent rejections. They needed a "bare minimum" about other things, too.

"I bet you'll be pretty happy to have the B&B to ground you," Dad suggested.

Guilt settled like a lead ball in Pippa's stomach. *That again.* Her brain switched gears and she thought about Finn's family. They'd really known him. They'd never expected him to take over the family business. It was all because he'd shared his dreams with them. It was time for Pippa to do the same.

"About that, Dad." Pippa drew a deep breath to prepare.

"I know, Pip." Dad offered her a second candy. She'd never gotten that as a kid. She must look seriously pathetic. "You don't want the B&B. You never have."

Pippa jerked her head to the side and met his eyes. There was no anger there. Instead, she was met with a patient sort of knowing. "How long have you known?"

"Oh, forever. I was just waiting for you to tell me. I wanted you to be honest about it." Dad stopped walking and wrapped his arms around Pippa, pulling her close into a bear hug.

A ball of warmth burst inside her chest. "You know why I took the internship in Ireland?"

"Because it's Ireland." Dad shrugged, as though no further explanation was needed.

"That, and it was because I wanted to get on the list. The New York Times Best Sellers list." She bit her lip as she remembered that one item on her literary to-do list. "I thought Finn Burke could help me do that."

"That doesn't seem like you, Pip. Was that really why you took it?" Dad frowned, his mouth flattening into an uncharacteristic line of disapproval, as they made a circle and began walking back to the B&B.

"I thought that if my book was a runaway success, that you'd see my writing as a real career and you wouldn't expect me to take over Yankee Hollow. I don't even know why I got that idea in my head." Recounting everything then for Dad made Pippa feel even more foolish than she had at the start of the walk.

"You are working on a real career, Pip. Your heart's in your writing. And though I worry about you eating, and being able to put a roof over your head, you're old enough to decide for yourself how you want to live your life. Your life isn't mine to control." He shook his head. "You don't need to get your name on some list to prove that to me."

Regret, harsh and brutal, slammed into her. Why had she thought lists and accolades were important? The only thing that mattered was that she kept putting words on the page.

A recommendation from Finn Burke couldn't help her with that. She had to help herself.

"What will you do? Yankee Hollow has been ours forever." Memories of Mom bustling down the hallway with home-baked sugar cookies with a hint of almond sprung into her mind. "And Mom—"

Tears formed in Dad's eyes, but they weren't the sad kind. They were the happy kind, or maybe, more accurately, the bittersweet kind. "Your mom loved this place. I grew to love it. But when I first came here, I hated it."

"Then why did you stay?" Pippa stopped walking and turned to face Dad. "Why didn't you tell her the truth?"

"Because sometimes, when we love someone, we take the time to help them find what matters most to them. A good relationship only happens when each person believes in himself or herself. Otherwise, one person is always struggling, trying to latch onto another for support. Your mom always wanted to do this, but without me, she might not have." Dad chuckled. "Oh, how I hated this place. At first."

Pippa stared at him in disbelief. All those years and she'd thought he'd loved Yankee Hollow. He'd done it for Mom.

"I don't know what's going to happen with you and Mr. Burke, but if you love him, maybe there's a way you can help him find his true potential. Then he can help you discover yours. The way your mother did for me."

"What do you mean?" How many more revelations had Dad planned for that day?

"She understood that what I really wanted to do was travel and see the world. She made me promise I would— right before she died. She even left me a travel fund in her will. It wasn't much to start with—probably enough to get me to Ohio—but I've added to it over the years."

"So what will you do next?" Pippa bit her bottom lip, waiting.

"I think I'll sell this place and take the trip of a lifetime. Maybe see Asia." He grinned, real enthusiasm in his eyes.

"But the B&B." Pippa glanced down the street. One of Mom's many handmade flags waved in the wind, resting on its flagpole near the mailbox. It'd been a wonderful place to grow up, but somehow, Pippa knew the answer. Mom would want Dad to let it go.

"Your mother isn't at the B&B, Pippa." Dad rested a hand over his heart. "She's here. She's ingrained in our souls. The B&B is just a place. If you leave it behind, life will go on."

"I love you, Dad." Pippa stepped forward and wrapped her arms around him.

Dad rested his chin on her head. "What are you going to do about Mr. Burke?"

"I'll think about it." It was all she could promise. At least until she could breathe again, *think* again.

Dad patted Pippa's shoulder. "Come on, let's head back. We're not doing much walking, and I could do with a fresh cup of coffee."

As she looped her arm through Dad's, Pippa felt fifty pounds lighter. Dad finally knew the truth: that she didn't want the B&B. And also, the other truth, that she was in love with Finn. She just needed to decide if that love was worth chasing, or if it was time to let it go.

"Go after her? You're joking."
—Finn Burke, *Lost*

Finn stood inside Pippa's empty room, her book in hand. Sweat broke out on his brow. The walls were closing in around him.

"She's gone, you *arse*."

Finn spun around at the sound of Zoe's voice. "Zoe."

Zoe and Bob stood just inside the doorway, and Zoe's eyes glittered with anger. He'd never seen her look that way at him in all of his years. Even that time he'd hot-wired her car as a boy and planned to take it for a spin in the village. "You're the one who scared her away."

"Now, Zoe," said Bob. "Give the boy a chance to speak." But it was clear from the harsh set of Bob's jaw that he didn't believe the words he'd just spoken. Finn didn't blame him—he wasn't convinced of his own innocence, either.

"Whatever you have to say to me, Zoe, it's nothing my

own Ma hasn't already said." And nothing he hadn't already been berating himself for in his own head. "I followed Pippa's advice and my agent bloody well hated the book."

"A pretty poor excuse for treating Pippa badly, if I do say so myself." Zoe began to pace the room in an uncharacteristic show of unease.

"But Phillip—"

"Phillip doesn't like *anything*. You should've gone into all of this expecting him to argue with you." Bob shook his head. "I mean, how many times have we talked about Phillip's piss-poor taste and off-the-wall ideas. I think you *bolloxed* it up, boyo."

Bob Hannigan telling him off? Bob was usually more of a silent influencer, happy to leave the telling off to Zoe whenever the occasion called for it. Not that day.

"I know. I know I made a right mess of things. But no matter what Pippa thinks of me, I owe her an apology." Finn scanned the room again, expecting some clue and finding none. "So where is she? Did she check into a hotel?"

"She left. Back to the States. She called me in tears, brokenhearted over your sorry *arse*. Didn't I drive her to Dublin airport three days ago?" Zoe said.

Finn's head reeled. Dublin airport. Pippa had gone. Probably as soon as he'd left, from the sound of it. He'd fallen in love with a woman, and once more, he'd been left behind. But that was only the case if he compared her to Amélie.

Pippa was nothing like Amélie.

"Look, Zoe. I know I screwed the whole thing up. But

you coming in here and giving me a lecture just like my Ma isn't helping things. Give me a chance to fix them. How do I find Pippa?"

"She deliberately asked me not to tell you where she is." Zoe shook her head, crossing her arms over her chest. "If you think I'm about to give that information away, you're mad."

"She's at Yankee Hollow Bed and Breakfast in Gettysburg." Bob grinned, taking a step back when Zoe whipped around and faced him. "What?" Bob shrugged. "She didn't ask *me* to keep quiet."

"Thank you, Bob," Finn said. Pippa had gone home. That was the last thing she'd wanted to do. Her dad would expect her to take over the family business. She might even decide it made more sense to work there than to write. He had to go after her. Not just because he loved her, but *for* her. "Can you give me the address?"

"What are you gonna do? Go after her?" Zoe asked, her eyes widening to saucers.

"Of course I'm going after her. Isn't that what happens in all those romance novels you read?" Finn grinned at Zoe and she blushed.

"You cheeky devil." She waved him off.

"I'm forgiven, then?" He held out his arms.

"Only if you promise not to make Pippa cry again, you hear?" Zoe asked as she stepped into his arms and he hugged her.

"I'll do everything in my power to keep our girl tear-free." Finn's phone began to ring. The second time in one day. He must be developing a social life. What the *feck*? He scanned the screen, which read: *Unknown caller.* "I gotta take this. It could be Pippa."

"Not bloody likely," Zoe said, moving to the door.

"Stop in to see us before you go. We'll have that address for you." Bob tipped his hat at Finn, and the pair turned, leaving Finn alone once more in Pippa's bare room.

Finn jammed his thumb onto the accept button and brought the phone to his ear. "Burke." He answered in his usual greeting.

"Is this Finn Burke? The author?" The caller on the other end of the line was a woman.

He hovered his thumb over the hang up button, in case he'd been tracked down by a reporter. But he didn't hang up. Something in his gut told him to stay on the line. "You're speaking to him."

"I'm so glad I caught you. My name is Marianne Henson, with Henson Literary Agency in New York."

Finn froze. A *fecking* literary agent calling him? He scanned the window, searching for any flying pigs among the clouds. Since there were none, he decided to give the woman the benefit of the doubt. "Are you now? It's a pleasure to make your acquaintance."

"Likewise. You're probably wondering why I'm calling." Marianne's voice was warm, with a note of patience in it. Finn found himself losing the tension he'd first felt when he'd picked up the phone.

"I understand that you might be looking for new representation." Her voice held a hopeful thread.

"Now, where would you have heard such a thing?" Finn asked. "I didn't query any literary agents."

"No, but your assistant did . . . a Pippa Darling? Great name, by the way." Marianne chuckled.

Finn found himself growing defensive on Pippa's behalf. Until what Marianne said began to sink into his brain. "Pippa queried you? With what?"

"Your latest novel, I'm told. She is on your payroll correct?" Marianne asked, her voice filling with as much confusion as Finn felt. "She said she was your P.A."

Damn it. What had Pippa been thinking? Querying his manuscript without asking him? Bloody hell. Still, he was a smart man. Smart enough to know an opportunity when it fell on his lap. "She is. She's just so proactive I wasn't aware she'd gotten started with the query process."

"I'm glad she did. After reading your second book, frankly, I'm blown away. This is exactly the type of manuscript I love to read, and you're the kind of author I've always hoped to represent."

Finn's mouth dropped open of its own accord. Surely, he was dreaming. "You're sure you're not just saying that because I've already written a best seller?"

"In all honesty, it doesn't hurt, however, and I hope you won't take offense to this, I was never really a fan of *Lost*. I found it to be a little, well, crass. I like this much better. You've found your voice."

Finn froze in place. Just when he'd thought it wasn't possible for him to be more shocked in one day, she'd let that news slip. "You don't say?" he asked, carefully leveling his voice.

"I know at least a dozen editors looking for this exact manuscript. I would love to represent you."

"Really?" He wished he could come up with a better

response, but it was impossible. After his shoddy relationship with Phillip, he'd believed he'd never find an agent who was excited about his work. Christ knew Phillip had never been—even at the beginning. Yet, there Finn was, having a conversation with an agent who was *enthusiastic* about his book.

"Why don't I send you some information and a contract? We can have a conference call next week to iron out the details."

"That sounds good." He forced the words out, flummoxed.

"Excellent. We'll talk soon."

Finn shook his head. It was all down to Pippa. He'd railed at her, walked out on her, and she'd helped him anyway, because it was what she knew he needed. His heart beat hard in his chest, aching with love for her. Pippa.

Finn agreed to contact Marianne immediately if he received any other offers of representation. Soon enough, they ended the call, Finn's head still spinning.

On a sigh, Finn turned, locking the door to the cottage behind him. He just had a few more things to take care of and some very important reading material to grab. Then he'd be off.

It was high time Pippa Darling came back to Ireland.

PIPPA

"I ache for her. My heart and soul broke the moment we parted."
—James Black, *To the Ends of the Earth*

*P*ippa sat on the side porch, typing away on her laptop. She was content, and it amazed her that she could even get to that place emotionally. Especially after Finn and everything that had happened between them.

Yet, writing had always been her refuge. Without writing time, Pippa began to wither the way Dad's flowers did without water. Dad must have seen it, because he insisted she spend more time actually working on her manuscript. It was due the next week, September 6th, so she was days away from having to turn it in.

She'd have to lie, of course. She'd have to say she'd gotten Finn's final feedback on that last rewrite. Somehow, she didn't think Finn would contradict her. If anything, Finn would be just as desperate to blight her from his life as she was him.

Thinking that way, however, only led to the painful path. The path of *what ifs*. Pippa couldn't risk that journey again.

Instead, she chose to work on her own story. She'd stuck a slew of post-it notes to the table beside her—color coded to reflect the changes she'd need to make. One by one she completed each. Her progress, along with the fresh tumblers of coffee Dad kept bringing her, and the *clackety-clack* sound of her fingers on the keyboard, cheered her.

Whether she wanted to admit it or not, she'd learned from Finn. He'd helped her find her voice. She finally knew what to do. And if Finn's advice kept filtering into her ear, she didn't ignore it. When she finished her novel, it would mean at least one positive thing came out of her time in Ireland.

Something besides a broken heart, at least.

She was halfway through her last chapter when tense voices cut into her world. Dad and someone else, who she couldn't make out. Pippa stood, set her laptop on the table, inched toward the edge of the porch, and then scanned the front yard.

"Look, I know I've no business being here. I just need to speak with her. I made a mistake. At the very least, I want to apologize."

Finn. Pippa's heart slammed in her chest. She couldn't believe he'd come to the B&B to find her, and in Gettysburg of all places. It seemed like a very un-Finn place to be, yet there he was, standing and talking to Dad.

The old hurt lodged itself in her throat, but it was quickly eclipsed by anger. How dare he? How dare he show up at her family's B&B and bring his drama with him?

The calm she'd felt all morning faded, as it swapped places with anger. She'd spent the whole summer pursuing her dream while giving her criticism on his work. And then the minute he heard something he didn't want to hear, he took off. Well, two could play at that game, and they had. She had a few things to say to Finn Burke.

She drew a breath to calm herself, and then rounded the corner of the bed and breakfast from the side porch. Finn and Dad stood right in front of the koi pond. It would be nice if Dad just shoved Finn into the water, but that wasn't going to happen. Too many witnesses.

Finn turned and met her eye, and her breath left on its own. It seemed like years, even though it had only been a few days since she last saw him. Her traitorous heart told her it might as well have been eons. Her emotions warred with one another. It was a toss-up between anger and bone-searing grief. She decided to front load with the anger.

Pippa stormed toward him. "Who do you think you are showing up here?" She came to a stop right in front of Finn and tapped him on the chest with her index finger. "You were a jackass, and now you have the balls to come *here*? You're delaying my writing time." She fought the urge to cover her mouth—no way was she apologizing for her feelings anymore.

"She's got a point," Dad said from behind Finn. "Maybe you should leave."

Pippa rolled her eyes. "Dad, this is my argument, okay? Let me have it."

Dad's eyebrows shot into the air. "Um, if you'll excuse me." But as he passed them on the way to the front door, she caught his smile. He was actually enjoying himself. Figured.

"Pippa, please." Anguish painted Finn's face. His usually neat beard hadn't been trimmed and had gotten a little bushy in the time since they'd been apart.

"No. You just stormed out because that asshat of an agent of yours had something to say that didn't match my feedback."

"Pippa, I know I've acted like an incredible *arse*. But I had to come and see you." Finn shoved a hand through his hair. His eyes seemed tired and red-rimmed. Maybe he'd been crying, or maybe he'd just worn himself out.

"I told you that I wrote the book for Amélie and that she left me." He ran a hand through his hair again. "What I never said is that she died. That very day, she'd been on her way home from seeing me and she got in a car accident. They said she'd been drinking. Then when the book did so badly, I just . . . stopped living."

"I don't know what to say." Pippa shook her head. "I'm sorry you went through all of this. I truly am. It doesn't excuse your behavior."

"I know. I'm deeply sorry. I should never have treated you the way I did. Especially after our night together."

"Yeah, you pretty much acted like a jerk."

"An immense jerk," he agreed. "I'm better off without Phillip. I believe in you, Pippa. If you come back to me, I'll prove it to you."

"Why? You don't need an intern now." She bit her lip on the inside, waiting.

"Marianne Henson called me."

Pippa's hand flew to her mouth. "What? She did?" Despite her anger at Finn, there was a part of her that was still rooting for him, wanting him to find success. "What did she say? What did she think?"

"That she loves it. She wants to rep me." Finn gave her a ghost of a smile. He rocked awkwardly back and forth, alternating feet.

"I wondered if she would. On her submissions page, she listed *To the Ends of the Earth* as one of her favorite books of all time." Pippa grinned.

Finn's mouth dropped open. "My book? You're joking?"

"Yes, your book. You never did see. You've never believed in yourself. You kept rewriting and second-guessing your work. If you do that, you'll never finish anything."

"I know." Finn nodded, the weariness in his eyes seeming to amp up. "Why did you query Marianne for me?" he asked.

Finn took a small step closer. It reminded Pippa of the way wranglers approached wild animals on jungle documentaries.

"I only contacted her because I think, at the very least, we should still be friends. I still want to see your book do well. That's why I submitted on your behalf." She linked her fingers together to still her hands.

Finn took another step forward, the expression on his

face familiar as desire slid into his eyes. A mirror image of the one he'd worn when she'd lain in his arms.

Please let him say the right words. God, I don't even know what they are, but please let him say the right words.

"I don't want to be your friend. I'm no good without you, Pippa. You've made yourself a part of my life and I don't know how to go back to how things were."

"But, Finn—"

"I need you. I'm in love with you, Darling."

His light green eyes, that she'd once compared to the hills of Ireland, burned into her. Had she actually heard him right? Finn was in love with her?

But should she believe him? After all, she'd trusted him once and it ended up hurting her. He'd thrown her under the bus when Phillip disliked the manuscript.

He took a final step forward, so that they were separated by mere inches. *"Trust is the greatest leap of faith we'll ever take. If we pass over the divide, we'll reap rewards just shy of heaven."*

Those words worked.

"Where is that from?" Pippa cocked an eyebrow.

"It's from a new book. One I'm going to write in the new year, in the style of James Black. After I rerelease *To the Ends of the Earth*, of course." He smirked, that smile of his worming its way back into her heart.

Her heart swelled in her chest. He was going to write the way he was meant to again. Could she really hope for anything more?

"Come away with me, Pippa. Come back to Ireland so we can give this another try. I promise I'll never make you doubt me again."

"Finn—"

"Unless . . . you don't love me?" Finn's eyebrows dipped to the center.

He was so cute, so endearing. He was everything she'd never known she needed.

"Yes, I love you. I don't know why, but God help me, I do." Pippa rushed forward into Finn's arms, relief swamping her as they closed around her. She rested her cheek against the soft cotton of his flannel shirt.

"And you'll come with me? What about the B&B? I'll understand if you have to stay behind for a while. I could work here if you need me to." Finn shot the questions at her rapid-fire. It wasn't like him. Maybe Pippa's speech patterns had rubbed off.

Pippa drew back, cupping his cheeks, the wiry whiskers of his beard escaping between her fingers. "I told Dad the truth. He's going to sell the place and see the world. And I can do whatever I want."

"And do you want to be with me?" he asked, his voice husky. "I've only started to get to know you. I want to know so much more."

"Remember, Pippa. The bare minimum." Dad's voice filtered out from inside the house, and she spotted him hovering near the window. "Don't forget that, Finn, when you take my daughter back to the Emerald Isle."

Finn grinned. "So, how about it, Darling?"

"When do we leave?" Pippa asked.

"Whenever you want. Oh, and"—he pointed to the backpack he'd set on the ground—"your manuscript's in there. I read the whole thing on the way here."

"And marked it up with a little red pen, I presume?"

"The whole damn thing. It was very gratifying." He grinned. "It's brilliant. Just tightening, is all. And we're going to get there. I'm going to help you as you helped me."

"You really liked it?" She almost lifted herself on tiptoe.

In answer, Finn drew Pippa into his arms. "Maybe we'll just tweak that kissing scene a bit, Darling," he whispered against her mouth.

Pippa pulled Finn tighter. This time, she wasn't letting go.

EPILOGUE
PIPPA

"Stardust drenches her, rendering her a magical creature. Not a figment or fairy, but a true woman of flesh and blood."
—Finn Burke, *Ingénue*, from the James Black Collection

One Year Later

"Where are we going?" Pippa asked as Finn drew her outside and down the walkway that led from their home.

"That's the thing, see. I've got a surprise for you. And that means you have to keep your eyes shut and wait for it." Finn Burke being playful and romantic. Who would have thought the crotchety urchin she'd first met had it in him?

But he had.

Finn was kind and caring and helpful and challenging. She'd loved every minute of that past year. She loved him.

It didn't hurt that, after nearly a year of working on her manuscript and polishing it, she'd just landed her own agent and a very nice book deal.

Would she make it onto the New York Times Best Sellers list when her debut novel got released? She didn't know, and she didn't care.

Sure, it would be nice, but it didn't matter if her book made it onto some list. The important thing was that she wrote something she could be proud of.

Because, in the end, she needed to believe in herself before anyone else could.

"I thank you for staying away while the construction team worked through the final stages on the keep," Finn said.

Pippa resisted the urge to peek through her fingers as she moved on. "Sure. I've been busy anyway."

"I thought today, I'd surprise you with a big reveal." Finn's voice grew as light as a boy's. She could almost feel the bounce in his step.

"That's awesome. When do I get to see it?" she asked.

Finn stopped, reached up, and then tugged her hand away from her eyes. "How about now?"

Pippa sucked in a breath. The sun was in the process of setting on the horizon. It turned the sky a heady mix of pinks and oranges and yellows. And there, part of one breathtaking panoramic view, stood the keep.

Its gray stone had been cleaned and cemented into place. Ancient-looking windows, some stained glass and some not, had been installed, but they were only ancient *looking*. Those babies were triple-paned. From where Pippa stood, it seemed as though there were lights coming from the inside.

"So beautiful. I thought there wasn't electricity in that place?"

Finn shrugged. "There isn't. Come on. Let's go in."

Together, they followed the walkway up to the keep entrance. Finn withdrew a large skeleton key and inserted it into the lock. He turned it and pushed the door open.

Pippa had been expecting bare stone floors and walls. Instead, Finn had placed an enormous desk in front of one of the windows, so that it looked out over the sea. There were several overly-large, comfy looking chairs positioned around the room, along with a bookcase that had been filled with some of Pippa's favorites, and Finn's, as well. Rich tapestries hung on the walls in colors of green and gold. Little knickknacks and trinkets filled the shelves and low tables in the space.

Lit candles were everywhere, giving off a soft glow, sending flickering shadows dancing in the twilight.

"When did you have time to do all this?" she asked. "Your book—"

"The book can wait." He shrugged. "I wanted to surprise you." He tugged her hand again. "Come on. Let's go upstairs."

Pippa grinned. If Finn wanted to show her something upstairs, she was more than for it. Not only was Finn a considerate lover, but his talents in the bedroom could have earned him a medal.

But he seemed to have something different on his mind as he led her along the stone spiral staircase. "Now close your eyes again. This is the best part."

She let him lead her. Two more steps, three, four more up the spiral staircase, and Finn stopped. "Open your eyes."

Pippa complied, but she fell back against him as her vision jumped into focus. "Oh my God!" she exclaimed.

Everyone she loved was there. Dad, Uma, Zoe, Bob, Caden, and Lila, Finn's mom.

"Welcome to your first Publishing Deal party, Pippa Darling." Finn grinned, releasing her hand so she could say hello, but she spun around and brushed her lips against his. "This is so thoughtful. Thank you."

"I'm glad you like it, Darling. Go. Go greet your guests." He beamed with what seemed like pride.

Squealing, Pippa ran across the room and straight into Uma's arms, holding her close. "I can't believe you're here. You didn't have to take a taxi from the airport, did you?"

Uma shook her head, releasing Pippa. Her blue color-coordinated pantsuit matched her blue boots to perfection. "Caden drove me. He's promised to take me on a tour of Ireland." As Uma glanced back at Caden, she wore an uncharacteristically shy smile. A faint blush covered her pale skin.

"I had no idea your American friends were so good looking, Pippa." Caden winked. "I might have to transfer to another university. Broaden my education."

Pippa grinned. "Cool. Caden's a great tour guide from what I've heard." She leaned closer to Uma's ear and whispered, "I want details, okay?"

Uma reddened and nodded, but she said no more as Pippa moved down the line.

Next, she found Lila and Dad chatting it up, each with a glass of white wine. It wasn't the first time they'd met, but Pippa couldn't help noticing Dad seemed different with Lila. Happier.

"Oh, Pippa, your father. You're a scandalous flirt, Jim Darling." Lila grinned before she pressed a kiss to Pippa's forehead. "Your book's going to be wonderful. I can't wait to read it."

"Thanks, Lila." Pippa hugged the older woman. Finn's mother had become more than just a friend. Along with Zoe, she'd filled a tiny piece of the void Pippa's own mother had left.

"Baby, I'm so proud of you," Dad said. He pulled her close. His familiar Dad smell—sandalwood—filled her nostrils. He'd been right. Even though he'd sold the B&B, Pippa hadn't lost her home. She could always find it in Dad. In herself. "I knew you could do it."

"As did we."

Pippa spun around at the sound of Zoe's voice. "Zoe!" She hugged first Zoe, and then Bob. Both had done more than their share to make Pippa feel at home. She'd be forever grateful to them.

"Okay, okay!" Finn cut into the reunions, thrusting a glass of champagne into Pippa's hand. He then passed a glass into the hands of each guest. "A toast to Ms. Pippa Darling's first book deal. May it be the first of many more. *Sláinte.*"

"*Sláinte.*" Everyone responded in unison, raising their glasses.

Pippa grinned from ear to ear before taking a sip from her own glass. The bubbles tickled the back of her throat, the dry liquid going down easily.

"And now, while we have you all here," Finn continued, "there's one more thing I want you all to be a part of."

Turning Pippa to face him, with the backdrop of the

crashing waves behind them, Finn Burke dropped to his knee. Reaching into his pocket, he withdrew a shining silver Claddagh ring.

All of the air left Pippa's body at once. He couldn't be. Could he?

"This ring is the same one my father gave to my mother. Will you marry me?" The man who was known for his words, whether they be crass or endearing, had kept his proposal simple. He didn't make any promises, for trust was a leap of faith. But, as Pippa had learned, when you believed in yourself and in the ones you loved, the jump didn't seem so impossible.

"Yes. Yes, I will." She held out her hand to Finn.

Finn's eyes widened as he slid the ring onto her finger —a perfect fit—and rose to his feet. "You'll marry me then, entitled American?" His lips twitched.

"Of course, I will," Pippa said. "Bloody *eejit*."

And she realized that every moment up until then had been moving her forward. To Finn Burke. To love. Toward the next chapter in her life.

THE END

YOUR NEXT FREE READ!

The most wonderful thing about writing is connecting with readers! I occasionally send out newsletters with details on new releases, as well as special offers and other news related to my books.

And if you sign up for my mailing list I'll send you another book for FREE.

Steph

DOWNLOAD YOUR FREE BOOK >
http://bit.ly/pippa-free-book

ALSO BY STEPHANIE KEYES

Young Adult Fantasy

The Star Child

Seventeen-year-old Kellen St. James has been haunted by the
same girl for half of his life. When they finally meet outside of
his dreams, he's thrust into the world of faeries, gods and
goddesses—and all at his college graduation.

The Spellbinder's Sonata

A brilliant concert pianist, a clarinetist with a history of magic,
and a haunted house. Beauty and the Beast meets The Phantom
of the Opera in a tale of magic, music, and one dark curse.

The Boy in the Trees

Part of the Blood In the Shadows anthology, Jemma's sketched
the same boy hundreds of times. The only problem? They've
never met.

New Adult Romance

The Internship of Pippa Darling

Pippa's one Irish internship away from graduation,
unfortunately it's with Finn Burke, the one author whose work
she hates.

The Education of Uma Gallagher

Uma Gallagher's thrilled to land a teaching position in Dublin, but the last thing she expects is to find rock star Caden Hannigan in the back of her class.

ABOUT THE AUTHOR

Stephanie Keyes is a geek, a dreamer, and an award-winning author. She's also a hopeless romantic who writes books ranging from young adult fantasy to adult contemporary romance.

Steph won the RONE Award for Best Young Adult Book of 2019 and took 2nd place in the Romance Writers of America Athena Awards (Paranormal Category) for *The Spellbinder's Sonata*. She also took the 2014 Dante Rossetti Award for *The Star Catcher*. In addition, she was a finalist in the International Book Awards, Readers' Choice Awards, and Kindle Book Review.

Keyes is a technical writer, teacher, and speaker. She lives in Pittsburgh, Pennsylvania with her husband and her two boys, and dog, Duncan MacLeod. Steph is a hopeless romantic and Whovian who's shamelessly addicted to Nutella. She has also written as Gemma McKay.

facebook.com/StephanieKeyesAuthor
instagram.com/stephkeyes38
pinterest.com/stephaniekeyes

ACKNOWLEDGMENTS

It takes so many people to write a book. I may have been the person putting words on the page, but this could never have been possible without the help and support of the following people.

To Susan Chapek, Marcy Collier, Mary Jo Glover, and Jenny Ramaley for being amazing critique partners. You helped shape Pippa and make the book so much better. I am truly grateful.

Dave Amaditz, you convinced me that I really have a flair for romance. Once upon a time, you helped me find my voice. I'll be forever grateful.

Grandma, I love our Tuesday trips. You gave me something to look forward to every week. Without your stories of Ireland, I probably wouldn't have started writing at all. Thank you.

To Ashley Turcotte, for being an amazing editor. You can take any text and make it sparkly in a fun and educational way. I think you love Finn just as much as I do.

Najla Qamber, you are the most amazing cover

designer. You have a way of pulling thoughts out of my head and turning them into a book cover.

For my boys, whom I affectionately call Hip-Hop and Bam-Bam, thank you for being patient with Mommy on all of those occasions she locked herself away in her office on a Saturday morning. I owe you guys a year's worth of ice cream.

For Aaron, who is everything. You've read this book more times than anyone. You're my ultimate litmus test. If I can make you cry, Mr. Keyes, then I know I've gotten something right. This book would not exist without you and your unwavering belief in me.

And thank you to my fans, especially Jackie Jackson, for asking when my next book was coming out. It may have seemed like a small question to you, but to me it was the motivation I needed to push through and finish this book.

www.ingramcontent.com/pod-product-compliance
Lightning Source LLC
Chambersburg PA
CBHW031035120726
47905CB00007B/2192